It is every parent's worst nightmare. Greer Dobbins' daughter has been kidnapped—and spirited across the Atlantic to a hiding place in Scotland. Greer will do anything to find her, but the streets of Edinburgh hide a thousand secrets—including some she'd rather not face.

Art historian Dr. Greer Dobbins thought her ex-husband, Neill, had his gambling addiction under control. But in fact he was spiraling deeper and deeper into debt. When a group of shady lenders threatens to harm the divorced couple's five-year-old daughter if he doesn't pay up, a desperate Neill abducts the girl and flees to his native Scotland. Though the trail seems cold, Greer refuses to give up and embarks on a frantic search through the medieval alleys of Edinburgh—a city as beguiling as it is dangerous. But as the nightmare thickens with cryptic messages and a mysterious attack, Greer herself will become a target, along with everyone she holds dear.

Books by Amy M. Reade

Secrets of Hallstead House

The Ghosts of Peppernell Manor

House of the Hanging Jade

Malice Series
The House on Candlewick Lane

Published by Kensington Publishing Corporation

The House on Candlewick Lane

A Malice Novel

Amy M. Reade

LYRICAL UNDERGROUND
Kensington Publishing Corp.
www.kensingtonbooks.com

Lyrical Press books are published by
Kensington Publishing Corp.
119 West 40th Street
New York, NY 10018

Special book excerpts or customized printings can also be created to fit
specific needs. For details, write or phone the office of the Kensington
Special Sales Manager:
Kensington Publishing Corp.
119 West 40th Street
New York, NY 10018
Attn. Special Sales Department. Phone: 1-800-221-2647.

First Electronic Edition:
eISBN-13: 978-1-5161-0014-9
eISBN-10: 1-5161-0014-X

First Print Edition:
ISBN-13: 978-1-5161-0017-0
ISBN-10: 1-5161-0017-4

Printed in the United States of America

Acknowledgments

There are several people who were instrumental in the evolution of this book, and I am deeply indebted to all of them.

My husband is always my first and last reader. And without him I wouldn't have made that first trip to Scotland, where my family and I fell in love with the landscape and the culture.

Sharon Aguanno, Kathleen Charon, and Missy Schenck found mistakes I didn't catch and asked probing and thoughtful questions that made me work harder to make *The House on Candlewick Lane* a better book.

Martin Biro and the many other talented editors, artists, and professionals at Kensington Publishing spend their days working with people like me to bring dreams to fruition, and their support is invaluable.

Many years ago I spent one semester as an intern at the National Center for Missing and Exploited Children in Arlington, Virginia. Until my time there, I didn't realize that familial kidnappings are by far the most prevalent type of kidnapping in the United States. Though it is essential to teach our children about stranger danger, it is also important to know that a child is far more likely to be kidnapped by a family member or close family friend than a stranger. You can learn more about the work done at the NCMEC on their website at http://www.missingkids.com.

Prologue

I must have fallen asleep, because I sat up with a start, not remembering where I was. But after a second it all came back to me in a sudden rush of fear and indignation. I was sitting on the twin bed. It was hot. My hair stuck to the back of my neck and my forehead. Gray light forced its way into the room through the small window that overlooked the fields behind the house on Candlewick Lane. The rain was still falling, smearing the glass. I wondered where Neill was. I knew pounding on the door would be of no use, but I had to do something. I had to try. My fists bore the bruises from my earlier futile attempts to be heard. There was nothing to do but wait to be released from this tower prison. Someone *had* to let me go.

They couldn't keep me here forever.

Chapter 1

The phone rang as I was gulping down my second cup of coffee, ready to head out the door to work.

"Hi. Is this Ellie's mom?"

"Yes."

"This is Maureen from the primary school office, just calling to confirm that Ellie is out today."

"No," I answered, setting the coffee cup down with a clunk. "She should be there."

"Okay. Mrs. Dennis probably just marked her absent by mistake. I'll call down to the classroom and get back to you."

"Thanks." I hung up, frustrated with Mrs. Dennis. This wasn't the first time she had been careless about marking Ellie absent when she was sitting right in front of her. And now I had to wait for the office to call back and was going to be late for my class.

I had folded half a load of laundry before the phone rang again.

"Dr. Dobbins? This is Maureen again. Mrs. Dennis said Ellie wasn't in the classroom, so I went down to check. She's not there."

"Is she in the bathroom?"

"Mrs. Dennis said there's no one in the class bathroom. I checked the bathroom in the hallway and she wasn't there. She's not in the nurse's office, either. The custodian is checking the other bathrooms and the gym to see if she's there."

It wasn't like Ellie to leave her classroom without telling the teacher. "Let me call my neighbor. She walked Ellie to the bus stop with her kids this morning. I'll call you back."

I hung up and dialed Dottie, my neighbor across the street.

"Hi, Dottie. It's Greer. Did Ellie get on the bus okay this morning?"

"Yeah. Why? Is something wrong? Is she sick?"

Dottie was known by all the moms in the neighborhood as a rabid worrier, and Ellie had been frequently sick this fall. The divorce seemed to be affecting her more now that she had started going to school.

"No, no," I hastened to assure her. "They marked her absent because she's not in the classroom."

"Oh. She's probably in the gym." Ellie's fondness for Mr. Leicester, the gym teacher, was legendary.

"You're probably right. Thanks, Dottie. Talk to you later."

I called the school right back. Maureen answered on the first ring. "My neighbor put her on the bus," I informed her.

"She's not in the gym, and Mr. Leicester didn't see her this morning. I was just going into Mrs. Ravell's office to see if Ellie's in there." I couldn't imagine why Ellie would have to see the principal.

"Call me back as soon as you've checked."

"Of course."

I finished folding the laundry and put my coffee cup in the dishwasher. I double-checked my makeup in the mirror and was standing in the front hall gnawing on my thumbnail when the phone rang again. It was Maureen.

"She's not in with the principal. I made an announcement on the PA system asking her to come to the office."

"When was that?"

"Right before I called you."

A small, cold pit of worry was beginning to settle inside my stomach. The school wasn't that big—even if Ellie were in the farthest reaches of the building, she should be at the office in under three minutes. "Can you just put me on hold until she comes to the office?" I asked Maureen.

"Sure." I heard a click, and my ears were assaulted by the very loud radio station the school used as its hold music. I held the phone several inches from my head while I waited. I bit a hangnail on my index finger, then shook my head. "Stop it," I told myself. I paced the kitchen and living room while I waited for Maureen to come back on the line.

About five minutes passed. I had practically worn a hole in the living room carpet when I heard another click, followed by Maureen's voice.

"Dr. Dobbins? She's not here yet. Are you sure your neighbor put her on the bus?"

The cold feeling in my stomach began to grow. "I'll call her again and double check, but she said Ellie got on the bus this morning, just like she normally does."

I dialed Dottie as quickly as I could. "Dottie, you're absolutely sure Ellie got on the bus this morning?" I blurted out before she could even say hello.

"Of course." She sounded a little hurt. "I remember specifically because I noticed as she climbed the steps onto the bus that her hair ribbon had come undone." I'd tied a dark blue grosgrain ribbon in Ellie's hair. "They haven't found her yet?"

"No."

"Is there anything I can do?"

"Not right now. I've got to call the school back." I gave her a perfunctory good-bye and hung up, my breath coming a little faster.

When I called the school again, Maureen put me right through to the principal.

"Dr. Dobbins, I don't want you to worry," she said soothingly. "I'm sure we'll find her. But do you mind coming down here? If she's hiding because there's something bothering her, it might be a good idea to have you nearby just in case."

I called the department chairman on the way to school and spoke to his secretary. I didn't tell her the real reason I was going to be late, opting instead to blame my tardiness on the alarm clock. She said she would relay the message. The chair wouldn't be happy to have to teach my class, but he would have to deal with it.

As I drove, my thoughts began to churn in sync with my stomach. What if Ellie had fallen asleep on the way to school? What if she were stuck on the bus in some parking lot, scared and crying? What if she were sick? Did the bus drivers check for sleeping kids when they finished their routes?

Worst of all, what if she had been kidnapped?

* * *

There was a bus in the parking lot when I got to the school. Walking past it, I tried to peer in the windows for a glimpse of Ellie. But I wasn't tall enough to see anything. I pressed the buzzer to be admitted to the main office.

Maureen sat at her desk, frowning at her computer screen and talking on the phone. She waved me right into Mrs. Ravell's office.

The principal sat behind her desk, also on the phone. Two women sat opposite Mrs. Ravell. I recognized one of them right away as Ellie's bus driver. It must have been her bus I saw in the parking lot. I nodded to her.

Mrs. Ravell put the phone down and motioned me into a chair between the other women. "Dr. Dobbins, I'm sure you know Mrs. Bennett, Ellie's bus driver." I nodded. "And this is Mrs. Garcia, this week's bus monitor," she said, indicating the second woman.

"Hi," I greeted her as I sat down. She flashed a worried smile at me.

Mrs. Ravell began speaking. "Mrs. Bennett has double- and triple-checked the seats, and the bus is empty of children. Mrs. Garcia is a first-grade teacher whose responsibility this week is to monitor the children getting off the buses. She got here only a moment before you did." She turned her attention to Mrs. Bennett.

"Did you see Ellie Gramercy get off the bus this morning?"

The bus driver shrugged. "I assume she did since the bus is empty, but I'm not sure that I paid attention to *her* getting off the bus specifically. There's a lot going on when the kids are getting to school, so it's hard to notice one particular child."

Mrs. Ravell nodded. "I understand." She turned to me. "Once they get off the buses, the kids line up and go into the school single file." She looked at Mrs. Garcia. "Did you see any child getting out of line this morning?"

Mrs. Garcia shook her head. "I didn't notice anyone out of line, but there was a commotion involving two kids getting off the bus behind Mrs. Bennett's. I suppose I could have missed something."

"Is there just one teacher out front to supervise all the buses unloading?" I asked.

Mrs. Ravell shifted in her seat, looking uncomfortable. "Yes. We've never needed more than that. I stand in the vestibule and greet the kids as they come in, but there's only one member of the staff out there. Plus the bus drivers, of course."

"There's another thing we can check. There are security cameras mounted by the front doors to the school, and they capture the buses loading and unloading. I'll have our AV tech pull those up and we can have a look at them." She picked up her phone and spoke to Maureen, asking her to find the tech and send him in.

Shouldn't that have been done already? A surge of anger flooded through me.

Mrs. Bennett and Mrs. Garcia left, leaving me alone with the principal. I caught myself biting my fingernail again and forced myself to stop by interlacing my fingers. "You've checked the nurse's office?" I asked Mrs. Ravell.

She sighed and nodded. "No one has seen Ellie this morning."

There was a knock at the door and it opened slowly. A bearded man peered into the office. "You called for me?"

Mrs. Ravell motioned in my direction. "Gus, this is Dr. Dobbins, Ellie Gramercy's mother. We can't seem to find Ellie in the building, and I'd like you to pull up today's video of the buses unloading to see if we can figure out where Ellie went after she got off the bus."

"Sure." Gus fingered his tie nervously.

Mrs. Ravell moved out of the way as Gus went around her desk and signed into her computer. I walked behind the desk and stood with the principal, watching Gus pull up the video from earlier that morning.

The screen was divided into quarters. Black-and-white images of children jerked across all four boxes. I recognized some of them as kids in Ellie's grade.

Ellie's bus pulled into view, and Mrs. Ravell asked Gus to slow down the video. I watched, unblinking, as kids piled off the bus one by one. I saw Dottie's three children and two other kids from down the block. A tall boy stepped down, and then I spotted her. My little girl was making her way in black and white down the bus steps, her big backpack slung over her shoulder.

"There she is," Mrs. Ravell and I said simultaneously. Gus slowed the video to an agonizing crawl.

We watched as she made her way toward the front of the school. I could see Mrs. Garcia in the background, hurrying over to the bus behind Ellie's to assist with the scuffle she had mentioned.

I kept my eyes on Ellie. She turned her head. She seemed to be looking for something. Then she kept walking across the screen in slow motion.

Then she turned her head again. It looked to me like her eyes narrowed. She stopped walking. The kid behind her walked into her. She looked at the boy, then back again at something off the screen.

She stepped out of line, looking behind her. I could see her eyebrows knit together as she shifted her backpack to the other shoulder.

"What is she doing?" asked Mrs. Ravell.

I shook my head, too intent on watching the video to answer.

"Gus, can you advance the video one frame at a time?" Mrs. Ravell asked.

The video stopped, then moved forward one frame as he pushed a button on the keyboard. Ellie was in mid-step, moving away from the line of students.

Another frame, and she set her foot down on the pavement. Another frame, and she moved again, this time farther away from the line.

Another frame, and now a dark image appeared in the corner. I couldn't tell what it was. But frame by slow frame, Gus moved the video forward, and we could all see that a car was pulling in front of the bus while Ellie walked toward it.

I started taking deep breaths. Mrs. Ravell must have thought I was going to faint, because she gestured to Gus and took my arm, lowering me gently into the chair Gus vacated. I sat down without ever moving my eyes from the screen.

"Do you know whose car that is?" I didn't even know who asked me the question.

I didn't answer. I was watching my daughter approach the passenger side of the car as Gus continued to tap the keyboard slowly. The window on the passenger side was rolled down. Ellie leaned into the window and, frame by frame, she opened the car door and got inside. The car drove off.

My hands were shaking. I pushed the chair back and leaned forward, putting my head between my knees so I wouldn't throw up or faint. Mrs. Ravell picked up her phone and said something to Maureen, but I couldn't hear her because the sound of blood rushing in my ears was too loud.

Gus reversed the video and stopped it again at the point when the car pulled up in front of the bus.

"I can't quite make out what kind of car that is," he said, grimacing and shaking his head.

Maureen came hurrying into the office with a glass of water. "Here, Dr. Dobbins. Drink this. It'll help."

Mrs. Ravell was on the phone again, this time talking to the police. She hung up and pushed another button on her phone. Suddenly I heard her voice over the PA system, announcing a school-wide lockdown. It was strange, hearing her voice over the intercom and also in person, directly in front of me. *Why the lockdown now, when Ellie is gone already?* I stared at her.

As if reading my mind, Mrs. Ravell said gently, "I have to do that. It's school procedure."

I looked away from her and tried again to focus on the black-and-white frames in front of me, but my peripheral vision was going black. I swayed, and Maureen knelt down on the floor between me and the desk, cupping my face in her hands. She spoke sternly.

"Dr. Dobbins, pull yourself together. We have a job to do. Focus now, and help us find Ellie."

Her stern words were exactly what I needed to hear. I sat up a little straighter. Mrs. Ravell spoke up. "The police are on their way. No one else can get in or out until I give the order."

I inched the chair closer to the computer screen, straining my eyes to see what kind of car had pulled in front of Ellie's bus. Maybe if we had that information… But only the front right side of the car was in the image. The make and model were impossible to determine. Tears blurred my vision. I cursed in frustration.

"Are there any other cameras outside the school?" I asked Gus.

"I'll pull up the one closer to the main road."

Ellie's school was in a bucolic setting, with a large park separating it from the road. Anyone driving out of the school's parking lot had to go past the park to get onto the main road. Gus's fingers flew as he pushed several buttons. Before long, a split screen appeared, this time in color. He pushed more buttons, and the frames reversed until the time-stamp on the new video matched the time-stamp on the bus video. He then moved forward through images for several seconds until the car that had been in front of the bus—the car containing my little girl—pulled into view.

It rolled quickly through a stop sign and turned right onto the main road leading past the campus. In a matter of seconds it was out of sight.

It was my ex-husband's car.

"That's Neill," I told Mrs. Ravell and Gus, my breath catching in my throat.

"Ellie's father?" Mrs. Ravell asked.

I nodded, transfixed by the sight of his car driving out of sight on the monitor.

Maureen had returned to the main office and buzzed Mrs. Ravell. "The police are here. I'm sending them in."

There was another knock at the door, and two police officers entered. Mrs. Ravell, who plainly knew both of them, introduced me quickly and outlined what we knew so far from the video surveillance. I stood up, still shaky, and offered her chair to one of the officers. He sat down and asked Gus to pull up the video from the line of buses. The other officer took out his phone and turned his back to the rest of us. I couldn't hear what he was saying. After a moment, he clicked off the phone and joined us around the desk.

The officer at the computer turned to me. "You're sure this is your ex-husband's car?"

"Yes."

"Do you happen to know the license plate number?"

I shook my head, mentally kicking myself for not memorizing Neill's license plate. The officer swiveled back to the monitor and watched the video several times, moving the frames backward and forward, with the second officer leaning over his shoulder. Finally he looked up at Gus and asked to see the video closer to the main road. Gus complied rapidly, and in just a moment, the officers were watching Ellie disappear over and over again as they reversed and forwarded the frames again.

"Wait." The second officer pointed to the screen. "Can you reverse that? Just one frame." We all crowded around the computer to see what the officer was pointing to.

"See that? It's a partial plate." We hadn't noticed it before. He turned to Gus. "Can you enlarge that frame?"

Gus pushed more keys and the frame appeared larger on the screen. If I stepped back from the computer and strained my eyes, I could make out four grainy letters on the license plate. The officer standing next to me got on his phone again, relaying numbers and letters to the person on the other end of the line. He clicked off the phone again. "We'll get that information disseminated right away. He won't be able to get far before someone sees him."

The two officers talked to each other in low voices while I stared at the computer screen. Mrs. Ravell gestured toward Gus and spoke to him privately next to the door. It was only a few moments before my phone vibrated. I yanked it out of my pocket, hoping Neill had come to his senses and was bringing Ellie back to school. But then I noticed that Mrs. Ravell and Gus were looking at their phone screens, too. We had all been contacted at the same time.

It was an Amber Alert. I should have expected it, but I looked at the screen in confusion. It took me a second to realize I was reading Neill's license plate number and physical descriptions of him and Ellie. My memory jerked back to the times I had received Amber Alerts for other missing children. I always felt a jolt of dread for the child and the parents involved. I would look at the cars and people around me to see if any of them matched the descriptions in the alert. But when they didn't, the Amber Alert would melt into the background of my mind as I returned to whatever task was at hand. I almost never gave the alert a second thought. It didn't involve me, so I never bothered to find out what happened to the child or the family who was the focus of the alert. And I felt a sudden stab of guilt and regret for all the times I didn't spare any more pain for those people. Suddenly that pain was fiercely personal. It didn't seem possible for this to be happening to my family. This was something that happened to other people. I wanted the nightmare to stop.

Chapter 2

"Is there a place where we can talk to Dr. Dobbins privately?" one of the policemen asked Mrs. Ravell. She showed us to a small conference room and departed, closing the door quietly behind her.

"I'm Sergeant Boyd," he said, "And this is Sergeant Templeton. Now I want you to start at the beginning and tell us what happened with you and your ex-husband."

I took a deep breath to try to steady my nerves. As horrified as I was, this was no time to lose control of myself.

"My ex-husband and I divorced about three years ago," I began. "I got primary custody, but he gets Ellie one night a week and every Saturday."

"Why did you divorce?" Officer Boyd asked.

"Irreconcilable differences," I said, hoping they wouldn't pry any further.

"Such as?" Officer Boyd prompted.

"I found out he had a gambling addiction," I stated. "It led to arguments, secrecy, you know. I couldn't take it anymore and I left him. I took Ellie with me."

"Has he ever abused Ellie?"

I shook my head. "No. Definitely not."

"So it's normal for her to go in the car with him?"

"I suppose so, but not on a weekday and certainly not at the start of the school day. He must have told her something that sounded urgent enough for her to leave the line of kids going into school. Maybe he told her I was sick. He could have told her anything. Do you think you can catch him?"

"I hope so." The full importance of what was happening hit me just then. I tried to catch my breath as I bent forward. The police officer grabbed my arm and helped me to slide to the floor, where I sat with my back against the wall. The sounds in the room seemed to subside into a murky black background.

The next thing I knew, Officer Templeton was bent over me saying, "Dr. Dobbins, stay with me. I need your help, Doctor. You have to help us." It was the second time that morning someone had reminded me to remain focused, remain alert. But I just couldn't bear the weight that was pressing down on my chest, making it hard to breathe and making clear thoughts impossible. Only one thing was screaming its way through my head:

Neill has Ellie.

Neill has Ellie.

I was living in a nightmare.

What did he want with her, anyway? Where could he be going with her? I looked up into Officer Templeton's face. I could see the concern in his eyes. He took my arm and helped me to sit up. Maureen appeared out of thin air with smelling salts and a glass of orange juice. I nodded my thanks, unable to speak, and tried to focus on what the officer was saying, but I realized he wasn't talking to me. He was talking to Officer Boyd. I could only hear snatches of the conversation.

"...check his last known address..."

"...find out where he works..."

"...issue an APB..."

"Dr. Dobbins?" Hearing my name jerked me out of my trance. It was Officer Boyd.

"Yes?"

"We need some information from you about your ex-husband."

I nodded. What followed was an exchange I barely could recall later. I dimly remember telling him that Neill was an English professor and that he had an apartment about thirty minutes away. I must have given him other information, too, but I don't remember what it was.

The police issued instructions to Mrs. Ravell to end the lockdown. They were quite sure this was an isolated event. "Domestic incident" they called it, though Neill wasn't part of our household anymore. As they prepared to leave the school, Officer Boyd asked me to accompany him to the police station to provide a list of Neill's family contacts.

"I'll have to stop at home to get my address book," I said.

"You don't have the contacts on you? On your phone?"

"No. I don't have anything to do with his family."

"I'll follow you."

We drove to my house, which was a short distance from the school. On the way I dialed Neill's mobile phone. No answer, as I suspected. As I pulled into the driveway, Dottie came running across the street.

"I've been waiting for you!" She glanced nervously at the police car out of the corner of her eye. "What on earth is going on?"

"Neill took Ellie from school."

She gasped, her hand flying to her mouth. "Where did he take her?"

"That's the problem. We don't know. Dottie, I'm sorry, but I've got to get numbers for Neill's family and get down to the police station. I'll tell you everything later." I was walking up the front steps and opening the front door as I spoke.

She nodded. "Let me know if you need anything, honey. Anything."

I closed the door behind me and ran into the office. I rifled through stacks of papers on my desk, finally locating the leather-bound book that contained the names and contact information of Neill's family.

I took the book with me and went out the front door, locking it behind me.

In my haste, I hadn't noticed anything amiss in my office. Knowing what I do now, I wish I had looked more closely.

Chapter 3

I followed Officer Boyd to the police station, and he ushered me into an office. Sitting down opposite me at a utilitarian table, he took out a pen and pad and waited for me to open the address book.

"Whose name do you want first?" I asked.

"Parents and then siblings."

I flipped through several pages. "His parents' names are Janet and Alistair Gramercy," I said as I ran my finger down a page. "They live outside Edinburgh, in Scotland."

"They don't live in the U.S.?"

"No. His whole family lives in Scotland."

"Is that where he's from?"

"Yes."

Officer Boyd jumped up and left the room. I waited nervously for several minutes until he returned. "Why didn't you tell me he's not from the U.S.?" he asked as he came back through the door.

I was bewildered. "I … I didn't realize that was important."

He rubbed his forehead. "That kind of information is always important."

"I'm sorry. I didn't realize."

"I notice you speak with an accent. Are you also from Scotland?"

"Yes."

"How long have you lived in the United States?"

"About seven years. Since before Ellie was born."

"And you've been divorced for three years?"

"Yes."

"Tell me more about your ex-husband's gambling addiction."

I tried to answer fully without telling him the whole story. "I didn't see it coming. We'd been having problems, and all of a sudden I found out that he owed money to people I'd never heard of. And he was afraid of them. It wasn't safe for me or Ellie anymore."

"Do you think these people may have had something to do with Ellie's disappearance?"

"I have no idea."

"What brought you to the U.S.?"

"My job and Neill's job."

"And what do you do?"

"I'm an art history professor." He scribbled something down on the pad in front of him, then gave me a hard look.

"I'm sorry," I repeated.

"Just give me the rest of the contact info."

I gave him the address and telephone number of Neill's parents. Officer Boyd glanced at his watch.

"What time is it there?"

"They're four hours ahead."

"I'll be back in a minute."

I listened to the sounds coming down the hall of the police station while I tried not to bite my fingernails down to the quicks. The air smelled of stale coffee and garlic. My stomach and head ached, and my breath came in shallow bursts. *Where did he go? What is he doing? Is he calling Janet and Alistair? Why doesn't he hurry?*

I pulled out my mobile phone and tried calling my own parents. No service. I slapped the phone down on the table in frustration.

Officer Boyd returned several long minutes later. "I've got someone trying to get in touch with Neill's parents."

"What's being done to find Neill and Ellie?"

Rather than answer my question, he posed one of his own. "Have you tried contacting Neill?"

"Yes. In the car on the way from the school to my house. He didn't answer. It didn't even go to voice mail." He furrowed his brow, and I repeated my question. "What's being done to find Neill and Ellie?"

"We've got a bulletin out for his car and we've alerted the airports in the area."

"Airports?"

"We can't rule out Neill taking Ellie to Scotland. Or anywhere else."

"He can't do that! I have her passport."

"On you?"

I hesitated. "No, I keep it in a safe in my house."

"Not in a safe-deposit box?"

"No."

"I want you to get that passport and bring it to me."

"Right now?"

He let out an exasperated sigh. "Yes. Right now."

I grabbed my handbag from the table and practically ran out of the room, down the echoing station hallway, and out into the parking lot, where the sunshine was rapidly being replaced by dark gray clouds.

I made it to my house in record time. Fumbling with the key to the front door, hot tears began to prick the insides of my eyelids.

"Greer, are you all right?" Dottie. I hadn't heard her coming. I groaned inwardly as I turned to face her. I didn't need an audience right now. "Hi."

She took one look at me and wrapped me in a big hug. I must have looked worse than I thought. I finally broke down and started to sob. "I'm sorry, Dottie. I'm just overwhelmed."

"Of course you are, honey," she said gently, smoothing my hair. "What can I do?"

I sniffled and wiped my eyes. "Nothing, I guess. I'm here to pick up Ellie's passport to take it to the police station."

"Why?" Dottie gave me a puzzled look.

"I guess they want to make sure Neill doesn't take her out of the country, since he's not from the U.S. and his family lives abroad. I'll call you the minute I know anything," I promised her.

She hugged me again. "Okay. Make sure you do. And let me know if you need me."

I had opened the door and dropped my purse on the hall floor. The safe was in a corner of my office. I switched on the desk lamp and glanced toward the corner.

The safe door was open.

"Dottie!" I screamed.

I heard her clattering back up the front steps a moment later as I sat on the floor, stunned.

"What is it?" she yelled, charging into the office.

"The safe door is open." I jammed my hand into my pocket and pulled out Officer Boyd's card. "Will you call this number? Officer Boyd is helping me."

She rushed over to the phone on my desk while I pulled everything out of the safe into a heap on the floor. Bank documents, gift certificates, receipts, Ellie's baby book, countless pieces of paper.

But no passports. Not hers; not mine.

I tore through everything again, hoping I had just missed the passports. Behind me, Dottie was on hold for Officer Boyd. After a moment, she handed the phone to me.

"Officer Boyd? Ellie's passport isn't here. Mine isn't, either."

"Are you sure?"

"Yes," I said, holding back a scream. Out of the corner of my eye, I could see Dottie, still as a statue, her hand over her mouth.

"Is there any other place they could be? A dresser? A desk drawer? Maybe you put them somewhere else and forgot about it?" Officer Boyd asked.

"No. I took Ellie to Vancouver two months ago, and I distinctly remember putting the passports in there after we got back. I haven't touched them since."

"Where do you keep the key? Or the combination?"

I groaned. "I don't keep the safe locked. I didn't want to have to worry about getting locked out of it if I forgot the combination or if I lost the key, so I just leave it unlocked."

I could practically see Officer Boyd shaking his head in disbelief. Dottie had come up behind me and put her arm around my shoulder.

"Officer? What now?"

"Sit tight and I'll call you back." He hung up.

"Dottie, what have I done?" I whispered.

"You couldn't have guessed this would happen," she said.

"I should have guessed," I insisted. "I should have known something like this was possible."

"Let me get you some tea while you get these papers cleaned up. I don't want to interfere with the things you have in the safe, or I'd help you."

"Thanks," I said listlessly. I began gathering papers into small piles, but I couldn't sit still. I paced across the front of the house, looking out each window in turn. Maybe I expected to see Neill drive up with Ellie, but the street remained empty of cars. I tried my parents again. It was early afternoon at their house. My mother answered the phone.

"Mum? It's Greer."

"What's wrong?" I could hear the alarm in her voice immediately.

"Neill took Ellie from school this morning. I don't know where they're going." I started to cry again.

"What? Are you sure?"

"Yes."

"Where could he have taken her?"

"I don't know."

"Are the police looking for them?"

"Of course."

"What can I do to help you?"

"I don't know," I managed to say, choking on the words. I wished for the hundredth time that my mother didn't live on the other side of the Atlantic Ocean.

"Do you want me to come?"

"I don't know," I said again. "I don't know if there's anything you can do."

"I can check flights. I doubt if I can get a flight out tonight, but there'll be flights in the morning. I can drive down to London and leave from there. Edinburgh is closer, but there are probably better flights out of London."

"Let me think about it and I'll call you back. Thanks, Mum."

Dottie came back in with two mugs of tea. She handed one to me. I couldn't drink it. The lump in my throat was too big. I thought I would be sick if I tried eating or drinking anything.

"Drink it," Dottie urged me. "It'll help. It's good and strong. And hot."

I took a tiny sip to make her happy and burned my tongue and throat. "Ouch," I croaked. I set the mug down.

"Sorry. Maybe a little too hot."

"That's okay."

"What are the police doing?"

"I have no idea. I'm waiting for them to call me back. Where do you suppose Neill took Ellie?"

Of course Dottie didn't know where they were, but I needed her opinion. She had been a good friend for the past six years, since we moved to her neighborhood several months before Ellie was born. She had supported me through my divorce and had always been a shoulder for me to lean on.

"I wish I knew," she answered, her mouth set in a grim line. "I'm sure the police are doing everything they can right now."

"I just wish I could do something. I can't stand this waiting."

"I know, Greer, but what if he brings her back here? You'll want to be here."

I seized on the idea. "Do you think he'll bring her home? Do you think he just took her to scare me but he doesn't really want to keep her?"

She shook her head slowly. "I don't know. But I hope he does. Maybe he'll wise up and realize he's made a mistake."

"Or maybe he'll figure there's no going back now that he's taken her and he'll dig in his heels," I countered.

"Let's not think about that possibility. Let's stay positive," she suggested.

"I'm going upstairs. I need to have a look around Ellie's room," I told her.

"Are you sure that's a good idea?" she asked. "What if the police want to have a look in there? You don't want to disturb anything."

I hadn't thought of that. "You're probably right. I won't touch anything."

I went upstairs and stood in the doorway of Ellie's room. Her bed was made, her stuffed animals in a heap on top. I scanned the room, looking for anything amiss, but there was nothing out of the ordinary. I walked down the hall to the guest room, which Ellie sometimes used as a playroom. Her toys were strewn about.

Suddenly my breath was coming in gasps and I couldn't stop it. I was in a full panic. Dottie was at my side in an instant. "I'll be right back."

She hurtled down the stairs and was back in a moment carrying a brown paper bag. I couldn't catch my breath.

"Here," she ordered, bunching up the top of the bag and handing it to me. "Breathe into this." She sat down next to me on the floor and put her hand on my back while I took huge, deep gasps into the bag, finally slowing my heart rate and my breathing. After several minutes I was breathing normally again.

Dottie took my hand and led me to the loft outside the guest room. She sat me down on the couch. "I want you to lie down right here."

I started to protest.

"No," she said, holding up her hand. "You need to calm down."

I couldn't rest. I sat on the couch, scrolling through texts I had received from Neill over the past several weeks. There weren't many. I was searching for any clue he might have let slip about his plan to take Ellie. I couldn't find anything. Dottie finally sat down next to me, watching me with pity in her eyes.

My stomach was in knots. My head hurt. I felt like I weighed a million pounds. "Dottie," I said, "I have to *do* something. I don't know where to start."

"Is it possible Neill contacted Ellie before he took her?"

I stared at her in confusion. "You mean, told her he was taking her somewhere?" I shook my head. "No. No. That's not possible. She would have told me."

Wouldn't she?

"I mean, maybe he told her they were going to do something fun, just the two of them, and maybe he told her not to tell you. Would she tell?" Dottie said.

Her suggestion threw me into a state of uncertainty and doubt. What if Neill had told Ellie not to tell me? She was still little. She knew about stranger danger, but she would trust her own father if he told her to keep a secret.

I jumped up and ran into Ellie's room. I didn't know what I was looking for—maybe a hint that she knew that Neill was going to pick her up at school that morning. Maybe she took a change of clothes with her. Maybe she took a favorite toy in her backpack. I didn't care if I was disturbing anything the police might want to see.

I tore through her dresser drawers, looking for anything that might be missing or out of place. She had more clothes than I did. I didn't keep a mental inventory of all of her outfits, but I knew her favorites. She had a pair of jeans that she would wear every day of the week if I let her, and I didn't see those in her room. I ran downstairs to the laundry room, where I dumped the baskets of dirty clothes onto the floor. Tossing garments aside, I went through all the laundry.

Her jeans weren't there.

I dashed upstairs to her room, where I went through her dresser again, double-checking for her jeans. They were gone. I rifled through the T-shirts next, but didn't notice anything missing. But then again, I probably wouldn't because she had so many. I yanked open the closet door, confident that I would immediately notice missing dresses or skirts. But they were all there.

"Are you all right?" Dottie said from behind me. I peered around Ellie's closet door.

"Her jeans are missing. Her favorite jeans. They're not in here, and they're not in the laundry."

"Have you called the police yet?"

"Not yet. I was looking to see if there's anything else missing."

"How about her toys?"

I scanned Ellie's bed. All her best animal friends were there, staring at me, watching me fall apart.

"They're all there."

"You'd better call the police and tell them about the jeans."

The phone rang. I jumped, startled, then looked at Dottie. "What if it's Neill?"

"Answer it! Talk to him!"

I grabbed the phone and answered it breathlessly. "Hello? Neill?"

"It's Officer Boyd, Dr. Dobbins. Have you heard from Neill?"

I let out a disappointed sigh. "No. I was hoping you were him."

"Sorry, ma'am. Have you located the passports?"

"No. They're gone. Neill must have taken them. He must be planning to take Ellie somewhere. Ellie's favorite jeans are missing, too."

"Are you sure? Have you looked everywhere for them?"

"Yes."

"I'm on my way over to your house right now with a detective. We're going to take a look around and see if we can find anything. You'll be there?"

"Yes, of course."

"We'll be right over."

Dottie helped me put Ellie's things back into her dresser, and then we went downstairs. The police arrived just a few minutes later. I introduced Dottie to Officer Boyd. He introduced us to the other officer, Detective West.

Officer Boyd took charge when we were all seated in the living room. "So tell me about the jeans," he said briskly.

"They're blue denim with Xs in bright green stitching on the back pockets. She loves them. I've looked through all her drawers and in the laundry and they're not here. She must have taken them."

"Which means that she knew Neill was planning to pick her up," Officer Boyd mused.

Detective West spoke up. "I'd like to go to Ellie's room with Dr. Dobbins and look for anything else that might be missing."

Officer Boyd nodded, looking at me. "I'm going to ask—Dottie, is it?—some questions. Then I'd like you to show me where you keep your safe, and I'll take a look around that room."

I showed Detective West where Ellie's room was, then opened the drawer where she kept her jeans. There were still several pairs in there, and Detective West took them out one by one and examined them.

"You're sure the jeans with the green Xs aren't somewhere else in the house?" he asked.

"Positive."

I watched as he looked through the rest of the dresser drawers, then started searching the closet. He made several notes in a small notebook he was carrying. "Have you gone through the pockets in all her clothes?"

"No. I hadn't gotten to that yet."

"Let's do that now. We'll need to know if he gave her a note."

The long minutes ticked by as we went through all the pockets in her clothing. Officer Boyd came to her bedroom door while we were working.

"Got anything?" he asked.

"Not yet," grunted the detective, reaching his thick fingers into a tiny hip pocket in a pair of Ellie's shorts.

"Dr. Dobbins, I'd like you to show me where the safe is now," Officer Boyd said.

He accompanied me to the office and followed me to the safe. I took out all the documents and set them on the floor as he pulled a chair over from the desk. I left him alone to meticulously go through each pile while I returned to Ellie's room.

Detective West stood up when I entered. "There's nothing in any of her pockets. Is there anything else I should see?" he asked.

I didn't know what might be important and what wasn't. "I'm…I'm not sure," I stammered. "Do you want to see the laundry?"

"Yes. We'd better go through that, too. Have you looked through her desk?"

I shook my head. "Not yet. Do you want to go through it?"

"Yes. Does she have a diary?"

An irrational surge of hope swelled up in me. I had forgotten about the diary she kept in the top drawer of her desk. I crossed the room in one step and pulled the drawer open, shuffling through the artwork, crayons, colored pencils, and paperback chapter books.

"Here it is!" I pulled out the lavender book with the small brass plate and tiny keyhole. I fingered the dark purple ribbon that acted as a bookmark. The key was attached to the ribbon. I handed the book to the detective.

He unlocked the book and leafed through it slowly, his eyes scanning each page. Too anxious to wait for him to finish reading, I looked over his shoulder and read the pages, too. A lump in my throat grew as I thought about Ellie's thin fingers, carefully printing the words in the diary. Words she thought were for her eyes only.

Her entries were sporadic; she only seemed to write when something exciting or fun or especially upsetting had occurred. She had written about our trip to Vancouver and drawn little pictures in the margins. She had written about the day we went to the zoo, and about the night her pet bunny died.

Nothing about Neill.

Detective West closed the book. "Do you mind if I take this with me back to the station?"

"Not at all. Do you think there's something in there that could help find Ellie and Neill?"

"I don't know yet, but I'd like to go over it again."

I led him downstairs to the laundry room, where he lifted up the dirty clothes one piece at a time, putting everything in neat piles on the floor. I watched him from the doorway. He finally turned to me and asked, "Have you noticed anything else missing besides the jeans? Maybe pajamas or socks and underwear?"

I hadn't even thought of looking for Ellie's pajamas. I ran upstairs and rifled through her dresser drawers again, looking for her two favorite pj sets. One set was missing. I looked around on the floor, where Detective West had left some articles of clothing during his search of the dresser drawers. They weren't there.

Carrying the other set, I returned to Detective West, who was going through all the pockets of the dirty clothes. "Her favorite pajamas are gone."

"What are those?" he asked, nodding at the outfit I held in my hand.

I held them up and looked at them listlessly, as though seeing them for the first time. "This is her other favorite set."

"Can I take those with me?" he asked.

"Go ahead."

He dropped them in a plastic bag, sealed it, and scrawled something across the front. As he was capping his pen, Officer Boyd came in.

"I got prints from the safe, though I'm relatively certain it was Neill who took the passports."

"So what next?" I asked.

"I'll contact the area airports again and we'll double down on watching out for them." The mobile phone on his hip beeped.

"Yeah," he answered.

He nodded while listening to the voice on the other end. Then he turned the phone off before saying,

"They have a lead on the car your ex was driving."

Hope surged in my chest and I took a sharp breath. "What lead?"

"Two officers found it parked in a lot downtown. It's being canvassed now for evidence."

"Any sign of Neill and Ellie?"

"No. The car was empty. But hopefully they left behind something that will give us a clue as to where they're headed."

The detective finished going through the laundry, and both men followed me out to the kitchen, where Dottie was preparing more tea. "I'm heading over to the station to talk to the officers who found the car and to have a look at it myself," Officer Boyd said. "It's in the impound lot. Dr. Dobbins, we'll be in touch soon. In the meantime, please let us know if you hear from Neill, Ellie, or anyone in Neill's family."

"Okay."

The officers left, and Dottie and I returned to the living room, where I sank into an armchair.

"How are you holding up?" asked Dottie.

"Not so well." Tears welled up in my eyes again and spilled slowly down my cheeks. "What if Ellie gets sick? She needs me when she's sick," I sniffled. I looked at Dottie. "Neill doesn't know how to take care of her like I do." The sobs came then. My body shook as I cried, my hands over my face, my body bent forward in the chair. I didn't care that Dottie was in the room with me, didn't care how I looked or how I sounded. Didn't care about anything except finding Ellie, wondering where she was and if she was okay. And through the pain, I felt the beginning of a hard, hot pellet of hatred for Neill. How could he do this to me and to Ellie?

When I had cried all the tears I could, I was exhausted. Over my protests that I wouldn't sleep, Dottie took me upstairs to my room, where she pulled the shades and helped me lie down on the bed.

"You'll tell me if you hear anything, right?" I asked her, my voice wild with panic and fatigue.

"Of course I will," she soothed.

She went into my bathroom and reappeared with a glass of water and a Xanax, an old one left over from the many sleepless nights I suffered following the divorce. I resisted, telling her that I wanted to wake up quickly if I needed to.

"That's why I'm only giving you one pill," she replied. "Greer, there's nothing you can do right now except rest and shore up your strength. The pill will help you sleep and help steer your mind from places it shouldn't go."

I was too tired to resist any longer. I reached for the pill and swallowed it quickly, then settled my head on the pillow as Dottie left the darkened room quietly. *How odd to escape a nightmare by going to sleep* was my last thought before the medicine started to work.

Chapter 4

I was jarred awake by the sound of my bedroom door opening. Dottie peered into the room. For a moment I was confused. Had I overslept? Why was she here?

But all too soon, the day's horrors came rushing back.

"Greer? Are you awake? Phone call for you."

I jumped out of bed, swaying with grogginess. Dottie hurried in and grabbed my arm, steadying me, then handed me the phone. I clutched it as if it were a lifeline.

"Hello?"

"Dr. Dobbins, this is Officer Boyd. Just checking in to let you know I had a look at Neill's car. It's been dusted for prints, but since we already know Neill and Ellie were in it, I suspect we won't get any more information from it. There was nothing else in the car to give us a clue as to their whereabouts. Have you heard anything?"

"No, no one has called. Is there something I can be doing to help you?"

"No. Just sit tight and wait for me or Detective West to call. Let me know if you hear anything."

I looked at my wristwatch. I hadn't slept very long. Now that I was awake, I knew I wouldn't be able to fall asleep again. I couldn't sit around and do nothing. I reached for my purse.

"Where are you going?" Dottie asked.

"Over to the school. I have to talk to Ellie's teacher."

"I'm sure the principal and the police have already done that." I knew Dottie wasn't trying to keep me from staying active and involved, but that's the way it sounded.

"I know," I replied crossly. "It's just that there might be something she forgot to tell them. Maybe I can get her to remember."

"Do you want me to go with you?"

"Can you stay here in case Neill or the police call? I'll have my mobile on, but the reception at the school is bad. If you hear anything from anyone, call the school and have them page me." With that, I ran out the door.

When I got to Ellie's school, there were two police cars in the parking lot. Maureen was back at the front desk. "Any word?" she asked anxiously as I walked in.

"No. I was hoping I could talk to Mrs. Dennis for a few minutes."

"Sure. Let me call her down. The police have already talked to her. They're in her classroom now." She dialed Mrs. Dennis's classroom and spoke for a moment. She hung up and said, "Mrs. Ravell is in the room with the officers while they're talking to the kids, so Mrs. Dennis can come to the office now. You can go into the conference room where you talked to the police earlier and have some privacy."

I thanked her and paced the office while I waited for Mrs. Dennis. When she arrived, she swept over and hugged me. "How are you doing, Dr. Dobbins?"

"Please call me Greer. And I'm not doing too well, as you can imagine."

She studied my face. "I'm so sorry about all of this. I don't know what I can tell you that I haven't already told the police, but let's go sit down and talk." She led the way to the conference room, and we sat down opposite each other at the table.

"What would you like to know?" Mrs. Dennis began.

"You can tell me everything you know about Neill."

"I've only talked to him a couple times," she replied, folding her hands on the tabletop. "I think all of our conversations have been about Ellie's progress. He seems very involved."

I nodded.

"I'm so sorry you're going through this," she repeated. "It's every parent's worst nightmare," she added unhelpfully. Maybe it was because we were talking about Neill, but Mrs. Dennis was starting to get on my nerves.

"Thank you," I said. "Does Ellie ever talk about her father?"

She was silent for a moment, then said, "She has mentioned him a couple times. I think the first time she said she doesn't see him very often, then another time she said he's from Scotland."

"But she never said that he tried to contact her?"

Mrs. Dennis shook her head immediately. "No. I'm sure of that."

"Did she ever say she had plans I might not know about?"

"Not that I'm aware of."

I tried another avenue of questioning. "Has Ellie ever spoken of her family in Scotland?

She thought for a moment before answering. "She's spoken before of 'Granny,' but I wasn't sure which set of grandparents she was talking about. I don't even know if there are two sets of grandparents."

"There are. Ellie doesn't really know Neill's parents, but we've spoken of them before. We call Neill's mother Granny and my mother Mimsy." Mrs. Dennis gave me a strange look. "It's what my mother wanted," I explained. "What did Ellie tell you about Granny?"

"Only that Granny has cows and sheep."

"That's right," I said, thinking back to the last encounter I had with my mother-in-law. "Has she ever spoken of any other family?"

Mrs. Dennis shook her head slightly. "No, I don't think so. If I remember something, I'll surely let you know."

"How about her artwork?" I pressed. I knew from anecdotal research that children often revealed themselves in astonishing ways through art. "Is there any indication in the artwork she does at school that would suggest that she had a secret? That she was going on a trip? That there was something I didn't know about?"

"I don't think so. Her pictures are very much like the pictures of most of the other children—sunshine, trees, families holding hands. That sort of thing."

"How many people are in Ellie's pictures?"

"Always three—Ellie and you and her father. You are always standing on either side of her, never together."

"That makes sense," I said wryly.

"She has mentioned that you and her father are divorced, but she told me in a whisper, like it's a secret. I already knew, of course," Mrs. Dennis said.

"I know," I sighed. "It never bothered her too much until she started school. I think she's sad because she hears the other kids talking about their parents and she wonders why her mum and dad don't live together. It's actually made her sick several times since school started."

"Poor thing," Mrs. Dennis clucked. "I'm sorry I can't be of more help."

I thanked her and went back home, where Dottie was waiting at the kitchen table.

"Anything?" she asked.

I shook my head and sat down across from her. She put her hands over mine. We sat in silence for several minutes.

I felt like I needed to go somewhere, do something, but I was stuck waiting, not knowing what to do or where to go. I went upstairs to Ellie's room to look around again and practically ransacked her drawers and closet, rifling through all the clothes Detective West had examined, hoping to find something we both had missed.

But eventually I had to acknowledge that we had missed nothing—there was no clue to suggest where Ellie and Neill might be.

I went to the bathroom and splashed cold water on my face. I was drying off when the phone rang.

"This is Detective West. I've spoken to Dottie's three children, the kids in Ellie's class, and several teachers. No one seems to know anything about Ellie going somewhere. I'm not surprised. In a situation like this, the non-custodial parent would be foolish to tell the child exactly where they were headed. It's not unheard of to tell the child they're going somewhere, but it's usually presented as a secret, something the child shouldn't tell anyone, even the custodial parent. Very often it's even touted as a surprise for the custodial parent, and the child thinks he or she is going somewhere special and that the whole family is going to be involved."

"Do you think that's what happened?"

"It's beginning to look that way. Now all we have to do is figure out where they went."

Chapter 5

For the next hour, I called Neill's colleagues in the English department at the university. They all seemed surprised he hadn't come to work without phoning anyone or notifying his students and his department chair, but no one knew where he was. One or two mentioned they had noticed that Neill seemed rather anxious lately, but couldn't shed any light on the reason. After I got off the phone, I wandered through the house aimlessly, jumping at every sound and looking through the curtains every time I walked past them, seeing no one. I had never felt so helpless. Waiting for news from the police was agonizing.

When they finally called, I snatched up the phone breathlessly. "Dr. Dobbins, this is Detective West. I think we've got a hit on them."

"Where?" I demanded.

"We think they've been spotted on video surveillance at the airport."

"Which airport?"

"Albany, New York."

"You think you saw them? Can't you tell for sure?"

"No, ma'am. Your ex-husband's head was down most of the time, and Ellie was dressed like a boy."

"But she has long hair. Couldn't you see that in the video?"

"The child had short hair, ma'am."

"Are you telling me she's had her hair cut since this morning?"

"Yes, ma'am. That is a possibility."

I closed my eyes, the silence lingering across the telephone line. I'd heard of things like this happening, but always on television. Never to me.

"Dr. Dobbins? You still there?"

"Yes, Detective. Sorry. I'm just trying to wrap my head around this."

"Can you come down to the station? Airport security in Albany has copied the video and sent it over. I'd like you to have a look at it and tell me if you recognize them."

"I'll be right there. Are there police at the airport to arrest Neill?"

"We don't know if he's still there, ma'am. We're continuing to piece together the videos."

I drove to the police station in a daze of confusion and disbelief. Detective West was waiting for me when I hurried inside the station. He led me to a darkened room with video equipment set up. I waited while he pushed some buttons on a machine in the back of the room. A screen against the wall flickered, and pictures began moving in front of me. People, lots of people, all moving in different directions. Much like the video surveillance at Ellie's school, this screen was divided into four sections. Each section was apparently footage from a different camera.

"Watch that lower left screen," Detective West said. The video slowed. People moved across the screen, slow and jerky. A few seconds passed, and I watched each person intently. Suddenly there was a tall man and a little boy walking hand-in-hand, a big backpack on the boy's shoulders. "Right there," the detective said tersely. I could hear him tapping buttons, and the video slowed.

The man kept his head down, as if he was trying to avoid being spotted on a security camera. The boy with him looked all around, though. At one point he looked directly up at the camera.

I gasped. It was Ellie.

"Stop," I ordered Detective West. The video halted immediately on the frame of the child looking at the camera.

"You see it, too?"

"That's Ellie. I recognize her even with that haircut. Why do you think he cut her hair?"

"So we wouldn't recognize them right away on security cameras."

"Where are they going?"

"We haven't determined that yet," he answered grimly. "We have to figure out their path through the airport using video from the security cameras, and then we'll know where they went."

"Can't we just call the airport and ask someone to look up their names?"

"We've started that process with airport security and the TSA, but getting that information requires special clearance and time. It's quicker to watch the cameras."

"But what if it's too late? What if they've already gotten on a plane and left?" I could hear the panic rising in my voice.

"Let's take this one step at a time. First we have to figure out where they went at the airport."

"How long will it take?" My voice was high and thin.

"We don't know. Why don't you wait out in the lobby, and I'll come for you as soon as I know something." I nodded, unable to say anything.

I sat in the lobby, my breathing shallow and irregular. The desk sergeant took pity on me and offered to get me a cup of coffee. I declined, figuring I would throw up if I put anything in my stomach. It wasn't long before Detective West appeared again. I jumped up at the sight of him.

"Come on back, Dr. Dobbins," he said.

I followed him to his cubicle and sat down across from him yet again. "What have you found?" I asked eagerly.

"The man and child we see on the video are indeed Neill and Ellie," he confirmed. My heart sank. Until that point, I had held out some hope that we were wrong, that the two figures were really a father and son jetting off somewhere. But now I knew for sure.

"Where did they go?" I managed.

"Looks like they went to the Bahamas. A small airport with limited video surveillance capabilities, to be exact."

"Why would they go there?"

"I would guess they're trying to shake the authorities. If that's what Neill is doing, he's done his homework. But they landed half an hour ago, so we've got the Bahamian authorities looking around the airport for them. The security footage isn't available to us yet."

"So what do we do now? Should I go there?" I started to stand, expecting him to tell me to get on the first plane to the Bahamas.

"I would wait. We need to figure out where they went once they got off that plane."

"Do you think they flew somewhere else?" I asked, sitting down on the edge of the seat. My leg jiggled up and down rapidly, almost of its own volition.

"We can't rule that out. They seem to be staying just one step ahead of us."

I sat back. He picked up his phone and punched a string of numbers. After a moment of waiting, he spoke. "It's West. Yeah. Got anything for me?" He nodded. "Uh-huh." Another silence while he listened. "Okay. Thanks." He hung up the phone. "The TSA is in contact with the authorities in the Bahamas. Why don't you go home and wait there? This could take a while."

My shoulders slumped. I wanted everything to happen quickly. I couldn't stand waiting another minute. But I did as Detective West suggested and went home, where I managed to clean up the stack of documents that I had removed from the safe.

It was nearing dinnertime, though I didn't feel at all hungry. When Dottie came over and insisted that I join her family for dinner, I didn't want to go. But she wouldn't take no for answer, so to make her happy, I went back to her house with her. Her husband and kids were there. They clearly didn't know what to say to me. Her husband hugged me at the door and then didn't say much after that. The kids just stared at me. I felt sorry for them. Any other time they would have been talkative and full of energy, but I seemed to have put a damper on dinner. When my phone rang and I took the call in the kitchen, I'm sure they were relieved. I could hear them whispering and Dottie's "Shhhh!"

It was Detective West. He was calling to tell me that Neill had again disguised Ellie as soon as they deplaned in the Bahamas. Their layover was very brief and they had again eluded the authorities. They were now on a plane bound for Edinburgh.

I was exasperated. "How could security let this happen?" I demanded. "How could they let Neill and Ellie slip by them? How many fathers with five-year-old sons could have been arriving in the Bahamas this afternoon?" I knew my voice sounded thin and angry, but I didn't care.

He evaded my questions. "All the authorities are doing everything possible. They'll get him in Edinburgh. The flight is long enough that airport personnel will have time to organize themselves and be waiting for him when he arrives."

"I should have known Neill would go there," I said.

"He did his homework if he wanted to elude police and airport security, but he's not going to give anyone the slip again," Detective West said.

I breathed a small sigh of relief.

It would be over soon.

Chapter 6

When I got home, I realized that I hadn't called my mother since the morning. She must have been beside herself waiting for news about Ellie. I called her right away. "Mum, they're on their way to Edinburgh."

"Thank God you know where they've gone," she said. "Why did it take you so long to call?"

"I've been dealing with the police all day long. I'm sorry." I told her the details of the flight Ellie and Neill were on. "Can you plan to be at the airport when they land? I'm sure they'll take Neill right into custody, and Ellie won't understand what's going on. I want a familiar face there for her."

"Of course," she assured me. "Are you coming, too?"

"Most definitely." I looked at my watch. There would certainly be no direct flights to Edinburgh from Albany, so it would be quicker for me to drive to JFK. "I'll be on the first flight out of New York. I've got to call the airline now and make my reservation. I'll talk to you soon." I called the airline and booked a late-night flight leaving JFK in four hours. The only seats left were in first class, but this was no time to grumble about the cost. I stuffed some clothes in a duffel bag and got in the car. I started the engine and put the car in reverse, then stopped short.

Neill had my passport.

I grabbed my mobile phone and dialed Detective West. He had gone home for the day. I left a message for him to call me as soon as possible and left for the airport. I would have to solve this problem there.

I sped all the way to JFK, and after parking ran into the building and stopped to talk to the first airport employee I found. I briefly explained the problem and asked to talk to someone in security. When I was ushered to the security office, it took some minutes before I found someone who knew about the search for Neill and Ellie earlier in the day. The woman who spoke to me was sympathetic about my missing passport, but there wasn't much she could do to help. She offered to take me over to customs to talk to a supervisor.

As I explained the problem over and over to the people at customs, the long minutes dragged by and my flight time grew closer and closer. I could feel myself getting more upset and weepy. Finally a woman came up to me.

"Are you Dr. Greer Dobbins?" she asked.

"Yes."

"Detective West talked to me earlier today and told me what's going on. He knew you'd have to fly out of JFK tonight. I can help you." I could have hugged her. In just a few moments, I was signing my replacement passport and running to catch my flight to Edinburgh.

I made it just in time. The attendant had finished stacking up her papers and turning to close the door to the Jetway when I ran up, breathless and sweating. "You're lucky," she told me with a smile. "You almost missed it."

I sank into the seat on the plane and ordered a whisky, neat, from the first attendant who walked past me. The man next to me smiled. "Tough day?"

"You have no idea." The attendant brought the drink, and I finished it in a few draughts. I ordered another and drank that one more slowly, holding it in my shaking hand as the plane took off for Scotland.

"Are you all right?" my neighbor asked. I looked at him as if noticing him for the first time. He looked genuinely concerned.

"I will be as soon as we get to Edinburgh," I replied with a wan smile.

"It won't be long now, then," he said. "I'm James Abernathy." His Scottish accent was strong and lilting. I introduced myself and then, hoping I wasn't being too rude, closed my eyes and waited for a small meal to be served. I hadn't eaten much at Dottie's house. All the tension from the day, all the stress and anxiety, began to recede a bit as I settled into my seat, secure in knowing I would be reunited with Ellie in just a few short hours.

I awoke when the flight attendant came by with our meals, complete with wine selection and bread basket. James held up his glass to me and, with a nod and a smile, said *"Slàinte!"*

"Slàinte," I responded, lifting my glass.

I was starving. I tucked into my meal with enthusiasm, not caring whether my neighbor wondered if I always ate like that.

After the flight attendant had cleared away the tray, I leaned back and looked out the window at the dark sky.

"Beautiful, isn't it?" James asked.

"It is," I agreed.

"Are you from Edinburgh?" he asked.

"No, I'm from Dumfries. I've been living in the States for years, but my mother still lives in Dumfries. I spent quite a bit of time in Edinburgh growing up, you know, school holidays and summers. We would drive up from Dumfries and stay often. Are you from Edinburgh?"

"I am indeed," he answered proudly. "A beautiful city."

"Gorgeous," I agreed.

"Are you visiting your family?"

"Sort of," I said. I saw his gaze flicker to my left ring finger, naked of jewelry.

He sipped his wine. "The weather in Edinburgh has been getting a bit cooler lately. Winter won't be long now."

"I love Scotland in the winter," I replied.

"You like it?" he asked incredulously.

"Love it," I repeated. "There's something about the city on the cold, dark, rainy days that I find irresistible."

He thought for a moment. "I agree that the city *is* especially beautiful during the dark season, but that cold...." He shivered for effect, a smile on his face. "Brrr. I prefer the warmth of summertime."

"The museums are always warm in the winter, so they're fun to visit when the weather is very ugly," I said.

"I know. I work in one of them."

"Oh? Which one?"

"The Artists' Museum."

"I've been there," I said excitedly. "It's one of my favorites. What do you do there?"

"I'm the collections curator."

"What a fabulous place to work," I exclaimed. "I'm envious."

"I've been working there for several years now, and it's the best job I've ever had. What do you do?"

"I'm a professor of art history."

"You're kidding."

"I work at a university in the Berkshires, in Massachusetts." I fished around in my handbag for a card and handed it to him. He glanced at it and put it in his breast pocket.

"I've never been to the Berkshires, but I understand it's lovely up there."

"It is," I agreed.

"So you probably know more than I do about many of the artists and artwork we display at the Artists' Museum."

I smiled. "I don't know about that."

"When was the last time you were at the museum?"

"It was several years ago, on a trip with some of my students."

"Then there are lots of new things to see. You'll have to make a visit while you're in Edinburgh."

I hesitated. "I'm not really sure how long I'll be there."

"Oh?" He clearly was looking for more information. *What could I say without opening the Pandora's Box of everything that happened today?*

"Yes, once I pick up my daughter I will probably make arrangements to go back home. This was a sort of a spur-of-the-moment trip."

"You're here to collect your daughter, you say?"

"Yes."

"How long has she been visiting?"

"A very short time, actually."

"Pity you can't stay longer and enjoy the city."

"I need to get back to work."

"Ah. Yes, well, I suppose that is important."

The conversation had become a bit stilted once I mentioned picking up Ellie. James opened a newspaper from the seat pocket in front of him. I closed my eyes again, knowing the time would go faster if I slept.

I was awakened by an announcement from the captain that we were beginning our descent into Edinburgh. James had lifted the window shade, and I could barely see anything in the dark gray sky. I searched for a glimpse of the city where, I knew, Ellie was waiting for me.

Smoothing my clothes and gratefully cleaning my face with a small hot towel the flight attendant gave me, I was anxious to deplane and see my little girl again. James smiled at me. "You must be chuffed to see your daughter. How old is she?"

"Five." He seemed surprised by my answer. "Do I look too old to have a daughter who's five?" I asked with a smile.

"No, no," he hastened to assure me. "Not at all. Has she been visiting your family?"

"Not exactly," I answered. "But my mum will be at the airport with her."

"Oh." He clearly didn't know what to say next.

Without warning, I suddenly found myself blurting out my whole story to my seatmate. He stared at me, mouth agape, while I talked in a rush. "So now you know why I'm in Edinburgh," I concluded.

"I'm *verra* sorry. I didn't know all that," he said apologetically, his accent becoming more pronounced than before.

"It's all right. But Ellie will be at the airport waiting for me. I asked my mother to meet her so she has family with her when the police take Neill into custody."

"That was a good idea. Lucky your mum's not too far away."

We sat in silence for a little while, until the familiar sounds of the plane descending and restless travelers told us it was time to start getting ready to go. The plane finally taxied to the terminal, and one of the flight crew announced that we could turn on our electronics. I reached for my phone and pressed it on. As soon as it came to life, it started buzzing and beeping with text alerts. My department chair, no doubt, wondering whether I would be able to teach my own classes tomorrow. Checking in my handbag for my small umbrella, I flipped through the list of texts.

They were all from my mother.

Neill and Ellie aren't here.

The airport police can't find them.

Are you sure they were on that flight?

Just confirmed they were on the flight.

When does your flight land?

Tell me what to do next.

I gasped. James looked at me with concern. "Are you all right?"

"My mother says Neill and Ellie are missing. The airport police can't find them." I was starting to panic. I texted my mother.

Just landed. Where are you?

In the office at customs, she immediately responded.

"Were they on the earlier flight?" James asked.

"Yes. But they disappeared sometime between getting off the plane and getting to customs."

"Can I help?"

I shook my head. "I don't think so. Thank you, though. I don't know what to do now."

He motioned to the flight attendant. "Can you bring the lady a glass of water, please?" He turned to me. "You're looking awfully pale." The flight attendant hurried back with a glass of ice water and stood there while I drank it.

"Can I get you something else?" she asked with concern.

"No, thank you. Can you just tell me where I can find airport security as soon as I get off the plane?"

"Certainly. Can I call someone and have them meet you?"

"Yes. Thank you."

She left, and I could see her talking on the phone up near the cockpit. She returned a moment later. "There should be a security officer waiting for you when you exit the Jetway."

I tried to give her a grateful smile, but it turned into a grimace. James fished in his jacket pocket and pulled out a business card. "I don't know how much help I can be, but please don't hesitate to call me if you need anything."

"Thank you."

The attendant hurried up to me again. "I've made arrangements for you to deplane first," she said quietly.

"Thank you. I appreciate that." I was starting to get looks from the other passengers. I turned to James. "Thank you for listening."

The door to the Jetway was opening, and the flight attendant held up her hand to the people in the front row. "Just a moment, please," she said. She motioned to me with her hand. I grabbed my duffel bag and stepped into the aisle.

A security officer met me at the gate and ushered me immediately to a small office in the terminal. I related the events of the entire day, ending with the texts I had received from my mother. He talked into a phone mounted on the wall while I waited.

"Your mother is waiting for you at customs," he told me after he hung up the phone. "Airport security is combing the area for your daughter and ex-husband."

"But they haven't found them yet?" I asked, my voice rising.

"No, ma'am. I'll take you to your mother now."

As we walked quickly through the airport, I scanned every face for Ellie's big brown eyes. "Have they checked the restrooms?" I asked my escort.

"Yes, ma'am. Those are the first places we checked."

They weren't in the airport. In the pit of my stomach, I knew they had managed to disappear again.

Chapter 7

At customs, my mother met me with a big hug, her eyes puffy and wet. I clung to her for a moment, then pulled away and got down to business. I spoke to the woman in the customs office. She told me she was working with airport security to pull up the video feed from the cameras outside the airport.

Mum and I waited in the customs lobby for the next several hours, while airport police, security, and customs officials came and went, looking for Ellie and Neill. There was no good news.

As time dragged on toward afternoon, a customs official came up to us. "You should probably find a hotel," she said. "It looks like you might be staying in Edinburgh for a while."

I spoke again to the police officers heading up the now formal investigation, and they confirmed their belief that Neill and Ellie had indeed somehow left the building without the knowledge of airport personnel or customs officials. The search would now expand into the city of Edinburgh.

My mother reached for my hand, and together we walked outside and hailed a taxi. I told the driver to take us to any hotel in Old Town Edinburgh, and eventually we pulled up in front of an inn along a cobblestone street. If I had been in Edinburgh under different circumstances, I would have found the inn quaint and charming. As it was, I barely noticed the stone facade of the building.

We checked into two rooms and unpacked. I wanted to return to the airport, but Mum convinced me to take tea with her in the inn's dining room. I sat with her, stiff and silent, sipping my strong tea and waiting for my mobile phone to ring. Mum offered theories on Neill's behavior. At that point, I couldn't have cared less *why* Neill had taken Ellie. I just wanted her back. I was jerked back into the conversation when I heard Mum mention the name "Sylvie."

"What about Sylvie?" I asked.

"I think she should come stay with you here at the hotel while you're in Edinburgh."

My sister and I, though close in age, had very different personalities. She was happy-go-lucky to my nervousness and reserve. She was a city person, while I was happiest in the mountains. She was a doer; I was a thinker. She still lived at home, and I had been on my own since college. I didn't really want her around with her carefree selfishness while I waited for news about Ellie and Neill.

"Why?" I asked.

"For moral support," my mother said gently, covering my hand with hers. "I think her presence could be good for you. Besides, she's between jobs right now, so she can take the time to come here." Which meant, of course, that Sylvie was unemployed again.

I wasn't capable of making any decisions just then. I didn't care whether Sylvie came or stayed back in Dumfries. Thinking about it was just too exhausting. I deferred to my mother.

"Do whatever you want," I said wearily. "I don't care if she comes or not."

Mum wasted no time taking out her mobile phone and dialing home. "Sylvie? No, they weren't on the flight. Yes, she's here with us. We're at an inn in Old Town. Waiting to hear. Sylvie, dear, I think it would be a good idea for you to come up here and stay with Greer for a bit. She could use your support."

I held my breath, hoping Sophie had better things to do than wait with me.

"Right, then. I'll text you the address of the inn, and we'll see you in a few hours."

So Sylvie was coming to stay.

"I don't know how much time I'll be able to spend with her," I cautioned.

"You don't have to entertain her. She's a grown woman. She's coming to be of help to you."

If she's so grown-up, why is she still living with you, then?

I looked at my phone as if it were a foreign thing, wondering why no one was calling me. I wanted updates from the airport, from the police, from anyone. I checked to make sure the volume was turned up so I wouldn't miss a call. "I'm going back upstairs," I told my mother. She nodded sadly, saying nothing, probably knowing I didn't feel like talking to anyone.

I returned to my room and switched on the television, hoping for news of a missing little girl and her father. But I knew there would be no news of them. They had melted into the city.

And as if to confirm my worst fears, my phone rang. I snatched it up. "Yes?"

It was an officer with the airport police. She informed me they had found footage of a child and a man matching the descriptions of Ellie and Neill getting into a taxi outside the airport.

"How were they able to leave?" I asked, my heart sinking.

"We think he must have bribed an airport employee to let them out through a restricted area to avoid going through customs. He probably knew we would be waiting for him."

"So if you have video of them getting into a taxi, then you can get the number off the taxi, find the driver, and ask where he took them, can't you?"

"I'm afraid not, ma'am. The taxi they entered was parked behind another, larger, van and the taxi went around other larger cars to exit the airport parking lot. So we are unable to identify the car they took."

Another dead end.

I groaned. "Now what?"

"Now we look for other leads," she said. "Don't worry, ma'am. We'll find your little girl."

Her words, spoken with the aim of making me feel better, somehow did manage to lift my spirits a bit. Those five words, "We'll find your little girl," gave me a hope I had no rational reason to feel.

"What should I do?" I asked her. "Should I go see Neill's parents?"

"Stay in the city for now," she advised. "Let the police talk to Neill's family first. At the moment, there's nothing you can do. We've got a team of people working on this, and they won't rest until they've found Ellie. I would recommend you get some food and rest, because without those things you'll be quite useless when we find her."

"Thanks," I said. I hung up the phone and dialed Mum's mobile. I repeated the officer's words and told her I would join her for dinner in a few hours. What I needed now, I said, was a brisk walk outdoors. She offered to join me, but I wanted to be alone.

I struck out alone onto the streets of Old Town, seeing but not really appreciating the cobbles below my feet or the centuries-old buildings surrounding me. I followed no particular route through the labyrinth of lanes and alleys that had existed since medieval times. The art historian in me would have relished such a walk at any other time, but I couldn't concentrate on anything except where Neill could have taken Ellie. I decided to return to the inn and make a list of the people whom I knew were acquainted with Neill from his days teaching at the University of Edinburgh. I planned to visit them the following day to see if Neill had told any of them he was arriving in town. And regardless of what the woman with the airport police had said, I knew a visit to Neill's parents was in my near future.

My mother was probably wondering what to do with herself in Edinburgh. I knew she was feeling as helpless as I was and wanted to help somehow. I knocked on her door when I got back to the inn and told her of my plan to make a list of Neill's university colleagues.

"I've thought of something you can do to help me," I said. "Come to my room and get on my laptop, will you? I'd like you to read me the names of everyone in the department of English literature at the university."

She was eager to lend a hand. She read the name of each member of the academic staff, the administrative staff, the honorary fellows, and even the tutors. Whenever she read a name I recognized, I wrote it down. I had a list a few pages long by the time we had completed the research.

"I am going to start calling each of these people tomorrow," I told her, looking at my watch. "I'm sure most of them have gone home for the day by now."

Armed with a plan, I felt a bit better. I couldn't just sit around and do nothing. I was sure the police didn't want me interfering, but I was determined to do whatever I could to find Ellie. I joined my mother for dinner that evening and ate more than I expected to.

As we were finishing dinner, Sylvie walked into the dining room. She greeted me with a long hug and wiped her eyes with her coat sleeve as she sat down at our table. As ambivalent as I had been about her coming to Edinburgh, I felt a surprising sense of relief that she was here. She ordered dessert and asked a thousand questions, most of which I couldn't answer. She wanted to know why Neill took Ellie, where I thought they had gone, why he left the United States to come to Edinburgh, and on and on. I wanted answers to all those questions, too.

Physically, Sylvie was practically my double—tall, with shoulder-length brown hair and big brown eyes. We had both been blessed with flawless skin from our mother's side of the family. People often mistook us for twins, though I was fourteen months older.

Sylvie would be sharing my room in the inn. We talked about my plans for the next day as we got ready for an early bedtime. Her job was to set up appointments for me to see some of the people on my list, the ones who weren't in their offices.

I slept better than I thought I would, probably because I was exhausted from the tension of the past two days. I awoke to a rainy day, so typical of the Edinburgh I remembered and loved. I watched wistfully out my window as people hurried by on the street below—tourists with backpacks slung under their ponchos, locals with Wellies and rain hats, and smartly dressed people going to work, juggling umbrellas and briefcases. Though I knew differently, it seemed that none of them had a care in the world except to get to their destination and out of the rain. I was pretty sure none of them was walking around in search of a missing child. Not surprisingly, Sylvie was still sleeping.

But I needed to stay focused. This was the day I was going to start taking concrete steps to find Ellie. I hurriedly dressed in a pantsuit, slipped into a pair of high heels, grabbed a neck scarf, and headed down to breakfast. My mother was already in the dining room. I ate a *tattie* scone, half a broiled tomato, and a handful of sautéed mushrooms. It was more than I usually ate for breakfast, but being back in Scotland made me nostalgic—and hungry. Mum and I planned what we would do that day. She would stay at the inn and wait for any word of Ellie or Neill, just in case the police came looking for me. I would go to the university. When Sylvie decided to get up, I would provide her with a list of the people not in their offices. She would call and make appointments for the next day or two. I hoped such appointments would be unnecessary, that I would have Ellie back with me by then, but I needed to have them set up just in case.

But my hope waned after a fruitless day of knocking on doors and finding no one who knew Neill was in Edinburgh. A second day of the same agenda yielded the same results. And Sylvie found it difficult making appointments with faculty members since no one knew who I was and I didn't have an academic interest in speaking to them. The first appointment she was able to make wasn't for another week.

And after two days Mum had nothing to report, either. No one had called—no police, no airport security, no customs.

Before dinner the second day I took a taxi to the airport. I thought they might pay more attention to me if I showed up in person. When I got there, I was lucky to be able to speak with two of the people who had helped me the day I arrived in Edinburgh to find Neill and Ellie gone. They had had no luck, they told me, in obtaining any other information about the taxi that took Neill and Ellie away from the airport. They didn't even know the name of the taxi company. They had been able to figure out how Neill had managed to elude customs officials before leaving the airport; the police had detained an airport employee for leading Neill and

Ellie through restricted areas to avoid the authorities. Apparently Neill had paid the man a large sum of money to help them escape. The man had no other information—Neill hadn't told him where they were going or why they were in Edinburgh.

I returned to the inn discouraged and upset. Mum and Sylvie were in the dining room. Mum and I picked at our dinners while Sylvie ate heartily. After dinner, Sylvie went to my mother's room. I sat in my own room scanning newspapers for any mention of a man and a child but, as I suspected, there was nothing. My mobile phone rang as I closed my third paper with a sigh.

"Hello?"

"Hullo, Greer? This is James. James from the plane. I was calling to see if there's any good news."

"Oh, James. It's nice of you to call. Unfortunately, there's no good news to report. I've been scouring the English literature department at the university to see if any of the faculty or staff have been in touch with Neill. He's still employed by the university even though he's been in the United States for several years. But no one knew anything. The only thing they've been able to figure out at the airport is how Neill and Ellie left without going through customs. It was easy enough—Neill bribed an airport employee."

"You sound rather done in. I'm going out for a *dram* after work. Care to join me?"

I wasn't sure I wanted to meet anyone for anything, but it sounded better than lying wide awake in bed, which had been my plan. So I agreed to meet him. When he learned where I was staying, he offered to meet me at the pub next door, since the museum where he worked wasn't far away.

We met in the pub a bit later. I was seated at a comfortable booth waiting for him when he arrived. I watched as he carefully shook the water from his Burberry coat and matching umbrella and hung them on a rack near the front door. He smiled when he saw me and made his way over.

"Nice weather we're having, isn't it?" he asked with a laugh. I gestured to the seat across from me.

"Sit down and warm up a bit," I told him.

"I will. I'll get our drinks first. What would you like?"

"A Balvenie 12 with a splash of water, please."

He looked at me with appreciation. "A woman who knows her whisky. I should have known that when I saw you on the airplane." He smiled and went over to the bar, then returned a few moments later with two glasses of amber liquid. He handed me one and slid into the booth opposite me.

"To Ellie," he said, lightly clinking his glass against mine.

"To Ellie." I took a tiny sip, savoring the warmth as it slid down the back of my throat, over the lump that had formed at the mention of her name.

"So tell me what's been happening," he said.

I related all the events since getting off the plane at the Edinburgh airport, ending with my unsuccessful foray onto the campus of the university to visit Neill's colleagues. "I have a few appointments next week," I told James. "Hopefully I can glean some useful information from one of those."

"Do you think there's anything I can do to help?"

"Not unless you know any faculty members at the university who knew Neill."

"Who've you spoken to so far?"

I pulled out my now-tattered list of faculty, staff, tutors, and fellows and showed it to him.

"You know, I deal a wee bit with members of the faculty for my job. I mostly speak with people in the art history department, but I have heard of a few of these people," he said. "I recognize a couple names because they teach classes that cross over between the two areas of study—literature and art." He took a pen from his breast pocket and checked two names. "Have you spoken to these people yet?"

I shook my head. "They're on the list for tomorrow. It seems some professors and faculty members don't take kindly to being approached by an outsider with questions of a personal nature." I smiled wryly.

"Before you go over, let me give them a call tomorrow and smooth the way for you. I know they'll be willing to meet with you if I talk to them first. I'll let you know when I've reached them."

"Would you do that?" I asked in surprise.

"Of course. I told you I'd do what I can to help you."

"Thank you very much."

He knocked back the last of his drink. "Can I get you another?"

"Sure."

We sipped our whiskies over a discussion of his job—how he went about procuring artwork for the Artists' Museum, how the staff decided which works to display and where to display them, and how his museum got its funding. It sounded fascinating.

"When you find Ellie, you'll have to come over for a look."

"We certainly will do that. It's been so long since I was there last. Can we get a private tour?"

"I would be honored."

We talked for a bit longer while James ordered a dinner of beef stew. The steam rose from his bowl, and the smell reminded me of Scottish winters, chilly and rainy. If only Ellie were back at the inn waiting for me, this would have been a comfortable, relaxing evening.

After James had finished his meal, I told him I needed to get back to the inn, where my mother and sister were probably wondering what had become of me. I hated to leave the cocoon of warmth and peace in the pub, the fire crackling in the hearth, and the low buzz of conversation all around us, but I had to get back to real life. The temporary break had been good for me. James walked me to the door, holding his umbrella over my head. "Would you like to get together for dinner later in the week?" he asked.

I thought a moment before answering. "I'd like to, but I can't make any plans because I don't know what might happen with Ellie and Neill. You're welcome to call me any evening and I'll let you know if anything has changed."

He seemed satisfied with my answer and bid me good night before hurrying up the street in the lamp-lit rainy darkness.

On my way back to the inn, I got a phone call from my department chair back in the States. He was wondering where I was and when I would be returning to school. I told him about Neill and Ellie, and we discussed possible solutions to the problem of my students having no professor for the rest of the semester if I had to stay in Edinburgh indefinitely. One option was to teach my classes remotely. It was a good idea, but I found myself leaning toward a different option—taking an emergency sabbatical, which would allow me the time I needed to find Ellie without having to worry about neglecting my classes. My boss said he would check with my colleagues in the art history department to see if they would be able to take over for me for the remainder of the semester, but he was quite sure they would be able to help out until I was able to return to campus.

When I rang off, I had a plan. My boss promised to keep me in the loop about my classes and other important events in the department, but otherwise told me he wouldn't bother me about work. I was free to use the emergency sabbatical as I wished.

And I wished to find my daughter.

I returned to the inn with a new optimism. I hadn't realized how much my work had been nagging my subconscious, and I felt a little lighter with the knowledge that I was free to spend my time looking for Ellie without having to worry about my students and my job responsibilities.

As it turned out, I had been right about my mother and Sylvie wondering where I was. They were frantic. And angry.

"Where have you been?" Mum demanded when I went into her room.

"Yeah!" Sylvie echoed.

"I'm sorry. I went out for a bit," I answered. "I had my mobile—you could have called me."

"I did," Mum seethed. "I got your voicemail."

I checked my phone. Dead. I would have to be careful not to let that happen again. "I'm sorry," I repeated. "I had no idea my phone was dead. Is anything wrong? Have you heard something?" My voice was rising.

"No, no, nothing like that," Mum answered. "We were just worried about you, that's all. Didn't know where you had gone. Tell someone next time, would you?"

"Yes," I replied sheepishly. It was foolish of me to have gone to meet James at the pub, even if I had needed a bit of time away from the inn.

I apologized again and returned to my room with Sylvie. She had news, though not news of Ellie and Neill.

"Seamus is coming for a visit," she said as we got ready for bed.

"Who's Seamus?" I asked through a mouthful of toothpaste.

"My boyfriend," she answered with a grin.

"He can't stay here," I pointed out.

"Why not?"

How callous. How typical of her. "What do you mean 'why not?' This is the first I've even heard of him. I don't want to sleep in the same room with a stranger."

She pouted. "But he's great. You'll love him, promise."

I glared at her. "Sylvie, no. He can get his own room if he wants, but I'm not paying for him to stay here."

"Oh, all right," she whined. "I'll tell him he has to get his own room and then I'll stay with him."

"Whatever," I said with a shake of my head. *Just what I need right now. I'll bet he's as lazy and cheap as she is.*

We went to sleep without speaking to each other. I knew she was angry with me, but I wouldn't back down. This wasn't a holiday pleasure trip. We were in Edinburgh for a specific and very serious reason—finding Ellie. I didn't care one wee bit about her boyfriend and thought she was unbelievably selfish for having the cheek to invite him.

My phone woke me in the middle of the night. I had a text. Bleary-eyed, I fumbled for my glasses on the bedside table and heard them fall to the floor. I reached for the phone and held it just a couple inches from my eyes. It took me a minute to focus because of the bright light of the screen, then when my eyes were adjusted I saw it was a number I didn't recognize.

I opened the text and gasped.

It's neill. I know u r in edin. Go home.

Where are you? I typed.

Ellie and I in danger. Don't lead them to us.

Lead who?

People after us. don't have long

Give me Ellie and we'll leave.

Can't. they'll find u.

Who's they?

People

What people?

I o them money

I didn't know what to say next. I couldn't think straight. Neill owed money? Again? And to whom?

Why did you take Ellie?

They'll find her and take her

A chill went up my spine. My fingers flew over the keyboard: *Why?*

To make me pay. Go home.

Tell me where you are and I'll pick her up. I'll bring the police.

No answer. I resent the text.

Tell me where you are and I'll pick her up. I'll bring the police.

Again, no response. I was in a panic now. My worst fears had hit me right in the heart and my stomach dropped. Ellie was in trouble from someone I didn't know. Strangers.

When Neill and I divorced, I knew his gambling problem was becoming more serious. But the divorce decree had required Neill to go through therapy to address his problems as a condition of him seeing Ellie on weekends. He had provided the court with the proper paperwork stating he had completed the therapy, and I had assumed his gambling problems were a thing of the past, or at least well in control.

I had obviously been wrong. I should have come right out and asked him about it, though I'm sure he would have lied to me. Now his gambling addiction had reared its ugly head again, and this time the stakes were higher than ever.

This time the loan sharks wanted Ellie. This time they were going to teach Neill a lesson he would never forget.

I couldn't breathe. I kicked off the covers and bounded to my feet, stepping on my glasses. Thank goodness they didn't break. All my movement woke Sylvie, who moaned and shifted in her bed. "Why all the noise, Greer?"

"I got a text from Neill. He and Ellie are in danger. I'm going to call the police."

She snapped on the lamp next to her bed. "What did he say?"

"That I am to go back home and he and Ellie are in danger."

"But why?"

"He owes money to people who are looking for him. They're threatening to take Ellie from him if he doesn't pay."

"Why doesn't he pay?"

I was exasperated. "I'm sure he would if he had the money, Sylvie. I'm sure he doesn't *want* this to be happening to Ellie."

"Why don't you pay?"

I hadn't thought of that, but it wasn't that simple. "He didn't tell me how much he owes. I don't know if I even have the money."

"Just ask him," she suggested unhelpfully. I struggled to remember why my mother thought it so important that she be here in Edinburgh.

"He stopped answering my texts. And I don't know where he is. That's why I'm going to the police," I tried explaining patiently, pulling on a pair of trousers. "I'm going to find out if they can do something to find the mobile signal and locate him that way. I've heard of that being done."

"Is there anything you want me to do?"

"Tell Mum where I've gone."

"You don't have to get mad, Greer," Sylvie said, a large hint of petulance in her voice.

"Sylvie, for God's sake, I'm not mad. I'm stressed! I'm upset! Have you any idea how difficult this is for me?" I responded in a loud whisper. I didn't want to wake other inn guests by having a row with Sylvie this late at night.

She turned away from me and pulled the covers over her head. Next time my mother wanted to make a helpful suggestion, I was going to ask her to keep her brilliant ideas to herself.

Downstairs, I woke the innkeeper, who was sleeping in a swivel chair behind the desk. I asked where the police station was. With an alarmed look in his eyes, he gave me directions. I could tell he was bursting to ask questions, but I didn't have time to engage in conversation with him and I left in a hurry.

It didn't take me long to get to the police station. I was ushered into a small room where I waited a short while for an officer to join me. When she finally arrived, I told her my entire story, beginning with the phone call from Ellie's school and ending with the texts from Neill. I had told the story so many times it was becoming automatic, almost like it had happened to someone else. I asked her if she could figure out where Neill was by triangulating his mobile phone signals.

Her eyes held a pitying look when she answered. "Yes, we can try that. But I want to give you fair warning: If you know mobile phone signals can be triangulated, so does he. I'm sure he was calling from a place other than where he's staying."

"But you can try?" I pressed her.

"We definitely can do that." She scribbled the mobile number on a pad of paper. "Why don't you head back to your hotel, and we'll have someone get in touch when we have an answer?" she suggested.

I returned to the inn with a heavy heart. Where there should have been hope, there was a growing feeling of despair. I had failed to keep Ellie safe back at home. What if I couldn't keep her safe in Edinburgh, either?

There were still a couple hours of darkness left when I returned to the inn. I slipped quietly into my room and crawled under the covers without even removing my street clothes. I lay awake until gray and purple began to streak the sky, listening to Sylvie's steady breathing, wishing I could sleep. I always suffered when I didn't get enough sleep. I had a hard time focusing. I'd been getting headaches, I was cranky and short with people. *Like I had been to Sylvie.* I felt sorry for the way I had spoken to her, though she had practically asked for it. I resolved to apologize to her when she awoke.

But when Sylvie woke up, she was in rare form. She stomped about the room, throwing clothes aside looking for the right pair of trousers, grumbling that she needed tea, complaining about the cold in the room, and insisting that my trip to the police station in the night had robbed her of an hour of sleep. I no longer felt sorry for her and decided to apologize some other time.

We met Mum for breakfast in the dining room, where Sylvie proceeded to explain to her why she was in such a foul mood. Mum looked at me with sympathy, but I didn't care any longer. I knew these moods of Sylvie's; it might take a day or so, but her good humor would eventually return and this rant would be forgotten. At least by Sylvie.

Mum announced that she was thinking of returning to Dumfries because she had a doctor's appointment the following day.

"Unless you want me to stay, of course," she said. "I'm really not that much help to you, I'm afraid. And as long as the police are looking for Neill, there's not much I can do right now. I'll come back as soon as you know something. And Sylvie will be here for support, won't you, Sylvie?" Sylvie looked up and nodded sullenly. I hoped she was feeling sorry for the way she had acted.

Part of me knew Mum was right, but part of me was reluctant to see her leave. She had been an important source of comfort during my discouraging days in Edinburgh.

"I've been thinking," I said to them, "I may look for a flat to rent for a short time. Just so we have a place to call home while we're in Edinburgh. This inn is nice, but it feels so…" I searched for the right word. "So itinerant. I'm living out of a duffel bag, Sylvie is living out of a suitcase. We need a place that feels more like home. More like normal. A place where I can wander around at night if I can't sleep. And a place where I can work if I feel like it."

Sylvie perked up. "Could Seamus stay there with us?" she asked, her eyes bright.

I nodded, resigned to the coming presence of Seamus. I had the feeling he was going to be around all the time no matter where we stayed, so Sylvie might as well have her own room to entertain him. More importantly, I might as well have a place where I could escape them. She grinned at me. "Thanks, Greer. That's great."

"Now, will you try a bit harder to help me?" I asked her. "You can be in charge of finding a place to stay."

She nodded, stuffing a rasher of bacon in her mouth.

Mum packed after breakfast and left later that morning, amid promises to return soon and good wishes for finding Ellie. She made me swear to update her twice each day, even if there were no news.

Sylvie, armed with a list of numbers to call for flats to let, left shortly after Mum did. I instructed her to take pictures of each place she visited and not to sign anything. Then I called the police station, hoping to speak with the officer I had seen in the middle of the night, but she had gone off shift early in the morning. The person who answered the phone promised to have her call me when she got to work that evening.

I took a bus out to the airport to see if the people at customs or the airport police had heard or seen or found anything that might be of help to me in finding Ellie and Neill, but that was another dead end. No one knew of anything else that could answer my questions.

I spent the rest of the day wandering the Royal Mile like any other tourist, popping into an occasional bookstore or tartan shop, thinking constantly of the things I would love to buy for Ellie. I ended up choosing a stuffed Scottie dog for her, as well as a packet of shortbread cookies and a children's history of Edinburgh. She would love them. I only wished she had been able to tour the Royal Mile with me. I kept a steady eye on the people milling about in case Neill had taken Ellie for an outing, perhaps to hide in plain sight. But no luck.

Toward the end of the afternoon, Sylvie must have taken a break from flat-hunting because I received fifty or so photos of places she had visited during the day. There were a few photos that caught my interest. I called her, asking questions about the ones I liked best. She sounded excited—I had known this assignment would appeal to her.

"There's one you would love, Greer. It's an old Georgian house divided into three flats, one on each story. It's across from a huge park and it's on a quiet street not far from the inn. It's a beauty! And it comes furnished!"

That sounded promising. I told Sylvie to call the estate agent so I could see the flat. She made arrangements for me to see it the next day.

There had been no further word from the airport or the police. The officer I had spoken to the previous night called and she had no information for me, either. I was at sea. I needed to *do* something, to feel like I was making every effort to find my daughter. Sitting in my room wasn't doing any good. Since Ellie's favorite thing was go to the playground, I had gone online to make a list of all the parks and playgrounds I could find in Edinburgh. There were so many. My plan was to visit each and every one, to look around, to perhaps find Ellie, just in case Neill had ventured out with her to give her some fresh air and time with other children. I didn't hold out much hope, but it was something and it would keep my body busy and my mind occupied. It was getting dark, though, and it wouldn't help to visit a park so late in the day. I wouldn't be able to see the children clearly enough to know if Ellie was among them.

James texted me to let me know he had paved the way for me to talk to two professors, so at least I had a plan.

I returned to the inn, where I met Sylvie in the dining room for dinner. Over plates of shepherd's pie with mashed turnips, we discussed the flats she had seen during the day. She was excited about a few of them and showed me endless photos on her mobile phone, more than what she had sent me earlier in the day. I was especially interested in the shots of the Georgian we were going to see.

I wasn't disappointed when I saw it the next morning. From the hilly street, which was narrow and cobbled, the very old, gray-stone three-story dwelling, named Bide-A-Wee House, was attached to its neighbors on either side. Each rectangular window was recessed in a large arch and the windows all sported wrought-iron plant boxes filled with greenery and winterberry boughs. I could see Sylvie watching me as I took in the breathtaking facade of the house. Through the gracious wooden front door of the flat was the faded sepia-toned beauty of what once had been a family home for a wool merchant, according to the estate agent. The first-story space echoed with high ceilings; dusty filtered light gave a golden yellow glow to the wooden floors and the ivory walls. The furniture didn't match the period of the house, probably because Georgian furniture would have been uncomfortable and fussy. Two long dark blue leather couches faced each other, flanking a huge fireplace with a white plaster surround. Between the two couches sat a large square coffee table topped with a large bouquet of heather and several stacked books. Three armchairs, a number of occasional lamps, and faded Persian rugs covering large swaths of the hardwood floors completed the setup. It was just the sort of place Ellie would love—comfortable, open, and bright.

The agent showed us the bedrooms next, and they were perfect. One for me, one for Ellie, and one for Sylvie. I could imagine Ellie in the room I chose for her, sitting on the ruffled white bed, staring out the window at the street below.

I signed the lease papers on the spot.

Sylvie and I didn't need much time to pack our belongings at the inn. We were moved into the flat by evening. I didn't know how long we'd be staying, but I wanted to feel like the flat was my home away from home, so one of the first things I did was put away my clothes. Then I went shopping at the Tesco grocery store nearby, and we finally had a home-cooked meal that evening.

The next day I began my search of the city parks. My appointments with the faculty members James had spoken to weren't until the afternoon. I would have asked Sylvie to help in the playground and park search, but I was afraid she wouldn't recognize Ellie from a distance. Sylvie had been traveling the last time I'd taken Ellie to Scotland, late in the spring, so she hadn't seen Ellie in person in almost a year. I e-mailed photos to Mum and Sylvie from time to time, but it wasn't the same as seeing Ellie in person. I wanted to be absolutely sure.

Before I left the flat, I spread out a large map on the kitchen table and made a red mark wherever I found a park. I decided to start right across the street from the flat and work my way outward.

One thought nagged at the back of my mind: I should be getting in touch with Neill's family. But after that last visit four years ago… I wasn't sure I could manage going to see them. Besides, I knew the police were talking to them and I didn't want to hinder the investigation. I was sure Janet and Alistair would share more with the police than they would with me.

The park across the street was large, but I was able to find the playground quickly and there were no children around. Walking to the next park on my map, I scanned the faces of passersby closely for any sign of Neill or Ellie. I spent my morning going from park to park, hoping in vain to find my little girl. I visited the faculty members early in the afternoon— another dead end. I did get a call from the police on my mobile phone, but only to be told that the mobile phone Neill had used to text me had been a throwaway. Indeed, the police had tracked its signal and found it in a rubbish bin on the street. I was encouraged by the find, though, since it indicated Neill was probably still in Edinburgh and hadn't tried fleeing his creditors any further. However, it probably also meant that he was deep in hiding somewhere and wasn't likely to risk taking Ellie to a public playground.

I had become more discouraged with each empty playground, but I needed to stay positive, to come up with a better plan that might help me find Ellie. I went online again that evening and looked for flats with private playgrounds and parks. There were only a few, so that narrowed my search considerably.

The next day I looked for Ellie again. The playgrounds and small parks I visited were each fenced in to ensure privacy, so my only choice was to peer over gates and through wooden slats for my daughter. I got some curious looks from people walking by, but I ignored them.

For a second day, I had no luck. I had ventured quite far afield from my flat and I walked all the way home to calm my restlessness, my feeling of dread.

When I got home, Seamus had arrived.

Chapter 8

I wish Sylvie had prepared me for Seamus. He was a giant of a man, with tattoos covering his thick neck and both arms. He wore a leather jacket and sported a long grizzled red beard. He was most definitely not what I expected. From what I could remember of Sylvie's past boyfriends, they tended to be mostly nondescript, with ordinary jobs and forgettable personalities. From the look of him, no one could accuse Seamus of having no personality. From the look of him, no one would dare.

Sylvie introduced us as soon as I got home. I assumed she had told him why I was in Edinburgh, because he expressed his sympathies. And as if he knew what would impress me most, he had prepared dinner for the three of us. He was a great cook. He had prepared a pot of cock-a-leekie soup, complete with julienned prunes, and set out a slab of Dunlop cheese for nibbling. I hadn't eaten Dunlop cheese in years. Despite his rough appearance, he was a keeper, as far as I was concerned.

Over the steaming soup, we talked about what I had done to find Ellie. Seamus wanted to know what he could do to help. Unfortunately, there wasn't much. My only hope was that the police would find some clue, some evidence that Neill had left behind somewhere.

After dinner, the three of us sat in front of the fireplace while Sylvie regaled Seamus with stories of our childhood, most of which involved great embarrassment to me. She told him of the time we switched classes and our teachers never realized the difference until it came time for Sylvie to take a test I had forgotten about. She took it and failed, and we had to tell the teachers what we had done. My punishment had been to keep the test grade.

Seamus had a deep, hearty laugh. He thought Sylvie's stories were hilarious. Like many people who saw us together or in photos, he couldn't believe how much we looked alike. We had switched places so many times as kids, it was a wonder we had such different personalities.

I went to bed that night feeling much less anxious about Seamus. It seemed Sylvie had finally found an interesting, likeable, useful guy.

The next several days went in much the same pattern: I would scour different areas of Edinburgh for Ellie during the day and go home to Seamus's cooking at night. Meals were the only bright spots of my days. Seamus was a master in the kitchen, and his specialty was traditional Scottish cuisine. We had everything from colcannon to *Cullen skink* to venison to *hairst bree*. Sylvie hadn't said how long Seamus would be staying with us, but I had the feeling if he stayed much longer I would need some new clothes in a larger size.

Seamus was an artist, so he could work anywhere. He found my job as a professor of art history endlessly fascinating and wanted to learn everything he could about my work. The three of us spent our evenings talking about art, artists, and technique. And though Sylvie found art tolerable, she joined in the conversations for Seamus's sake. She had asked me before Seamus moved in if he could usurp part of our living room for an "art studio," and I had reluctantly agreed. I found I enjoyed watching him work, though. His tastes ran to impressionism, portraiture, and the more traditional forms of painting and subjects, and I found that surprising. I had expected him to pursue more industrial types of art.

"How did you become interested in art, Seamus?" I asked him one evening while we ate dinner.

He glanced sideways at Sylvie, then turned his attention back to me. "It's something I've always liked, ever since I was a wee *bairn*. And I taught art for a while."

"Oh? Did you teach in a school?"

"Nope. Just grown people who wanted to learn."

I sensed this was a direction Seamus didn't want to take in our conversation. I changed the subject. "Do you get to museums very often?"

"*Och*, yes. I go to all the museums and galleries I can. Got to get my creative juices flowin' somehow, right?"

"I should introduce you to a new friend of mine. His name is James and he's the collections curator at the Artists' Museum." I sobered, remembering James's promise to show me around the museum with Ellie sometime.

Seamus's eyes lit up. "That would be *braw*!" I returned his smile and said I would try to arrange a time for James to show Seamus around.

I called James the next morning, and he agreed to give Seamus a guided tour of the Artists' Museum the following week—on the condition that I would join him for dinner that night. We arranged to meet at a tiny, chic bistro near the museum, and I went through the sad motions of another day spent in vain searching for Ellie. I missed her so much. By the time I met James that evening, I was dejected and losing hope. He took one look at me and suggested we ditch the restaurant and head to a neighborhood pub instead. I sighed with relief, wanting nothing more than comfort food and a dark, cozy place to sit and talk. We ate at a booth next to the window, where I could feel the warmth from the fireplace and watch the lights of nighttime Edinburgh twinkling to life. Staring out the window, I spoke to James of the things I missed most about Ellie: her high-pitched laugh, her habit of talking with her hands, the way she named inanimate objects. When I told him how her hair always smelled like honey and almonds, I couldn't help letting out a choked sob. He put his hand over mine, waiting until I was able to compose myself. Smiling my thanks through moist eyes, I reached for a tissue and blew my nose loudly. I looked around in embarrassment, and we both laughed self-consciously, momentarily lifting me out of my black mood.

We lingered at the pub for a few hours before heading out into the chilly evening. I'd had a few drams, so I was feeling a bit more relaxed and unguarded. When James reached for my hand while we walked to my flat, I didn't think twice about putting my cold hand into his warm one. Though I hadn't come to Edinburgh looking for a romance, it seemed I might have found one without looking. It felt good to have someone besides my family supporting me, someone encouraging me while I searched for my daughter.

But those warm feelings came with a strong sense of guilt. How could I be so selfish as to spend time with James when I should be concentrating all my energy on finding Ellie?

James must have read my mind, because he solved my dilemma for me. "You know," he said, squeezing my hand, "I don't want you to feel obligated to be spending time with me. I know you want to concentrate on finding Ellie. But you do need a break every now and then, and I'm happy to provide a distraction for you."

I looked up into his brown eyes and smiled my thanks.

My flat wasn't far from the pub. I invited James inside, and the two of us joined Sylvie and Seamus, who were enjoying a pint in front of the fire. We joined in their spirited debate about Scottish politics, and our comfortable evening lasted a few more hours before James reluctantly left, reminding us he had to get to work in the morning. James had been right—the evening had indeed provided me with a much-needed respite from the constant tension I felt when I was searching for Ellie. And though she was always in the forefront of my thoughts, it was nice to talk to other people about something other than my fear and grief.

By the time James left, Seamus had had quite a few pints. He went to bed, leaving Sylvie and me sitting on the floor in front of the fire, chatting quietly. Sylvie had also had a bit too much to drink. She rested her head against the couch cushions and sighed. "I'm so glad you like Seamus. And James seems to like him, too. He's tried so hard to be accepted again."

I jerked my head toward her. "What do you mean by that?" I asked.

"By what?"

"What do you mean when you say 'accepted again'?"

"Oh, nothing." She laughed lightly and spoke again in an exaggerated whisper. "Seamus got out of prison not too long ago. He doesn't have too many friends who aren't real *scunners*."

"Prison?" I said a little too loudly.

"Shh!" she hissed. "D'ye want him to hear?"

"Why was he in prison?" I whispered, almost afraid to hear the answer. She looked around the room, finally speaking into her glass. "The truth is, he beat up a man pretty badly in a bar fight. Almost killed him. Seamus didn't mean to, though. The other guy started it."

"He actually went to prison for assaulting someone?" I asked in horror.

"I told you, it was an accident. Self-defense, really. He doesn't want people to know, though, so don't tell him I told you."

"No, I won't," I said in a low voice, wondering how I had gotten myself into this mess. My entire world was upside-down. My daughter and ex-husband were missing, I was thousands of miles from home trying to find them, and now I had a houseguest who had been imprisoned for nearly killing a man.

"Anyway, he's paid his debt to society. He even taught art classes to the other inmates. He's focused on his painting now," she said in a quiet, dismissive voice.

"And you see nothing wrong with this?" I whispered, unbelieving.

"No," she answered. "He's really just a big teddy bear, Greer. You just don't know him well enough. He'd never have hurt anyone on purpose."

I rubbed my eyes. "Sylvie, I can't deal with all this right now. I'm too tired. Let's talk in the morning. I'll have to decide what to do then."

"What's to do?" she asked. "Surely you're not going to throw him out?"

"I should," I replied. "I don't need that kind of drama right now. Not with Ellie and Neill missing and in danger."

Sylvie got up from the floor and looked down at me. "You're an elitist, Greer. You think people can't make mistakes. Or if they do, you think they can't be forgiven. It's sick, that's what it is. Well, if Seamus leaves, I leave with him." She spun around, wobbled for a moment against the side of the couch, and left the room, swaying a bit as she walked. I was sure she hadn't meant to let slip the information about Seamus's past, but everything was out in the open now and had to be addressed.

Still, I couldn't reconcile the Seamus I had gotten to know over the past several days with the Seamus who had been in prison.

That night, I slept with my bedroom door locked.

When I awoke the next morning, both Sylvie and Seamus were gone. Sylvie obviously wasn't keen to talk about Seamus's past again, and she was likely feeling guilty for having told me about it without his permission. I wasn't surprised to find a note saying that she was headed home to Dumfries to get some of her things from Mum's house and that Seamus was out for the day, painting in a park somewhere.

It was just as well. It was a conversation I wasn't ready to have, either. But as I got dressed, I couldn't help wondering how well I really knew Seamus. He was brawny, that was for sure, and I shivered at the thought of being on the receiving end of that strength.

* * *

I spent part of the morning on the phone with my department chair. He had, indeed, found several other professors who were willing to teach my classes until the end of the semester, if that turned out to be necessary. I gave him all the information he needed to find my lesson plans and grades, then thanked him profusely for his time and efforts on behalf of me and my students. I rang off with a feeling of relief.

After talking with my boss, my thoughts returned to Seamus and Sylvie. I didn't know what to do. My heart told me Seamus was a good person. My head told me to get him out of the flat as soon as possible and let Sylvie deal with the consequences. I wanted to bounce my thoughts off an adult other than Sylvie, a person who could look at the situation with objective eyes. I could always call Dottie back home, but she hadn't met Seamus. That left James. I was torn, though. Even though Sylvie had revealed information to me about Seamus's past, I was uncomfortable sharing it with anyone else. After all, she hadn't meant to tell me. I left my flat and walked to Princes Street, then wandered through the gardens, lost in thought. Without realizing where my feet were taking me, I had wound my way up a hill, around a bend, and arrived at St. Giles Cathedral.

I walked into the magnificent building, my low heels clicking on the stone floor, sending echoes tumbling through the soaring space and into the vaulted ceilings. Though I had visited St. Giles countless times, it never ceased to inspire awe, hope, and amazement in my heart. Tourists were clustered in various parts of the enormous nave, speaking in hushed tones, pointing out the architectural wonders in every direction. They walked about quietly, some listening to an audio tour on headphones, some obviously following one of the maps the docents distributed, others sitting in the simple wooden chairs and listening to an organ recital, and the rest looking upward and trying to take it all in.

I preferred to stroll at my own pace, not looking at a map or listening to anyone in particular. I liked to experience the High Kirk in my own way and at my own pace each time I visited. And each visit was different for me. This time, I took in the splendor of the cathedral in a circle, walking slowly and trying to drink in each architectural detail, each sculpted frieze, each magnificent stained glass window. I ended up in Thistle Chapel, my favorite place in the giant church.

Thistle Chapel was tucked away in a corner of the building. A magnificent monument to the highest order of the Scots Knights, the chapel consisted of sixteen splendid stalls carved with cherubs, crosses, and Scottish emblems. Gorgeous stained glass windows depicting Scotland's past, Biblical saints, and other scenes filtered the light that streamed into the chapel.

I liked to go into the chapel because, despite its soaring height and splendor, it seemed cozy and intimate. As an art historian, I found an endless font of fascinating material in this chapel, but as a Scot I found inspiration, hope, and a deep spiritual connection with Scotland's history.

Miraculously, I had the chapel to myself, with the exception of the ever-present guard. I stood for a moment in the center of the room, the echoes of footsteps in the cathedral's nave receding into near silence. I closed my eyes and let the history of the place envelope me, filling me with a sense of peace and hope, a feeling I would need to sustain me through the coming days as I continued to search for Ellie and Neill, and as I dealt with the issues surrounding Seamus and Sylvie.

I spent several long minutes lingering in the chapel, marveling at the skill of the people who had carved the stone and wood long ago, wondering about the knights and ladies of ancient families who had occupied this space.

When several tourists entered the space and broke the spell the chapel had yet again cast over me, I finally turned to go. I felt restored, stronger, and more energetic. I left the chapel and made my way out into the cathedral's nave, barely looking where I was going as my eyes turned skyward to take in the view above me.

It was only when I looked down at my phone to see if I had any texts that something moving in the corner of my vision caught my attention. I glanced up when the image grew larger and larger. I was startled to see a stocky, burly man just inches away, a hat pulled down low over his eyes and a tan trench coat cinched at the waist. His shoulder rammed into me, knocking me backward. I dashed my head on a massive stone pillar as I fell to the ground on my back. Several people had seen the incident and came rushing to my aid.

"What happened, dear?"

"Are you all right, lass?"

They crowded around, all talking at once, all solicitous and kind. I craned my neck around their legs, trying to catch a glimpse of the man who had hit me so hard, but all I saw was his retreating back as he hurried down an aisle of the nave toward one of the exits.

Two men helped me to my feet and led me to a nearby seat, where their wives tended to the bump that had erupted on the back of my head. One of the men fetched a docent, who used his radio to request an ice pack.

"Did you see that man?" I asked one of the women.

"No, I'm afraid I didn't. He was gone before we realized what had happened."

I winced as I touched the back of my head, thinking he was probably some troubled individual who had committed a random act of violence or who didn't know right from wrong. I certainly hadn't recognized him. I barely knew anyone in Edinburgh. Another docent appeared with the ice pack, which I placed gingerly against my head. I assured the kind women and their chivalrous husbands that I would be fine, and they walked away to continue with their tour of St. Giles. My faith in the kindness of strangers had been rekindled.

My feeling of calm, of peace and hope, had evaporated. All I wanted to do was get back to my flat and rest. My head and back were in crippling pain, and I knew wandering the streets looking for Ellie and Neill today would be useless.

I left the cathedral and was returning slowly to the flat through Princes Street Gardens when I got the feeling someone was watching me. Wheeling around, I was just in time to see movement behind a grouping of trees nearby. I was suddenly afraid. Looking about for other people, I noticed for the first time that I was quite alone in the gardens. Only a few tourists strolled the grounds in the distance. No busy corporate types were taking a shortcut through the gardens to their next meeting. No lovers, no students, no children.

Just the person behind the trees.

Trying to pick up my pace, I limped along through the gardens, looking ahead to the closest route back to the street. But I wasn't fast enough. Someone grabbed my elbow and jerked me around.

I gasped. The man wore a plastic tan-colored mask, but I could tell it was the person who had pushed me in the cathedral. His trench coat was still tied tightly around him. I felt my eyes widen and I knew instantly that he was no stranger to the fear staring back at him.

"What do you want?" I demanded, hoping he would mistake my loud tone for bravado.

"Where is he?" the man growled.

"Who?" I asked, bewildered.

"You know who. Where is he?"

I shook my head. "You've mistaken me for someone else," I said, trying to ease my arm from his grip.

"Oh, no I haven't. We know he's here in Edinburgh. Tell me where he is or when we find him—and we *will* find him—we'll make sure you never see your daughter again."

Neill. I should have known. Neill was the only person I knew who might have a thug like this looking for him, except perhaps for Seamus.

"I-I don't know where they are, I swear," I stammered. "I'm looking for them, too."

"Bollocks," he answered with a snarl.

"No, it's true," I insisted. "He took our daughter and came here and I followed them. Does he owe you money?"

"None of yer business."

"Please let me go. I don't know where they are. But don't hurt our daughter, I'm begging you. She hasn't done anything wrong. She's just a little girl. Take me instead of her." I was babbling, terrified.

"We'll take you both. We know where you live. If I find out you've lied to me, I'll…" He trailed off as he looked up. There was a couple strolling toward us. He dropped my arm suddenly and took off running, back toward the grove of trees where he had been hiding, watching me.

I bent over, putting my hands on my knees, and took several deep breaths. Neill had been right—he was in danger, and more importantly, so was Ellie. I could only assume the man was looking for Neill to enforce the terms of a gambling loan, but it didn't matter. The fact remained that this man, and the people who had sent him, were serious and didn't care whom they hurt to get their money back.

I wanted to call the police, but I was afraid the man who had grabbed me would see what I was doing and come after me again. As quickly as my injured back would allow, I returned to my flat, making sure no one was following me. Once through the front door, I made it as far as the couch before I pulled out my phone and, fingers trembling, dialed the police station where I had gone for help once before. I spoke to the woman who had taken Neill's mobile phone information earlier. She promised to send an officer to Princes Street Gardens to look for the man in the plastic mask. When I told her he had attacked me at St. Giles Cathedral as well, she assured me she would send a second officer to the cathedral to look at the security footage.

After I talked to the police officer, I left the sofa momentarily to double- and triple-check the locks on the front door. As much as I wanted to go looking for Ellie, I couldn't move. I was starting to stiffen up, and the pain in my back was agonizing. I swallowed two aspirin and lay down against a heat pack.

I was awakened by the sound of the front doorknob rattling. Someone was trying to get in. Panicked, I sat up with a start, my back sharply reminding me not to move so quickly. I limped to the door and peered through the peephole.

Seamus. Now what do I do? My thoughts were still groggy. I had to let him in—all his stuff was still in the flat.

He had unlocked two of the locks while I slept. It was the chain that stopped him from getting in. I opened the door and he stood staring at me.

"What happened to you?" he asked.

"Good to see you, too. Come in," I snapped, stepping aside to let him in.

"I'm sorry, Greer. I didn't mean that. I meant, are you all right? You look like you're hurt."

"I know, Seamus. I didn't mean to bark at you. I've had a bad day."

"Tell me what happened."

"I was knocked down at St. Giles Cathedral, and then the same man who knocked me down followed me through Princes Street Gardens and grabbed me there, too."

"What?! Why?"

"I don't know, other than it has something to do with Neill."

"Have you called the police?"

"Yes. I called them as soon as I got back here."

"Did the man follow you here?"

"I was checking the whole way, so I don't think so. It doesn't matter, though, because he said he knows where I live."

"He's pullin' yer leg, Greer. Of that I'm sure."

"What makes you think so? I'm inclined to believe him. It's safer to believe him, don't you agree?"

"I don't understand."

"I mean, we'll be more careful in the future. You know, locking the doors, making sure no one is following us when we go somewhere, that sort of thing."

"Hopefully the police'll catch him, and you won't have to worry about him at all. Would you recognize him if you saw him again?"

I grimaced. "I'm not sure. He had a hat pulled low over his eyes at the cathedral when he pushed me down, and he wore a mask in Princes Street Gardens. I would definitely recognize his voice, though."

"Good lass. Have you heard from Sylvie?"

"No. She was gone when I got up this morning."

Seamus chuckled. "She was gone when *I* got up this morning. And I got up early. She must have had lots to do today. Now, I want you to lie down again and I'm going to fix you a snack. Have you eaten today?"

"Just some toast for breakfast."

"You must be half-starved. I'll be in soon with a tray. Lie yourself down."

I limped back to the couch and leaned back against my pillow. Seamus had somehow earned back my trust, just in the time it took for a quick conversation and an offer to make me lunch. He wasn't a threat to me or to Sylvie.

Chapter 9

Sylvie was laden with grocery bags when she came home a bit later. Seamus unchained the lock to let her in.

"Why was the chain pulled?" she asked crossly. "I couldn't get in, and this stuff is heavy."

"There's been a problem," Seamus said. "Greer will tell you all about it." He took the bags from her and went into the kitchen.

"What's going on?" she asked, easing herself into a chair opposite me and crossing her legs. She gave me a questioning look while she nodded her head toward the kitchen. "Does he know I told you?" she whispered.

"No. At least, I don't think so. I didn't say anything."

She noticed the heat pack I was pressing against my back. "What happened to you?"

I told her all about my encounter with the man at the cathedral and again in the gardens. She listened, her mouth agape.

"Who was it?" she demanded. "Have you told the police?"

"I don't know who it was, and of course I've told the police. I'm waiting to hear whether they find anything on the cathedral security footage or in the gardens. I called them as soon as I got home."

"But you must know the man from somewhere. Strangers just don't go around attacking people."

"He obviously knows Neill. He thinks I know where Neill is, and he's trying to scare me into telling him."

She thought for a moment. "It seems like the police should have found something by now, don't you think?"

I shrugged. "It'll take them a while to go through security footage and to scour the gardens for evidence."

"What happens now?"

"I'm going to rest for a bit, then I'll go back out and look for Ellie again."

"But aren't you afraid that man will find you again?"

"A little, but I can't stop looking for Ellie just because I'm afraid of some man I don't know."

"You're braver than me," she said.

Seamus came in, bearing a tray of teacups and saucers. "Thought we could all do with some tea," he said with a wide smile.

I drank the hot, strong brew and settled onto the cushions so my back would be more comfortable. Seamus offered to reheat the pad for my back and I gratefully accepted. Before long, I was asleep again.

But the caffeine in the tea had produced its intended effect and I woke up a short time later, restless and ready to get back to looking for Ellie.

I lumbered up from the couch and made my way to the kitchen, where Sylvie and Seamus were talking quietly. "I'm going out for a little while," I announced.

Sylvie gave me an incredulous look. "What?! Why? You're hurt, you're scared, and it's getting dark. What can you possibly accomplish?"

"I'm not trying to accomplish anything. I just want to go for a short walk. I've been thinking my back might hurt less if I got off the couch and exercised it a bit."

"Whatever you say," she said with a sigh. My mum used to say that when I was a teenager. It was bad enough coming from my mother, but it was almost unbearable coming from my little sister.

But when I stood on the sidewalk in front of the flat, I was too scared to go anywhere. I looked up and down the narrow street, seeing only threats: a person could be hiding between those parked cars; someone could be watching me unseen from the park across the street. Dozens of other scenarios crowded my mind, and I couldn't bring myself to venture any further for a walk. But I didn't want to go back inside, so instead I went around to the garden at back of the house.

I passed through a wrought-iron arbor at the entrance to the patio, then followed the meandering stone path, looking at the foliage and berries hanging from the shrubs and trees all around me. This was a huge garden for the center of Edinburgh. There were browning clusters of rudbeckia, several acer trees with fiery red leaves drooping gracefully toward the cold ground, and Black Lace berries clinging to branches naked of leaves. Where the berries hung, there would be gorgeous pink flowers in the spring.

There was a large fireplace at the back of the garden, almost hidden by trees and evergreen shrubs. I knew the owner of Bide-A-Wee House kept seasoned firewood in the basement. A cluster of small tables and matching chairs dotted the ground in front of the fireplace, inviting residents to relax. I couldn't wait to bring Ellie out here and enjoy a crackling fire with her.

My heart constricted as my thoughts turned to Ellie. I was getting nowhere in my search for her. Wherever Neill had taken her, they were hidden well if the thug who accosted me was also unable to find them. I suspected people like the loan sharks looking for Neill had ways that were, at best, illegal and at worst, dangerously effective to find their borrowers. Of course, most of my information about such criminals came from television and movies, but it seemed logical.

I circled the garden several times before going back into the flat. Seamus was directing dinner preparation, and Sylvie was happily following his instructions.

"Look, Greer! Seamus is teaching me how to make *stovies*. We've got corned beef, potatoes, carrots, and onions in this."

"It smells wonderful," I complimented her. "Do I have time for a shower before dinner?"

"Sure," Seamus answered.

The hot water on my back felt so good, I didn't want to get out. But when I did, I was surprised to find James in the kitchen with Sylvie and Seamus. I smiled at him, embarrassed because my hair was still dripping wet and I was dressed in pajamas.

"Why didn't you tell me you were coming over?" I scolded. "I would have at least put on street clothes."

James grinned. "It's fun to see you relaxed and sloppy for once. I stopped by to see what was going on, and Sylvie and Seamus invited me for dinner. If it's all right with you."

"Of course it's all right. I won't bother changing, now that you've seen me in pajamas." I poured four glasses of wine and handed them around to everyone. James looked at me, narrowing his eyes.

"Are you limping?"

"Yes. I was trying not to."

When he asked what happened, I was forced to retell my story. His look changed from interest to concern to horror as I told him about the events of the day.

"Why didn't you call me right away?"

"Honestly, all I wanted was to come home and sleep. I was exhausted. I called the police, but then I just wanted it all to go away for a while."

"I'm so sorry this happened," James said earnestly. "I would have come to help you. I could have stayed with you this afternoon."

"You wouldn't have enjoyed watching me sleep. There was no need for anyone to be here."

"I most certainly would have enjoyed watching you sleep," James retorted. Seamus whistled through his teeth and Sylvie started to laugh.

"Och, Greer, this is getting serious!" she said with a grin.

I could feel my face turning a hundred shades of red. I rolled my eyes and changed the subject. "James, are you working tomorrow?"

"I have to go in for a little while in the morning, but I won't be long. Why? Do you have plans?"

"I was going to go out looking for Ellie again, and I was wondering if you could go with me. If you do, I'll buy you lunch."

"How can I refuse an offer like that?" he asked with a grin. "Of course I'll go with you. I'll come by and pick you up when I'm done at the museum, and we'll go together. That way you don't have to go by yourself to meet me. I think you should always have someone with you when you go out, at least until the man who hurt you is caught."

Sylvie agreed. "And if James can't be with you, then you need to ask me or Seamus. You shouldn't even have left the flat tonight to go for a walk by yourself."

It was nice to hear Sylvie say that. She didn't often give the impression that she cared about people other than herself.

We enjoyed the stovies Sylvie had made. The corned beef was delicious, tender, and perfectly spiced. "Ellie loves stovies," I told them while we ate. "She's a big fan of Scottish food." Then, suddenly and to my great embarrassment, I started to cry. James jumped up from the table and came to put his hands on my shoulders. Sylvie put her hand on mine and Seamus looked around the kitchen awkwardly.

"Greer, you're going to find Ellie. We're going to find her. I just know it. I feel it," James said, leaning over to kiss the top of my wet head.

"He's right, Greer. We'll find her, of course we will," Sylvie agreed. "She can't stay lost forever."

Forever. The word made me cry harder. James rubbed my shoulders and Sylvie apologized for her word choice. "Och, what I mean is, she's got to be in Edinburgh. Between the four of us and the police, there's no way she can stay hidden."

I wiped my eyes, sniffling, and tried to smile at her. "I know. It just seems so hopeless sometimes." I glanced up at James, who was looking at me with concern. "I'm okay. Really. I'm okay now."

He sat down again, and we finished our dinner. Seamus, obviously relieved my crying jag was at an end, changed the subject. He was a great storyteller, and he regaled us with tales of how he got each of his tattoos. Listening to him and the others laughing made me feel a bit better. I finished my wine and began to feel a bit groggy again, so I went to bed shortly after dinner ended. James left after promising to pick me up mid-morning. But I had started to change my mind about the next day's plans.

Chapter 10

I knew when I first met Alistair and Janet that they didn't like me. Nor did Gerard, Neill's brother. Beatrice, his sister, didn't seem to care about me one way or another, but she always followed her parents' lead. Neill had assured me they would "warm up" to me, but if anything, their warming up turned into more of a white-hot hatred.

Alistair and Janet had apparently always been old-fashioned, even for folks in their small rural village. Modern attitudes toward women were something they couldn't accept and they didn't seem to be interested in trying to understand. They were convinced that Neill's marriage to a university professor would bring nothing but heartache to him. They believed I would be a shrill, demanding, unsatisfied shrew who would cause Neill no end of misery with my nagging. They had fervently hoped Neill would marry a good village girl and told me so on many occasions.

I tried to be a good daughter-in-law, but they weren't interested in listening to anything I had to say or seeing any of the tender things I did for Neill in their presence. I talked to Neill about it several times, explaining why I didn't like to visit them or talk to them on the phone or even talk about them when they were an ocean away. But Neill never understood. He never believed his parents treated me poorly when he wasn't looking.

And before long, he began to believe the things Alistair and Janet told him. He began to think I was too smart for my own good, too talkative, too pushy. He would bemoan my "feminism" and remark that he wished I would stay home and raise our daughter like other good mothers. He would say I wasn't doing the family any favors by continuing to work after Ellie was born.

We visited Alistair and Janet when Ellie was a year old. We were spending the summer in Scotland, visiting friends and family. Although I had taught summer courses until Ellie was born, I took that summer off to spend with her and Neill. I didn't want to visit Alistair and Janet, and I didn't think it was a good atmosphere for our baby. I wanted to stay in Dumfries, and I told Neill I thought it would be a good idea if he visited his parents by himself.

He insisted that Ellie and I go with him, and rather than putting up a fight, I relented and drove up to Glensaig with him at dawn one day during a raging summer storm. Rain lashed the car, and the wind tried its best to blow us off the road. Neill was exhausted and cross when we reached his parents' home, but he seemed to cheer up when we saw his family. They greeted him with hugs and slaps on the back, fussed over the baby, and had nothing but scowls for me.

I tried not to let it bother me. I even offered to help make the noon meal, but Janet told me she didn't want my help. I was sure she'd want me to help, if only to mock my kitchen skills. Besides, that's where the Gramercys believed a woman should be. Instead, I took Ellie to the third floor, where it would be quiet and far away from the family, and sang to her in one of the small bedrooms in the back. A beautiful painting by the Scots landscape and marine impressionist William McTaggart hung on one wall, and I stared at the painting while I cuddled Ellie. The ceilings in the room sloped steeply, and there was only one small window. It was a strange room, with a thick wooden door I assumed was a relic of the ancient past.

I assumed wrong.

I didn't hear the key turning in that thick soundproof door to lock us in. I didn't hear a person stealing away down the back stairs, leaving me and Ellie alone in the farthest bedroom where no one would hear my cries for help. It was a little while before I realized we were trapped, prisoners in my husband's childhood home. I tried banging on the door, but to no avail. I realized with a groan that I had left my mobile phone with my purse in the sitting room downstairs, so I couldn't call or text Neill to let him know where we were.

Holding Ellie in my arms, trying to stay calm so she wouldn't sense my distress, I walked to the window, where I could see, three stories down, Neill and his father walking out to one of the barns on the property, their heads protected by umbrellas, their Wellies squelching through the thick mud. I set Ellie down on the floor and tried banging on the window, but with the rain and the distance to the ground, neither of the men heard me.

Did Alistair know I was up here? I knew they couldn't keep us in that room forever, but I was furious. I fumed for hours, getting up every few minutes to pound on the door and yell for Neill. Ellie started to cry eventually, sensing my growing alarm. I was still nursing her, so she wasn't going to go hungry. But *I* was hungry and I had to use the bathroom.

I ended up having to use a ceramic chamber pot I found in a closet.

I peered out the tiny window every few minutes, watching and waiting for Neill to come back from the outbuildings with Alistair. When I finally saw them trudging toward the house through the rain, I tried pounding on the window again, but to no avail. Neither even looked up.

When I was sure Neill was in the house again, I tried pounding on the door. Ellie cried when I yelled for my husband, but the room had been soundproofed so thoroughly that my fists made only dull thuds on the door. I knew no one outside the room could hear me.

While Ellie dozed, I got up and crossed the room to examine the painting under the eave more closely. I was stunned that such a beautiful piece of art would be hidden from view. Art was meant to be shared, and it deserved a place of honor in the house.

Suddenly Ellie woke up with a sneeze, which was not surprising, as the room was covered with dust. I sat down on the bed with her as she drowsed, waiting for her to go back to sleep. When she slept again, I stayed there with her, keeping watch over her as the sliver of gray daylight coming from the window moved across the floor, eventually fading to a gloaming light.

I was checking the window again when I saw Neill pull away from the house in our car. I wondered where he was going, what he was thinking. Not long after that, I heard a soft scraping noise again and knew the key was being turned in the lock. Leaving Ellie asleep on the bed, I tiptoed to the door and opened it, but no one was there. I looked in both directions down the long, dimly lit hallway, but there was no trace of anyone. I went back into the room, gathered Ellie in my arms, and stole quietly downstairs and into the sitting room. Beatrice walked in a few minutes later.

"Who locked us up on the third floor?" I demanded angrily, trying to be quiet because Ellie was still sleeping.

Beatrice gave me a blank look. "I *dinnae* know what yer talkin' about," she said. "Is that where you've been? We've been wonderin."

I stared at her. My hands shook and I could feel my face turning red with anger. "Where's Neill?" I asked through clenched teeth.

She shrugged. "He took off. He was so mad that you left with Ellie and dinnae tell him where you went all day."

"You know exactly where I was all day." I stopped, knowing I wouldn't get anywhere with her. "Where's Janet?"

"In the kitchen, still working. You should probably offer to help since you've been gone for so long." She turned and left the room. I was sure she knew full well where I had been and I knew I was helpless to prove it to anyone.

I got the same treatment from Janet when I went into the kitchen after Ellie woke up. She offered me nothing but a scowl and questions about why I left "poor Neill" without telling him where I was going and why I couldn't be a "good and proper wife."

And it only got worse when Neill came back. He stormed in the front door, letting it slam behind him. Ellie, on the floor in the sitting room, let out a scream and began to cry. I was sitting next to her and I gathered her into my lap. Neill came to the door and stared at me, his left eye twitching and his nostrils flaring.

"Where've you been?" he yelled.

"I was locked in the third-floor bedroom all day," I answered quietly.

Neill snorted. "You don't really expect me to believe that, Greer. Now, dammit, tell me where you went with Ellie!"

I stood up, my fists clenched by my sides. I left Ellie on the floor at my feet, where she continued to scream. "I am telling you the truth, Neill. One of your delightful family members locked me in the room upstairs. Do you know it's soundproofed? I tried banging on the door, but no one heard me. Or at least *you* didn't. I tried banging on the windows when I saw you and your father go out to the barns, but the rain made it impossible for you to hear me."

"That's a load of rubbish!" he yelled, taking a step closer to me. "And of course I know it's soundproofed. Mum likes to read in there. She needs total silence when she reads."

"You need to drive me and Ellie back to Dumfries. I cannot stay here another minute."

"I will do no such thing," he said.

"Where have you been, anyway?" I asked him.

"Out looking for you!" he bellowed, his eyes bulging and the vein in his neck protruding.

"I was here all the time. All you needed to do was ask your mother or your sister. They knew very well where Ellie and I were. Check the chamber pot. I had to use it while I was stuck up there."

He turned on his heel and ran out of the room. I could hear him charging up the stairs, then up the second flight. He came rushing back down just a few moments later, holding the chamber pot in his hands.

"See?" he demanded. "Clean! You lying *bampot!*"

I walked over to where he stood, looking into the chamber pot. He was right—it was spotless.

"Someone washed it out," I told him.

He scoffed. "Sure, Greer. Your phantom strikes again. Now, I'll only ask you one more time. Was it another man? Is that where you've been?"

"Neill, I insist that you take me back to my mother's house."

"You are not leaving," Neill said. "You will stay here with my family until I am ready to return to Dumfries. And you are not leaving my sight."

"Neill, why don't you believe me?" I asked lowering my voice so his family couldn't hear our conversation.

"Greer, I know you hate my family for reasons that no one else understands. They have always been perfectly pleasant to you."

"Perfectly pleasant?!" I hissed, practically choking on the words. "They've been perfectly awful from the day I met them!"

"You are too sensitive, and you're also wrong. Just this morning I heard my mother tell you that she didn't want you to help in the kitchen. She was just thinking of you and Ellie. That was very thoughtful of her, and you repay her kindness by accusing her of imprisoning you!"

"Neill, she wasn't being kind. She was being rude. She didn't want me in the kitchen because she can't stand the sight of me."

He stared at me as if he were looking at a stranger. "You are denigrating my mother, and I will not listen to it. You owe her an apology."

"You're mad if you think I'm going to apologize to any of the nutters in your family."

That's when Neill reached out and slapped me across the face. I put my hand up to my stinging cheek and blinked. Ellie was still screaming, but her cries faded to silence as the blood rushed to my ears, and all I could register was my own anger and shock. It took me a moment to gather myself and reach down to pick up our daughter. I knew he wouldn't dare hit her, so I didn't worry for her safety. But I was furious.

It was then I knew, long before the gambling started, that my marriage to Neill was not going to last.

I grabbed my handbag so I wouldn't be caught again without my phone and stalked upstairs to the second floor bedroom where we had stayed in the past. I put Ellie down on the floor and reached for my phone. I called my mother.

"Mum? Can you come get me and Ellie?"

"Why? What's wrong?"

"Just typical Gramercy stuff." I was telling the truth, just not all of it. Neill's assault had been anything but typical.

"Greer, you may want to reconsider and stay there. You married into that family and you're stuck with them now. Why don't you try to make the best of it?"

Even my mother wasn't going to help.

I sighed. "Okay, Mum. I'll try." She would have driven up in an instant if she had known Neill had struck me, but I didn't want to tell her. I didn't want to worry her.

I hadn't eaten all day and I was starving, but I refused to go looking for food in the kitchen. I dug around in my handbag and found a cereal bar and a small piece of chocolate. Though I still nursed Ellie, she was eating solid food and she was probably hungry, too. I tore off small pieces of the cereal bar and gave them to her. She reached for them with her chubby little hands and put them in her mouth. As she chewed, a smile began to spread across her face. It was the first smile I had seen on her in hours and suddenly I began to cry. I buried my face in my hands and cried for several long minutes until the tears dried up by themselves. Ellie seemed to sense my frustration and anxiety because she climbed into my lap and snuggled against my chest, not making a sound, sucking her thumb.

Scooping her up again, I returned to the sitting room downstairs and retrieved our overnight bag. I put her in pajamas, and she fell asleep while I was rocking her in the bedroom on the second floor. My argument with Neill played itself over and over in my head until I couldn't bear to think about it any longer. When he eventually came upstairs to go to bed, I didn't speak to him or even look at him. I sat in the rocking chair with my eyes closed, Ellie in my lap. I waited for him to come over to me, to whisper an apology, to say he realized how difficult it was for me to be in his parents' house, but he did nothing. When his breathing became regular and shallow, I put Ellie in her bed and stole upstairs to the third floor bedroom where I had been imprisoned for so many hours earlier.

I don't know what compelled me to go, but I had to see that painting again. The McTaggart.

I propped open the door with a chair, which I carried across the room so no one would hear it scraping the floor. I wasn't taking any chances on being shut in that room again. I switched on a small lamp on the bedside table. As the dim light swallowed a bit of the darkness, it shone a small puddle of light toward the wall where the McTaggart painting hung, its wooden frame gathering dust and cobwebs. I stared at the painting for the next hour, trying to imprint on my brain every nuanced brushstroke, every hint of light and shadow. I had studied McTaggart for my Ph.D., and I remembered being thrilled when I learned Neill's family owned an original. Surprisingly, having been locked in the room with the painting didn't lessen the thrill. I still felt chills when I looked at the work.

Eventually I walked over to the painting to examine it more closely and to brush off the dust and cobwebs. That such a magnificent work of art should be hidden away like this, let alone covered in filth, was unthinkable.

I inhaled sharply when I heard a soft sound directly behind me. I wheeled around and stood face-to-face with Gerard, Neill's older brother. I had only seen him a few times since marrying Neill, and he scared me a bit. Under bushy eyebrows knit together in a frown, his glittering eyes stared at me.

"Hello, Gerard. Nice to see you again."

"Why are you in here?" he asked, obviously feeling no warmth toward me.

"I was just having a look at the McTaggart. I studied him when I was in school."

He scowled. "It's a wee bit suspicious that you're in here by yourself late at night."

"I couldn't sleep and I thought it would relax me to look at the painting."

"Are you done?" he asked, clipping his words.

I nodded. "I guess I am now," I said.

"Good. Don't be sneaking around the house at night anymore."

I quickly ducked out of the room, feeling his eyes boring into my back as I hastened, shivering, down the hallway.

Chapter 11

As hard as I tried, I couldn't dislodge the memories of that trip to Candlewick Lane. I fell asleep with ugly thoughts pricking the back of my mind. The events of the long day, coupled with the knowledge of what I would have to do in the morning, made me uncomfortable and restless, even as tired as I was. I tossed and turned during the night, wincing from the pain in my back every time I moved.

I was up long before the sun. The late fall days in Scotland were getting shorter and shorter; I had already noticed a difference in the daytime light just in the week or so I had been in Edinburgh. I moved slowly to the kitchen to make tea and found Seamus making breakfast.

"How are you feeling this morning, Greer?" he asked as I limped over to the sink. "Och, lass, have a sit and I'll bring you tea."

I sat down gingerly and waited for my tea. "How are you feeling?" Seamus repeated.

"Pretty sore," I replied. "I didn't sleep very well."

"I expect not. The pain must have kept you awake."

"It did, plus I'm a bit nervous about today."

He put the tea in front of me and handed me the sugar bowl and cream pitcher. "Why nervous?"

"I've decided to pay a visit to Neill's family this morning. They're farmers outside Edinburgh, and they don't like me."

"Where do they live?"

"Glensaig, in East Lothian."

"Why don't they like you, if you don't mind me asking?"

I sighed. "It's a long story. I'll tell you about it sometime, but I'm not ready yet."

He seemed to understand. "And James is going with you?"

"I think so. I'll tell him about the change in plans when he gets here."
He stood up and stretched. "I'm in need of a shower. Can I get breakfast for you first? There's broiled tomato, mushrooms, and beans."

"Thanks, Seamus. You take your shower, and I'll get the food myself. You're too good to me."

"I appreciate your letting me stay here with you and Sylvie, that's for sure. And I love to cook, so I'm glad to do it for you lassies!"

When I talked to James mid-morning, he said he'd be happy to accompany me to Neill's parents' farm. He offered to drive, and I told him a bit about my former in-laws as we drove out of Edinburgh and into the surrounding countryside.

"They're not very nice people," I told him with a sigh. "They never did like me, and I suppose the feeling was mutual."

"What don't you like about them?" James asked.

I didn't know how much to divulge. "They always hoped Neill would marry someone else." I laughed wryly.

"And what didn't they like about you, may I ask?" He hastened to add, "Not that there's anything to dislike, mind you." He grinned.

I smiled. "They thought Neill would be better off with someone who hadn't, uh, hadn't spent as much time in school as I had."

"They thought he should marry someone who wasn't as smart as he?"

"Exactly. They thought I was too big for my britches."

"Huh?"

I laughed at his unfamiliarity with the American phrase. "They didn't think I was a proper lady for Neill. They thought one professor in the family—Neill—was enough. Turns out they were right, but not for the reasons they thought."

We drove in silence for a while. James had put the Gramercys' address into his navigator, but I didn't need the car to tell me how to get to their farm. I would never forget the way.

The road straightened out ahead of us as we descended a steep hill into a valley. Farmland stretched along both sides of the road. This was a quieter time of year for farmers in Scotland, as the harvest was over and new crops wouldn't be planted until close to spring. Herds of woolly sheep munched grass just on the other side of the fences that kept them safe—sometimes—from motorists. Occasionally one would raise its head and, chewing contentedly, watch us drive past. James loved seeing them. "I don't get into the country outside Edinburgh often, so this is a treat! I could watch the sheep grazing all day."

I agreed with him. If I hadn't been so nervous about visiting Janet and Alistair, I would have enjoyed the sheep much more.

James slowed as we entered the village of Glensaig. Though the navigator told James where to drive, I couldn't help pointing him in the direction of the home, at the end of Candlewick Lane. There were only a few homes on the narrow road, and Janet and Alistair's house stood isolated. A stone fence bordered the Gramercy property. It was a large farm, mostly lying fallow now, but in the spring and summer it would be covered with fields of barley and several types of vegetables. Part of the land was covered and produced strawberries, and there were a few dozen head of cattle and about twenty sheep making this place their home.

My eyes followed the fence to its end in front of the farmhouse. I was suddenly hesitant to see Janet and Alistair. James must have sensed my apprehension, because he put his hand on mine and said, "You don't have to go in there, you know."

I shook my head. "Yes, I do. They may have heard from Neill. Not that they'll tell me, but maybe they can get him a message."

"Do you think he'd get in touch with them?"

I shrugged. "They're his family. I would contact my family if I were in trouble. Then again, I think Neill has shown us that he and I don't think the same way."

We had driven slowly up the rutted path to the circular drive in front of the house. It was an imposing structure, made of stone so dark brown it was almost black. It stood three stories tall, with only a few windows on each level. It had been built a very long time ago, when the government imposed taxes based on the number of windows in a home. Though some modern homeowners had renovated their old homes and added windows, Janet and Alistair had opted to keep the place dark. Taking a deep breath, I reached for the door handle.

"Want me to come with you?" James asked.

"I think you'd better stay in the car. I'll let you know if I need you. The last thing they'll want to see is that I've brought a stranger with me. They're very suspicious people."

He shook his head, and I gave him a quick smile. I walked slowly up the stone path to their front door, looking up at the forbidding facade of the house. A curtain in a downstairs window twitched, and I knew someone was aware of my presence.

I lifted the large iron knocker and released it, the metallic ring jarring my hand. I waited for a full minute before I heard the metal rod being slid out of place on the inside of the door. The door opened slowly, and I was staring into the dark hazel eyes I remembered so well. And the memories came rushing back.

Chapter 12

In the room I shared with Neill and Ellie, they were still sleeping soundly when I returned from my encounter with Gerard. I thought briefly about trying to find the car keys and steal away with Ellie back to Dumfries, but searching for the keys would wake Neill instantly. I couldn't bear the thought of crawling into the bed where he slept, snoring lightly, without a care in the world, so I sat in the rocking chair, eventually dozing with my chin resting on my chest. When Ellie began to stir sometime before dawn, I lifted my head to gaze at her, the pain in my neck excruciating. Neill still slept, so I picked her up and took her downstairs to the sitting room, where we played until everyone else began to move around. As hungry as I was, I hesitated to go into the kitchen. When I heard someone come downstairs and go in there, I was suddenly nervous.

It was the knowledge that I needed to eat in order to nurse Ellie that eventually forced us to go into the kitchen for breakfast and tea. Janet was in there, putting on the teakettle. She turned to me with a frown. "Are you going to disappear again today?"

"Janet, why do you and Beatrice insist on pretending you had nothing to do with locking me in the third-floor bedroom yesterday? You and I both know what really happened, even though you've somehow convinced Neill that I went out somewhere."

She gave me a sly grin. "The bond between a mother and her son is unbreakable. Ask him if you disagree. Ask Gerard."

A chill snaked up my back. *Is Janet trying to prove Neill loves her more than me? Is that what this has been about?*

My eyes narrowed as I stared at her. "Janet, I would never try to take Neill from you. Is that what you're concerned about? That I would try to take your place?"

She didn't answer. She turned around and busied herself at the sink. "Janet?" I said.

"You remember this, Greer," she said through gritted teeth, not facing me. I had to strain my ears to hear her. "Neill is my son and my flesh and blood. You will never be that to him." She turned to look at me, pointing at my chest with a shaking finger. "You can never love him as much as I do. Never."

The woman was mad. Love like that was suffocating, unhealthy. I backed away from her, wondering briefly when I might be able to eat again. Ellie was whimpering, burying her face in my shoulder. I took her to the sitting room and cooed to her while we waited for Janet to go back upstairs. Unbelievably, I was going to have to sneak around behind Janet's back to get a meal in this house. As soon as I heard Janet's tread on the back stairs, I hurried into the kitchen with Ellie and poured myself a cup of tea. I took a few pieces of fruit, several biscuits, and some bannock, wrapped them in a plastic bag I found, and took Ellie back upstairs. I left her in the crib while I changed my clothes in the bathroom, which was next to our bedroom. I didn't want to leave her alone, but I didn't want to be changing when Neill awoke. If he never saw me undressed again, that was fine with me.

After Ellie and I were both dressed and I shared some of the fruit with her, I put her in the stroller and we headed outside. The heavy front door protested when I pushed it open, the noise echoing through the house. I listened for a moment;there was no sound from upstairs. It was ridiculous that I had to be so furtive in my in-law's house. I pushed Ellie outside. We walked down Candlewick Lane and toward the village.

We had gone quite a distance when we got to the village proper. I wheeled her into the first little restaurant we came to and ordered strong tea, a traditional Scottish breakfast, and extra milk for Ellie. The traditional Scottish breakfast in a restaurant is a bit different from the traditional Scottish breakfast in a home, but I was famished and ate almost everything on the plate, including the tattie scone, the mushrooms, the tomato, the beans, the bangers, and even the blood pudding. I gave Ellie tiny bites of everything except the blood pudding, and she chattered away happily as we sat in the warm café, enjoying our time away from the Gramercy house.

But reality intruded when my mobile rang. It was Neill, angry again, wondering where we had gone. I told him he could find us at the café in the village, and he promised to be there to "bring us home" in a short while. I hoped "home" referred to Dumfries, but I had a sinking feeling he meant Janet and Alistair's house.

When he was arrived, he parked the car directly in front of the window where I sat feeding Ellie the remainder of my egg. I knew he saw me, because instead of getting out of the car and coming into the restaurant, he honked the horn and made angry gestures for me to hurry and come out.

I took my time paying the bill and getting Ellie strapped into her stroller, though she would be getting right into the car when we went outside. I wasn't deliberately trying to ruffle Neill, but I didn't mind making him wait, either.

I knew I would pay for it, though. And when I got in the car, he lit into me with a long string of epithets I was thankful Ellie didn't understand. She did understand, however, that Neill and I were very upset with each other, and she started crying almost immediately.

We both knew our marriage had taken a dramatic turn for the worse, and as far as I was concerned, it was the fault of him and his family. As far as he was concerned, it was entirely my fault. Why couldn't he see how manipulative, how dangerous, his mother and sister were?

When we got back to the farm, Neill pulled the car to a stop but didn't turn off the engine. When he turned to me to speak, his tone was low and measured.

"Greer, please try to behave while we're with Mum and Dad. For some reason you have convinced yourself that they hate you, but you're not giving them a chance." He hesitated. I thought he might apologize for hitting me.

"I just don't know what to do with you anymore," he said with a sigh. "It's like you're a stranger."

"Me?" I demanded. "If anyone has become a stranger, it's you. And it's happened just since we got to this Godforsaken house."

"Don't talk like that, Greer, I'm warning you."

"Neill, don't you see what your mother is doing? She's trying to prove to me that she has you wrapped around her finger, that you'll believe anything she says, and that she can do no wrong as far as you're concerned. It's sick!"

"Just go in the house," he commanded. "It's nearly time for lunch."

"I'm not hungry. I just ate." I know I sounded petulant, but I wasn't about to sit down to a meal with Neill or his parents.

We were still glaring at each other as we walked through the front door, Ellie asleep in my arms. I guess she had tired of the fighting in the car and decided her own dreams were a better place to be.

Janet met us in the front hall. "Neill, we have to discuss something," she said, ignoring me. Neill's eyebrows furrowed.

"What's the matter, Mum?"

She tilted her eyes in my direction, jerking her head toward the kitchen. I knew I wasn't invited. I didn't care what she had to say to Neill, anyway.

As I put Ellie down in her crib upstairs, though, I began to wonder what Janet wanted. She obviously hadn't wanted me to hear their conversation, so it seemed logical that they were discussing me. I crept down the main stairs and stood outside the kitchen door listening, straining my ears to hear my husband and my mother-in-law.

"...worried about her," Janet was saying in a low voice.

Who's worried? About whom?

"I am, too. I just don't know where this is coming from," Neill replied. "Do you think you should make an appointment for her to see a doctor?"

"Yes, I suppose I should. For Ellie's sake."

They *were* talking about me. It sounded like they were discussing my mental health. *How dare they?*

"I'd just like to know where she went yesterday with Ellie," Neill continued.

I was torn—should I storm in there and confront them? Should I go back upstairs where I knew I would fume and speculate?

Beatrice solved my dilemma for me. I hadn't heard her come up behind me. "Hi, Greer," she said in a loud voice, loud enough for Neill and Janet to hear and come out of the kitchen.

"You see?" Janet asked Neill, pointing at me. "Listening behind doors, disappearing with the child, refusing to eat the food I make just because I made it? It's alarming."

Neill nodded, his fingers raking through his thinning hair. "Greer, Mum is right. You've not been yourself the past few days. Maybe you should take a rest. Maybe you should see a doctor."

"She's not going to see a doctor just because you suggest it to her," Janet chided him. "You need to make the appointment. You need to go with her to make sure she gets the help she needs."

I looked at Neill in horror. Was this really happening? Was Janet trying to get him to believe I was mentally ill? Was he actually going along with it?

"This is absolutely ridiculous," I said a little too loudly. "There is nothing wrong with me that can't be solved by leaving this place. Neill, your mother is trying to sabotage our marriage and my relationship with Ellie. How can you let her do this?"

"Hush. You're being very rude, Greer. My mother only has your best interests at heart. Don't you, Mum?"

She smiled sweetly at him. "You know I do, Neill." She avoided looking at me. I turned suddenly and fled upstairs, locking the bedroom door behind me. I didn't stop to think how such actions would look to Neill. If I had thought it over, I wouldn't have done it.

Hands trembling, I fumbled around looking for my mobile phone, trying to be quiet so Ellie wouldn't wake from her nap. As soon as I found it, I called my mother.

"What is it, Greer?"

"Mum," I whispered, "please, please come get me and Ellie. Things have gotten very bad up here and we need to leave right away."

Now I had her attention.

"What happened?" she asked, her voice rising.

"I can't get into it now, but I need you as quickly as you can get here. Please come. I don't think it's safe for us here anymore."

"I'll leave in five minutes."

All I had to do was pack up a few of Ellie's things and wait for Mum to arrive. I could do that with the door locked, then I could leave quickly once she arrived. I would only have to speak to Neill long enough to tell him where he could find me when he was ready to leave his family and their insane ideas behind.

It wasn't long, though, before I heard a knock at the door.

"Greer? Let me in. We have to talk."

I had nothing to say to Neill. Let him talk through the door until his throat ran dry.

"Greer, please answer me. I'm worried about you. There's someone out here who would like to speak to you."

What!? How could he have gotten someone here so quickly?

In spite of myself, I answered him. "Neill, you and I both know this is crazy. Who's out there with you?"

Neill cleared his throat. "Dr. MacDonald is here. He just wants to talk to you. Please come out now."

"I'm not coming out to talk to some stranger about problems that do not exist. So you may as well tell him to leave."

I could hear murmuring on the other side of the door and then a voice. Not Neill's.

"Dr. Dobbins, I am Dr. MacDonald. Dr. Iain MacDonald. I'm here to help you."

"I don't need your help."

"Your family is very concerned about you and feel you might need someone to talk to."

"Ha! My real family is on its way here right now to pick me up. All I need is to get away from this house." *Sod it. I hadn't meant to tell anyone Mum was coming.*

"Greer? You called your mother?" Neill asked.

"I certainly did. You don't expect me to stay here, do you?"

"I was hoping you would, since we brought Ellie here to visit my parents and Beatrice and Gerard."

"I'm leaving. And if you think I'm going to let Ellie stay here with these people, you're the crazy one, Neill. I'm taking her with me."

Dr. MacDonald spoke again. "Greer, what I'm hearing is a resistance to interact with your in-laws. Is that a fair assessment?"

"I would say they have a failure to interact with me. To the point where they locked me and the baby in an upstairs room yesterday without food or bathroom facilities."

Silence on the other side of the door, then Neill again.

"Greer, we've been through this. You and I both know my parents would never let that happen to you or to Ellie. Nor would Beatrice or Gerard. Wherever you went yesterday, we can discuss that another time. What's important right now is that you are mentally healthy enough to take care of Ellie. And, frankly, I don't think you are. Please come out."

I rubbed my face repeatedly, almost clawing my eyes as my hands raked down my cheeks. *They're trying to get me to think I'm going mad.*

"Neill, I'm not coming out."

I could hear heated whispering on the other side of the door. Ellie was starting to fuss. It was funny how babies could sleep through all kinds of noise, then wake up in the silence following the noise. I picked her up, cooing to her, making her smile in her groggy way, and we sat down in the rocking chair to wait for my mother to text me that she was waiting for us outside. It would be a couple hours before she would arrive.

I sang to Ellie, quietly so I could hear anything—or anyone—outside the door, but there was no sound for a while. After about an hour of singing and playing, during which I nursed Ellie, I sat up straight, startled to hear a key sliding into the door. I thought the only key to this bedroom door was safely in the nightstand.

But I was wrong. The door swung open and Neill and a man I didn't recognize stood in the doorway. *Dr. MacDonald.* Neill's mother stood behind Neill, craning her neck so she wouldn't miss the show.

"I thought there was only one key to this room," I informed Neill, looking down at Ellie. I wanted to avoid looking at his face for as long as possible.

"Mum found another one. It was on a shelf in the cellar."

The doctor cleared his throat. "Greer—" he began.

"It's Dr. Dobbins," I interrupted.

"Dr. Dobbins, what happened to your face?"

I put a hand up to my face, where there must have been marks remaining because I had rubbed my face so hard earlier. I suppressed a groan. *How must that look to him? Not good, I'm sure.*

"Dr. Dobbins?" He was waiting for an answer.

"Ellie reached up and clawed at my face," I answered, realizing as I spoke how pathetic I sounded. Dr. MacDonald nodded, his calm demeanor doing nothing to soothe my nerves. I wanted him to stop judging me, to go away. I wanted him to turn to Neill and his interfering, miserable mother and tell them I was nothing but a harried wife and mother who was being mistreated by her in-laws.

But he didn't say any of those things. In his quiet voice he started to talk again. "May I come in, Dr. Dobbins?"

"I'd rather you didn't."

"Please? I just want to talk." I began to relent. Maybe if I talked to him, I could get him to understand the lunacy of what was happening.

I waved my hand toward the bed, where he sat down lightly, folding his long, slim fingers together in his lap. Neill and his mother watched from the doorway, but Dr. MacDonald nodded at them and said, "We'll be fine in here. If you could just close the door? Thank you."

I could see the reluctance on their faces as Neill turned and pulled the door shut behind him. I wondered if they were standing on the other side of the door, listening.

"Why don't you tell me what's been going on?" Dr. MacDonald asked, tilting his head and nodding toward me, encouraging me to let down my guard.

When I related the events of the previous day and overnight, the doctor raised his eyebrows several times and nodded often, but remained silent. I couldn't tell if I was persuading him of Janet's madness or mine.

Mine, as it turned out. When the story had tumbled out, I sat rocking Ellie in silence, watching her look around the room. She was such a good, quiet baby.

Dr. MacDonald cleared his throat. "What you've told me is extraordinary."

"Yes, I know that. It's almost too much to believe, and I understand if you have a hard time accepting it as the truth. But you have to believe me. I have to leave, and I have to take Ellie with me, so Janet cannot imprison us in this house again."

"I've known the Gramercy family for many years, and it just doesn't seem like the type of behavior they'd engage in," he said, his eyes searching mine.

I cursed myself for not asking him if he knew the Gramercy family before I started talking to him. Of course he knew them—how else could they get a doctor to the house on such short notice? I wondered how he knew them. I wondered if any of them were his patients.

But it didn't matter, because I was alone with him now, having told him my whole story. It was too late to retract it, to tell him it was a joke or I was mistaken. I could tell by looking at his erect bearing, his steady dark gaze, that he didn't believe a word I said and that he was going to take it upon himself to see that I was treated for my mental illness.

There was a slight noise at the door, and my earlier question was answered. Of course Neill and Janet, and God only knew who else, was standing on the other side of the door, listening to my ramblings.

My breath started to quicken and my palms were sweaty. I hugged Ellie closer to me, realizing as I did so that these things all made me look anxious and irritated. I could practically see the wheels turning in Dr. MacDonald's brain, debating where and how I would best be treated.

A soft knock at the door. "Greer?" It was Neill's voice. I didn't answer.

"I've just called your mother and told her you're sick. I advised her to turn around and head back to Dumfries until you feel better. She's worried about you, too. I just didn't want you thinking she was coming for you."

He sounded so reasonable, so rational. But everything was spinning completely out of control.

"Please, Neill, call her back. I need to leave. Ellie and I need to leave," I said. I hated myself for the begging tone in my voice.

"We'll go back when you feel better."

I looked at the doctor, who was staring at me with pity. "Don't look at me like that," I growled. "I'm not sick. Why won't anyone believe me? I'm perfectly healthy. I just want to leave, that's all."

"If you're not sick, then why the marks on your face? I don't think your daughter put them there. People don't scratch themselves like that. And look at your fingernails," he continued. I curled my hands into balls so he couldn't look at them again. I had tried so many times to stop biting my nails, but they were bitten right down to the quicks. "It's clear you're very anxious about something, and I'd like to help you figure out what that is." "I *know* what it is. I've been trying to tell you. My in-laws hate me and they imprisoned us. What more can I do to get you to believe me?" He stood up and held out a hand to me. "Come with me and we'll have you feeling better in no time."

Ellie started to cry, and I stood up and walked around the room with her under the doctor's watchful eye. I tried giving her toy after toy to play with, but nothing seemed to satisfy her. Finally I asked the doctor if I could have some privacy to nurse her and he agreed to wait in the hallway.

I thought furiously while I fed Ellie. How was I going to get myself out of this? I tried calling my mother's mobile, but there was no answer. There was a knock at the door. "Dr. Dobbins? Are you done yet?" asked Dr. MacDonald.

"Yes."

Without waiting for permission, he came back into the room, Neill fast on his heels. Neill came toward me and reached for Ellie. "Would you like to come play with Daddy, darling?"

"No, Neill. Please leave her here with me." I was begging again. I realized with a sinking dread how this was going to end. He was going to take Ellie away and I would be alone with the doctor, helpless to get him to believe me.

"You can have her back as soon as you're better," the doctor said. Though his tone might have sounded soothing to anyone listening, to me it sounded patronizing, grating, and terrifying.

"You're not taking me anywhere," I told him.

"You're going to come back with me to the place where I work, and we'll have you all checked out there."

"You can't do that!" I cried, my voice cracking as it rose higher.

"Neill has already given his permission, and that's all we need at the moment to get the process started."

"What process?" I asked, my eyes darting from the doctor to the window. Could I jump out? I was only two floors off the ground.

But the doctor saw my eyes and read my thoughts. He put his hand on my arm. "Don't do it, Dr. Dobbins. You'll hurt yourself, and it'll only result in you being away from Ellie longer."

And in that moment, I knew Neill and his family had me trapped. My only choice was to accompany the doctor wherever he was going and do my best to behave just like any normal person in order to get my daughter back. I couldn't bear the thought of her staying in this house without me. I was terrified of what Neill's family would do to her. I began to wonder if Ellie was old enough to be poisoned against me by hateful things she heard. My heart started beating faster, and I couldn't seem to hear anything.

Please, God, do not let me faint in front of this man. I sat down on the edge of the bed and took several deep, slow breaths. My vision, which had become dark and blurry around the edges, began to clear.

I stood up and faced Dr. MacDonald. "Where are we going?"

"A facility where I can help you get better quickly."

"Will I be able to come back here later today?"

He shook his head. "I'm afraid not. You'll have to pack a bag and bring it with you."

My knees began to shake. I sat down again. "Just one night?"

"Just as long as it takes."

"What about nursing Ellie?"

"Your husband can buy some formula and give it to the baby. Don't worry."

I held my head in my hands and started to rub my face again, but remembered suddenly that Dr. MacDonald found that behavior suspiciously unhealthy. I stopped abruptly and looked up at him. "Can I talk to Ellie on the phone tonight?"

"You won't be able to have your mobile phone with you, but you can use one of the phones at the center."

"What center?"

"That's where we're going. Pack a bag and we'll get started."

He left the room again, but didn't close the door behind him. *He's watching to make sure I don't jump out the window.*

I felt around in my handbag for my mobile phone, but it wasn't there. Neill must have taken it when I wasn't looking. I couldn't even call my mother and ask for help. I wondered if I could call her from the center. I could pretend I was talking to Ellie and hopefully she would realize something was wrong. I felt a glimmer of hope.

Once my bag was packed, I left with Dr. MacDonald. He must have believed I wasn't a physical threat to him because I sat next to him in the front seat as we drove away down Candlewick Lane. Tears streamed down my face as I imagined how Ellie would react when she realized I wasn't there at bedtime. I made a choking sound trying to stop crying and the doctor glanced over at me.

"Don't worry," he said. "Everything will be fine."

But everything wasn't fine.

Chapter 13

Neill's mother stood in the doorway, blocking the narrow space between the door and the jamb.

"What'dye want?"

"Hello, Janet. I've come to talk to you and Alistair about Neill and Ellie."

"We haf not heard a word. So be off wi' yourself." She began to close the door. I reached out and stopped her.

"Wait, Janet. Please. I'm sure you know they're in Edinburgh. I'm trying to find them."

"And whit d'ye want me tae do about it?"

"I want to know what you've heard, what Neill may have told you or Alistair, where they may be staying. Anything."

"We don't know anything. And we wouldnae tell you if we did."

"Janet, your granddaughter is in danger. And so is your son. If I can find them, if I can learn more about the reason he's in trouble, then maybe I can help him."

An ugly scoffing sound erupted from her throat. "You? Help him? He wouldnae want your help."

"I think he does. He's in real trouble this time, Janet, and he has Ellie with him. If I can help him, he'll be off the hook, and Ellie will be safe."

There was a faint noise behind Janet, and she bent her head around the door to talk to someone.

She turned her baleful gaze toward me again and opened the door a little more, sighing. "Ye may as well come in." I cast a backward glance toward the car before disappearing into the gloom of the old house.

"Who's that?" Janet demanded, following my gaze.

"A friend from Edinburgh who's helping me look for Ellie and Neill."

"A friend, eh?" she sneered.

"Yes. A friend." I stopped myself from rolling my eyes.

I followed her to the sitting room, a cold, dank space to the left of the front door. She gestured toward the horsehair couch, which I remembered as being unbearably dusty and uncomfortable. I sat down on its slippery surface and glanced around, noticing with surprise the painting that hung over the mantel. I knew that painting—it was the McTaggart. The one from the third floor.

Janet sat down in a straight-backed ladder chair across the room from me, staring at me, obviously waiting for me to say something.

I cleared my throat. "As I said, I'm sure you know Neill is hiding somewhere in Edinburgh. It seems he's gotten himself into more trouble gambling. And the people who loaned him money are after him. And Ellie.

"I've been attacked twice now by the people who are looking for him. They think I know where he is. But even if I knew I wouldn't tell them, because Neill has Ellie and I won't do anything to put her in further danger."

I waited for her to say something. She glanced sidelong to the doorway. I knew someone—probably Alistair—was over there, but I didn't say anything.

"Well, I already told you I don't know anything," she said.

"Have the police been here to see you?"

"That's none o' yer business."

So the police had paid the Gramercys a visit.

"Have you tried looking for Neill and Ellie yourself?"

"No."

"But Ellie is your granddaughter. How can you live with yourself knowing she's out there somewhere, in danger, and you're not doing anything to help?"

"I live wi' myself just fine, thank ye verra much."

She glanced again at the doorway. "Is someone out there?" I asked.

"I'll be right back. Don't move," she cautioned abruptly. She got up and stalked out without a second glance at me. As the minutes passed and she didn't return, I decided to ignore her warning. Walking quietly over the worn rugs scattered on the stone floor, I stood in front of the mantel to gaze at McTaggart's painting.

It was called The Village, Whitehouse. Several white cottages, some with thatched roofs, were portrayed along a dirt lane. A group of languid children sat on the ground at the end of the lane. The painting had been done in shades of tan, brown, yellow, chartreuse, ivory, white, and green.

It was a perfect rendition of a lazy summer's day, and I could practically feel the children's lethargy.

Though the painting itself was in pristine condition, the frame was a dusty mess. I could see fingerprints in the dust and wondered why no one bothered to clean the frame around such a beautiful piece of art.

Eventually I heard a step in the hallway outside and I hurried to sit down again on the couch. Janet appeared in the doorway with my ex-father-in-law, Alistair. Both stared at me suspiciously for a moment, then Alistair crossed to a small old-fashioned settee, his tall, lanky frame folding in upon itself as he sat down.

"Have *you* heard from Neill?" I demanded, staring at Alistair.

"No," Alistair answered.

"If you know anything and you haven't told the police, there'll be no end to the headaches for both of you."

Alistair let out a noise that was something between a growl and a cough. "Don't threaten us, lass."

Janet had been looking at Alistair, but she turned her baleful gaze on me. "What have you heard from the police?" she asked.

"I thought I made it clear that I don't know anything. If I did, you can be sure I would have Ellie back by now." So that's why they invited me into the house. They wanted information from me. "Could you do something for me? Could you give Neill a message if you hear from him before I do?"

"I don't know about that. I don't think he wants to hear from you," Janet replied.

"He texted me!" I was losing my cool and needed to keep a level head to talk to my former in-laws. I knew what they were capable of doing, and I didn't want to experience it again. "I know he wouldn't ignore a message from me. Would you just think about it? Please? Tell him I can help him by giving him money or anything else he needs. Tell him I just want Ellie back so I can take her home. She'll be safe there. The loan sharks want him. He's the one they really want."

Alistair looked at me from under his shaggy eyebrows. "We'll think about it. Now you'd best be off before I change my mind about being so nice."

Janet had other ideas, though. She stood up and blocked my path to the front door. "Not so fast. Who is it in the car out there?"

Alistair sidled up to the small window overlooking the drive in front of the house and peered through the dingy curtains. "Well?" he asked.

"His name is James Abernathy and he is helping me look for Ellie and Neill. He drove me out here today because I don't have a car in Edinburgh. He's harmless, I guarantee you."

Janet looked at me through narrowed eyes, doubt written all over her face. "Does he know Neill?"

"No."

"Couldn't you have gotten a car for hire?"

"Yes, but James offered to drive me and I accepted."

"Hmm," Alistair commented.

"Excuse me, please," I said to Janet as I approached the front door. She stepped out of my way, and I reached for the doorknob, then turned around and tried appealing to her one last time. "Please, Janet, whatever has gone on between us, it has nothing to do with Ellie. I hope you'll give my message to Neill if you hear from him."

"We'll think about it."

"Thank you," I said, nodding my head toward her. "I would appreciate it."

"Don't bother coming back," Alistair warned as I stepped out into the bright sunlight.

I didn't answer—I couldn't make such a promise—and I walked quickly to James's car. He started the engine when he saw me coming, and I slid into the front seat with a sense of relief.

"How'd it go?" he asked, easing the car down the drive.

"It was awful," I answered. "They're the most disagreeable people. I'm positive they know something, maybe even where Neill is staying, but they're not telling."

"What makes you think they know something?"

"Just a strong hunch. For one thing, Janet told me they haven't tried to find Neill and Ellie. Even as awful as Janet and Alistair are, they wouldn't just sit and wait for the police to find their son. They would look for him, too. Not only that, but they were pumping me for information. They want to know what I know. I'm guessing they want to report back to Neill. They can't stand me. They have never forgiven me for eloping with Neill, though it was his idea."

"You eloped?" James asked in surprise.

"Yes," I said with a tired grin. "I don't seem the type, do I?"

"Well, you rather strike me as the kind of woman who would like a proper wedding."

"I did want one, but Neill talked me out of it. Said we could save the money for a down payment on a house."

"And is that what happened?"

"Eventually. We lived in this squalid little place until we had saved enough money to buy a nice house just off campus where we both work. When he moved out, I took over the mortgage and Ellie and I still live in that same house."

James nodded. "Is there anywhere else you'd like to go?"

"No, we can just head back into Edinburgh if you'd like."

"Well, you promised me lunch, remember?" he asked.

"I did, didn't I? Well, let's stop somewhere. I'm starving!"

"I know just the place," James said, pulling to a stop in the Gramercys' driveway before turning onto Candlewick Lane. He punched some numbers and letters into his navigator and watched as a map popped into view.

"Where are we going?" I asked.

"You'll see. But first, a stop at a market to get food. We'll eat it when we get to the place I have in mind."

I related the highlights of my visit with Neill's parents as we drove. James didn't pry into the reasons behind the acrimony between us, and I didn't volunteer the information. We stopped at the local Sainsbury's and bought food to share, then headed east. James finally revealed where we were headed—Inveresk Lodge Garden, a property maintained by the National Trust for Scotland and a place I'd heard of but never had a chance to visit.

We entered the charming village of Inveresk, where ages-old mansions hid behind tall stone enclosures resembling ancient fortresses. Shrubbery cascaded over the walls from green groves barely visible over the height of the stone. Tree boughs canopied the sidewalks, making the footpaths slightly mossy and damp-looking. We drove slowly, watching as the high walls came to an end and homes changed from the large seventeenth- and eighteenth-century dwellings obscured by trees to smaller and more humble houses of timber and stone built close to the road.

After our quick tour of the village, we turned around and easily found the Inveresk Lodge Garden entrance. Gathering our lunch, we ventured into the secluded garden with its conservatory, aviary, magnificent sundial, pebbled paths, and delightful border gardens. With our visit arriving on the cusp between autumn and winter, many of the plants and flowers were dormant, but we did glimpse a variety of yellow, orange, red, and purple berries waiting to be plucked by eager birds. I noticed the winter honeysuckle and Christmas box, which would soon fill the air with unexpected and luscious fragrances. James and I found a bench, and we sat and ate our lunch. The birds flitted around the gardens as the sun disappeared and reappeared again and again around the dark clouds scudding across the sky.

"Want to take a walk down the path?" James asked as we put away the remnants of our meal.

I really wanted to get back to Edinburgh to see if anyone had called or visited Bide-A-Wee house with information about Ellie, but I agreed. The gardens had a calming effect on me, and I didn't mind lingering a bit to prolong that feeling of serenity.

James took my arm as we made our way down the sloping woodland path. At the bottom was a pond with several ducks gliding along its surface. A small family of rabbits loped in the grass nearby, probably readying their burrow for the coming winter.

Only one other person shared the idyll with us. She sat on a bench overlooking the small pond, a book in her hands and her head bent away from us. Her profile looked familiar.

As we walked slowly around the pond, James pointing out various birds in the nearby trees, I found myself casting several glances toward our fellow nature-lover. At one point she looked up toward James and me, startled by a sudden loud cry of a duck, and I was shocked. I must have let out a quiet gasp.

It was Neill's sister, Beatrice. I stared at her as recognition slowly dawned on her face.

"What's the matter?" James asked, following my gaze to the stranger. "Who is that? Do you know her?"

"Yes. That's Neill's sister," I whispered.

"Is that a problem?"

"A wee one," I answered. "She likes me about as much as her parents do."

Beatrice had obviously decided against ignoring me. She reached into her handbag for a bookmark, placed it carefully in the book, and walked toward us, her face an unreadable blank canvas. Her brown hair hung in a long bob, framing her thin face.

"What are you doing here?" she greeted me, not even looking at James.

"My friend and I stopped here for lunch. I've just been to see your parents."

"What did you want with them?" she asked, her eyebrows furrowing.

"I wanted to know if they have information about Neill and Ellie."

"Hmm," she replied. "And did they?"

"If they do, they're not willing to share it with me."

"Did you really expect them to?" she said, shaking her head. "You're not exactly high on their list of favorite people, Greer."

"I hoped they would," I answered. Then I ventured to ask her, "Have you heard from Neill?"

"Och, you know how angry my parents would be if I *had* heard something and I told you," she replied lightly.

Suddenly my heart started thudding against my rib cage. My breathing became shallow. My sweater felt too tight around my neck. I wheeled around, shook my head at the arm James offered, and ran off by myself. I could hear his hurried footsteps behind me on the grassy path, but I didn't slow down.

"Greer, wait," he called. "Are you all right?"

I stopped abruptly and turned to face him. He was so startled, he almost ran straight into me. "I'm sorry, James. I'm just feeling overwhelmed. I keep hitting dead ends. Neill's family will stand shoulder-to-shoulder against me because I divorced Neill. Beatrice actually used to be nice to me, but she won't do anything against her parents' wishes. If they won't tell me anything, she won't either." I wiped a tear from the corner of my eye, willing myself to calm down.

"Out of all the places we could have eaten lunch..." James began. "I wish we had just gone back to Edinburgh."

I could see he was distressed over my chance meeting with Beatrice. I did the best I could to cheer him up. "Beatrice really isn't so bad. She just needs to get a backbone. She's a teacher, you know. I don't know how she handles an entire classroom full of kids without the ability to stand up for herself. At least Neill's brother, Gerard, wasn't with her. Now *that* could have been unpleasant."

He nodded. "The brother's that bad too, eh? Well, I *am* glad you didn't have to face that beastie alone." We walked in silence for a few moments, then James turned to look at me.

"Was Neill's family nicer before you married him?"

I shook my head ruefully. "I doubt it. If you can believe it, I never met them before eloping with Neill. After I met Janet and Alistair—and Gerard, of course—for the first time, I was convinced he wanted to elope just so I wouldn't meet his family before getting married."

"I'm sure you're right."

"He always denied it, but I never believed him. Let's stop talking about Neill and his family, shall we?"

"With pleasure," he said, reaching for my hand.

We walked in silence back to the car, then headed back toward Edinburgh under the darkening afternoon clouds. Before long rain was slashing at the car's windscreen, making it difficult to see the road and the cars ahead. The weather matched my foul mood. James seemed to understand I didn't want to talk, so he hummed quietly to himself most of the trip. We were driving into the city proper when the rain stopped, the clouds cleared, and the sun shone onto the streets of the city, wet and glistening.

James turned to me at a stoplight. "See? Sun's out. It always comes out, you know."

I smiled at his poetic attempt to make me feel better as he drove me back to Bide-A-Wee. When we got there, he said he had to drop off his car at home and then run some errands near his office. He invited me to go with him, but my back was hurting again, and I wanted to lie down. I thanked him and promised to call him later.

As I walked up the front steps to Bide-A-Wee, I noticed the door was slightly ajar. A small piece of wood in the door jamb was splintered and broken. I pushed the door open tentatively.

Chapter 14

The living room of Bide-A-Wee was a shambles. Sofa cushions were scattered across the floor, a chair was knocked over, and the desk drawers were all pulled out, their contents strewn about the room.

"Sylvie? Seamus?" I hurried to the bedrooms, which were in the same condition. No one else was home. I ran back into the living room, fumbled in my handbag for my mobile phone, and called the police, quickly followed by Sylvie, then Seamus. They promised to come home as quickly as possible.

The police arrived first. I was sitting on the front steps when two officers pulled up to the curb. They went into the flat ahead of me, one of them taking photos of the front door, the rooms, and the mess, the other asking me questions.

When they asked where I had been earlier in the day, I intentionally misled them. I didn't want them to know where I had spent my morning. I didn't want them bothering James with their questions, and I didn't want them to know I had visited Alistair and Janet. I also didn't want to be accused of interfering with a police investigation. And though I hadn't had a chance to look around yet to see if anything had been taken, I couldn't imagine robbery was the motive for the break-in and vandalism. I told the officer and his partner—who by then had finished photographing the damage—about why I was in Edinburgh and the attacks on me in St. Giles Cathedral and Princes Street Gardens.

"So you think one of the people looking for your ex-husband could have broken in here to find information on his whereabouts?"

I nodded. "Absolutely. The man from St. Giles told me he knows where I live. I guess this is proof he wasn't bluffing."

Sylvie arrived then, followed a few minutes later by Seamus. They were shocked when they saw the condition of the flat. The officers questioned them extensively, asking them many of the same questions they asked me. When asked where they had been, Sylvie said she'd been job-hunting and Seamus had been sketching at one of the museums along the Royal Mile. Both, of course, denied knowing who might have broken into the flat.

Sylvie turned to me. "Do you really think that the person who did this is the one looking for Neill?"

"I do," I answered. "The man, or the people he works for, must be desperate to find Neill. I don't have any information that would help, though, so he wasted his time coming here."

I was surprised by my own reaction to the break-in. I wasn't afraid, just angry. Angry that someone would violate my home and my personal belongings. And a small part of me was glad—glad that whoever came into my flat had wasted precious time looking for Neill when I had no information that could help. Glad that the person's goal was thwarted.

But my thoughts quickly snapped back to Ellie. As much as I didn't care what happened to Neill after the harrowing events he'd put me through recently, anyone who was able to find Neill would probably find Ellie, too. I blinked, coming out of my thoughts about Ellie, and realized Sylvie was speaking to me. "Hmmm?"

"I said, were you able to find out anything when you visited Neill's parents today?" I looked daggers at her. I hadn't wanted her to say anything about my visit to their farm.

The officers looked at me. "You didn't say that's where you were," the lead officer said.

"I didn't get out there today," I lied, staring at Sylvie.

The officers stared at me for a moment. I don't think they believed me, but they asked me no further questions. They did warn me, however, against contacting the Gramercys and interfering with an ongoing case.

They finally left with a promise to be in touch as soon as they were able to investigate the break-in further and with an admonition that if we found anything missing from the flat, we were to notify them immediately. I couldn't imagine what further investigating they could do, but I assumed I would hear from them again at some point. And as for items missing, I knew nothing would be. I already knew who had broken in—the man who had attacked me in St. Giles Cathedral and again in the Gardens. Whatever he was looking for, he wasn't going to find it in my flat.

Sylvie turned to me after the officers had left. "Och, Greer, I'm sorry I mentioned Alistair and Janet's farm. I didn't realize you wanted to keep that a secret. Why didn't you go out there?"

"I did."

"Greer, you should have told the police."

"If the police find out I was there, they'll say I'm interfering with their investigation, and they might not be as interested in helping me or in sharing any information with me. I need to know everything I can."

I picked up the books that had fallen to the floor, stacking them neatly on one of the side tables. Sylvie and Seamus joined me, making piles of mail and papers. As we worked I told them of the events at the farm and of running into Beatrice.

It took a few hours to clean up the mess, which had probably taken our intruder minutes to create. Whoever he was, he had gone through the kitchen cupboards, probably just for spite, and knocked down tins and bags of pantry staples. Seamus found this especially offensive. He shooed Sylvie and me out of the kitchen while he cleaned up the mess. We could hear him muttering to himself as he went about his work. It brought a smile to my face, the first in hours, to know how intent he was on having a clean and orderly kitchen.

I sat with Sylvie in the living room, lying on a heating pad as my back was in agonizing pain. My mobile phone rang. It was James.

After I filled him in, he couldn't believe what I had found in my flat just after he dropped me off. He chided himself aloud for letting me go inside alone. "I should have walked you to the door, especially with your back bothering you," he said.

"How were you to know what would be inside? And I was perfectly capable of getting into the flat by myself, thank you very much," I said, hoping he could hear the smile in my voice.

He obviously couldn't. "Greer, I'll never forgive myself. What if that person had still been in there? What if he attacked you again?"

"James, you're really making too much of this. Come over and see for yourself. The flat is cleaned up, and I'm all in one piece."

"Invite James for some dinner," Seamus called from the kitchen.

"Did you hear that?" I asked James. "Seamus wants you to come for dinner."

"I'll be there," he promised.

A short while later, James arrived. When he first came in, he scanned the room slowly, as if trying to imagine the damage, or perhaps trying to divine the identity of the culprit. But he relaxed when he saw that my back was feeling a bit better—thanks to pain medication and the heating pad—and that the flat wasn't in as bad a condition as he expected.

The four of us ate a quiet dinner together around the kitchen table. James had brought a bottle of wine, and Seamus had prepared a luscious salmon with whisky sauce, swedes and tatties, and a beet salad.

There was no fire in the fireplace that evening. Everyone was tired from a long and stressful day. I was still surprised that I wasn't more worried about the break-in. I doubted it wouldn't happen again, since there was nothing valuable or even interesting in the flat. No appreciable amount of money, no valuables except Seamus's paintings, which were untouched, no documents of any kind that would be of interest to an intruder. I kept all my identification, including my driver's license and temporary passport, on me at all times.

But as I lay in bed, I found that my brain wasn't prepared for sleep in the way my body was. I stared at the ceiling, doubts beginning to creep into my thoughts from the darkness surrounding me. What if the man or people looking for Neill hadn't ransacked the flat? What if it was someone completely unrelated to Neill's disappearance with our daughter? What if the person was actually looking for Seamus?

That thought worried me the most. I found myself wondering about the people Seamus had known in prison, the people he had dealt with in his violent past. Could they have come looking for him? Could the ransacking have been a message directed at him? I had no way of knowing. He hadn't told the police about his past, though I was sure it would be easy enough for them to figure out on their own with the click of a mouse.

And I couldn't discuss it with Seamus—that was the worst part. I wasn't even supposed to know about his stint in prison. He would likely be furious with both Sylvie and me if he realized she had told me. I didn't want to discuss it with Sylvie because I didn't want her to worry. She, too, seemed quite convinced the break-in was related to Neill, so I didn't want to upset her unnecessarily with dire thoughts about Seamus that might not even prove to be true.

I finally fell into a fitful sleep and woke feeling groggy and agitated. When I stumbled into the kitchen to make a pot of tea, Seamus was already there, whistling softly and emptying the dishwasher. I stood in the doorway in the still-dark living room, wondering whether Sylvie and I were really safe with him around. I felt suspicious, confused, and unsettled, but above all, angry with myself for feeling that way about Seamus. He turned to me with a smile, scratching his unruly red beard, when I stepped out of the shadows and into the kitchen.

"Mornin' Greer! I've a pot of tea on. Care for a cuppa?"

"Yes, thank you," I replied, my mistrust evaporating again in the face of his kindness and cheer.

He poured me a cup and sat down across from me with his own tea. "Were you able to sleep last night?"

"Yes," I lied.

"I don't believe you. You look awful this morning."

"Thanks," I said, grimacing.

"You know what I mean. You have dark circles under your eyes, and you have that tired look about you. You worried about yesterday?"

I sighed. "A little. I'm starting to have doubts about who broke in. Maybe it wasn't someone looking for information about Neill, after all."

He leaned back and looked at me. I stared into my teacup, feeling uncomfortable. Did he know what I knew?

"You mean like a random stranger?"

I shrugged. "Yeah, I guess."

"But why would a stranger choose this flat? It doesn't stand out. There are plenty of other flats on the street, and lots of cars parked right outside. It doesn't make sense."

"Nothing about it makes sense," I replied.

"Why don't you go over to the police station and see if they've found anything?"

"I suppose I could do that," I answered slowly. Maybe he didn't know Sylvie had told me about his past. He wasn't acting like someone who was trying to hide something. He seemed sincere in his suggestion. He was really trying to help.

I pushed back from the table. "You're right, Seamus. I will go over there to see if they've found anything. Maybe they've interviewed the neighbors, and one of them saw someone."

"Aye, perhaps they have. Want porridge? I've got some on the stove."

After Seamus's hearty breakfast, I showered and made my way to the police station. Seamus went with me, then continued on to his errands. My back still hurt, but it was better than yesterday. At the station, I asked to see the lead officer. When the receptionist told me he was in a meeting, I decided to sit and wait for him, no matter how long it took.

To my surprise, I didn't have to wait long. He came out to greet me fifteen minutes later and led me back to his "office," which consisted of a desk that he shared with another officer inside what looked like an old coat closet.

"I came to see if you've found anything more since yesterday."

"As a matter of fact, I have," he said.

I raised my eyebrows, waiting for him to speak.

"It seems one of your neighbors, a woman who lives down the block a bit, saw someone— a man—knocking on your front door yesterday. She heard him calling your name. She might not have noticed him except for that."

"Calling *my* name?"

"Yes. Could it have been Neill?" the officer asked.

"I suppose. There was no child with him?"

"No. He was alone."

"Then I hope it wasn't Neill, because that would mean Ellie was alone somewhere. Besides, why would Neill ransack my flat?"

"You probably know that better than I would. Has he ever done anything like that in the past?"

"No," I said, before I remembered something. "Wait. He did make a mess in my house back in the States. He was looking for passports in the safe I keep in my office."

"What does Neill look like?"

"Tall, thin, brown hair, wears glasses."

"Hmm. Probably not him, then. According to your neighbor, this man was heavy-set and balding."

"Definitely not Neill, then," I said, not knowing whether to feel relief or frustration. While I would love to find him, I didn't want to think he had left Ellie alone somewhere. But the man who had accosted me at St. Giles and at the Gardens *was* heavy, and balding, at least a little.

I shared this with the policeman. "Do you think it was the same man?"

"Quite possibly."

"So where do you go from here?"

"Keep asking around. Someone else may have seen him leaving, may have gotten a better look at him. We'll keep you posted," he said, pushing back from his desk.

Apparently that was my cue to leave. I walked slowly back to the flat by myself, my thoughts churning. I didn't want to be out walking alone, but I didn't want to bother Sylvie or Seamus or James and ask for an escort.

I didn't know what to do next. The few leads I had followed had been unsuccessful. I still planned to follow up with Alistair and Janet, but I knew they wouldn't tell me anything. Yet. And if they thought I alerted the police, they would never give me the information I wanted. I needed to bide my time, to wait until they were ready.

For the next few weeks things were relatively quiet while I waited to hear news of Neill, Ellie, and of the person who had broken into my flat. It seemed the police were no closer to finding any of them. It was December, and Edinburgh was getting colder and colder with each passing day. Every morning I was finding it harder and harder to get out of bed. I was depressed and listless, and Sylvie and Seamus and James were at a loss in trying to buoy my spirits.

That Christmas was the worst of my life. I had bought small gifts for Sylvie and Seamus, and they had also bought some nice things for me. But opening gifts was the last thing I wanted to do. I cried easily that day, feeling hopeless and sorry for myself. I'm sure I was a damper on Sylvie and Seamus's spirits, but I couldn't help it. I was miserable and lethargic, wanting nothing more than for the day to end. I wondered constantly what Ellie was doing and whether Neill had given her any Christmas presents.

And New Year's Eve wasn't much better. James and I spent the evening in the flat while Sylvie and Seamus went out with friends. James had asked me to go out to dinner, but I simply couldn't bear the thought of seeing all the people of Edinburgh out celebrating while my heart broke.

My research was one of the only bright spots during the long, dragging days of winter. In an attempt to stay busy and keep my mind occupied, I had decided to spend my idle time doing a wee bit of research on Scottish art. I made several field trips to nearby museums, where I had obtained special permission to access some of the galleries that were closed to the public.

It was an especially dark, rainy day when I packed up my computer and headed off to the City Art Centre, where a magnificent collection of fine paintings by Scottish artists rivaled any collection in the world. I had done quite a bit of research on McTaggart and his paintings, including the one hanging in Janet and Alistair's home. The son of a *crofter*, McTaggart had left home at sixteen to pursue his art in Edinburgh. I got goose bumps when I looked at McTaggart's paintings, not just because I was mystified by the haunting, almost ethereal, beauty of his work, but also because of the ugly memories that the painting in Janet and Alistair's house represented.

I strolled around the museum, listening to snippets of murmured conversations about art, the weather, the architecture of the building, the items available in the gift shop, and places to get lunch along the Royal Mile. It was just another outing for the people milling around me. None of them seemed to be suffering, to be missing their little girl, to be wondering when they might see her again. None of them seemed preoccupied with fear and desperation, with depression and longing. I felt alone in a sea of happy faces, and I began to feel ill.

I knew seeing James would lift my spirits, so I called him and suggested we meet for lunch. He agreed readily, and a short while later we were each tucking into a hot bowl of lamb stew at a cozy pub not far from the museum. My mood, like the day, had been growing darker and darker, and it was nice to see a friendly face across the table. I instructed him to talk about his work so my mind would stay focused on something other than my own troubles. He obliged, telling me about a young boy who had wiped his peanut-butter-covered hands all over a priceless painting and an artist who demanded that each of her paintings be hung in a room by itself to allow the viewer to see each painting without being distracted by any other works of art. He rolled his eyes at the eccentricities of some of the artists he dealt with regularly, but concluded by saying that those "quirks," as he called them, drew visitors to the galleries. His eyes crinkled in the corners when he laughed. I felt better after our lunch together and went home in a lighter mood. I stopped at the police station before going home, just to check in and remind them I was still waiting for news of Ellie and Neill. I hadn't expected them to have any new information, but I did like to stop there every few days to keep my case in the forefront of their minds.

When I got home, I found the front door unlocked. This was not unusual, since Seamus often painted in our living room "studio" during the day when he wasn't visiting a museum or gallery, and Sylvie, having found temporary work as a receptionist at a private school nearby, sometimes came home for lunch.

But when I called out, no one answered. Their bedroom door was open so I peeked in, hoping I wouldn't see anything which would embarrass them. But no one was in there.

I was stepping warily, remembering the day our flat had been ransacked. I would have to remind those two to be more responsible and make sure the door was locked every time they went out. I moved through the living room cautiously; there seemed to be nothing amiss.

Until I went into the kitchen.

Chapter 15

Sylvie lay motionless on the floor, face up, her eyes closed. A thin trickle of blood flowed from the back of her head into a small pool. Her neck was covered with fresh purple bruises, and there were bloody, angry scratches on her hands and arms. It was horrifying. Suppressing a scream, I whipped out my mobile phone. I called the police and told them what I had found. They promised to come quickly, then the dispatcher stayed on the phone while I checked for Sylvie's pulse. My fingers sticky with her blood, I felt around her neck until I found a faint pulse. Letting out a cry of relief, I told the dispatcher she was still alive. She stayed on the phone with me, trying to soothe my nerves, until the police officers and an ambulance arrived just a few minutes later. If she hadn't been on the phone, I think I would have fallen apart. All the nasty things I had said about Sylvie since my arrival in Edinburgh—indeed, all the nasty things I had *ever* said about her—rushed into my head in a flash flood. I silently begged forgiveness for all those times I had entertained unkind thoughts about her, promising God and myself that if she lived, I would never be anything but the model sister to her.

I stood a few feet away while the paramedics triaged her and evaluated her most immediate needs. While they worked, the police took turns asking me questions.

I could barely concentrate on what they were asking, preoccupied with trying to hear the paramedics. I watched as they put a head brace on her, slid a stretcher under her body, hoisted her up, and wheeled her through the front door, telling me the location of the hospital where they were headed. I pleaded with the police officers to let me go with her, and they let me ride in the ambulance. They followed us to the hospital. It didn't occur to me at the time that they wanted to keep track of my whereabouts.

Sylvie regained consciousness in the ambulance. She screamed when she discovered she couldn't move her head, but the paramedic gave her a mask with flowing oxygen. That seemed to calm her quickly. I held her hand and explained what had happened. Her eyes grew wide, and tears started to flow.

"Am I going to die?" she cried.

"No, you're going to be fine, lass," the paramedic replied. His eyes held mine for a moment, and I knew better than to say anything. I hoped he was telling her the truth. I pulled out my phone and called Seamus, telling him tersely what had happened and the name of the hospital where he could find us. Then I called my mother, who promised to be there before evening. She had to throw some clothes in a bag, and then would get right on the road.

When we arrived at the hospital, the paramedics whisked Sylvie into the emergency department, while the police asked me to stay with them in the waiting room. I was impatient to get back to my sister, but they insisted I stay to answer a few questions.

Their questions were polite enough, but it slowly began to dawn on me that they were asking more about my comings and goings during the day than about the unlocked apartment door, Sylvie's actions, or her relationship with Seamus.

"Wait a minute," I said after they asked me what my relationship with Sylvie was like. "Do you think *I* did this to her?"

"This is just protocol, ma'am," replied one of the officers.

"Why would I do that to my own sister?" I asked. "My relationship with her is just fine."

The officer wrote something in his notebook and flipped it shut. "We'll be in touch, Dr. Dobbins," he said.

As the officers were leaving, Seamus came running into the emergency department. The police turned to look at him and when they saw he was headed straight toward me, they followed him.

"Where is she?" he asked me, breathless. "What's going on?"

"I was just on my way back to see her," I answered him. "The police have been talking to me and they kept me out here in the waiting room."

"Sir?" One of the officers tapped Seamus on the shoulder and Seamus whipped around, clearly on edge.

"What?" Seamus demanded. "Oh. Sorry, officer. I haven't got my wits about me, I suppose," he said, his face reddening.

"We have just a few questions for you before you go back to see Miss Dobbins," the officer said.

I moved away to give Seamus some privacy while he answered questions. It took much longer than I expected. Perhaps he had told them of his history and they had further questions for him, or perhaps suspicion naturally fell on a boyfriend in the case of an attack on a young woman. Whatever the reason, both officers had taken out their notebooks and were scribbling furiously. I wanted to ask Seamus about it, but when he finished talking to the police, he was anxious to see Sylvie for himself. He clearly did not want to answer any questions from me after his grilling.

"Did they tell you what they think happened?" I asked him.

"Not a word," he answered gruffly. "I don't want to talk about it." I frowned, taken aback by his brusque attitude. He saw the look on my face and his tone softened. "I'm sorry, Greer. I'm quite worried."

I was worried too, but I wasn't being rude to him. My thoughts began to reel. Was it possible he knew something about Sylvie's injuries? Was that the reason he didn't want to answer my questions?

A nurse took us back to the room where Sylvie was being examined by two doctors. He asked us to wait outside until the doctors had finished. I couldn't even tell if she was conscious. Seamus stood on tiptoe and craned his neck to see over the doctors' heads. He turned to me in disgust, his fists clenched. "I can't see a thing. Why can't they just let me look at her?"

"I'm sure they will," I said in what I hoped was a soothing voice. The truth was, he was beginning to scare me a bit. If I hadn't known him to be a gentle soul, I would have been afraid of him. Between the tattoos, the bushy beard, and his very thick neck, he was a formidable-looking Scot.

Several long minutes passed, during which Seamus paced the small hallway outside Sylvie's door. I watched him warily, looking at the clock again and again. Finally, one of the doctors came out and introduced himself as Dr. Yarbrough. Seamus whipped around at the other end of the hall and hurried over.

"Are you the family?" Dr. Yarbrough asked.

"I'm Sylvie's sister. Our mother is on her way here now from Dumfries. This is her boyfriend," I said, pointing at Seamus.

"How is she?" Seamus asked.

"She took rather a hard hit on her head and blacked out, but she's conscious now and talking a bit. She's quite frightened because she doesn't know what happened," the doctor answered.

"Is she going to be all right?" I asked, glancing at Seamus.

"I think so. We're going to run some tests and keep her here for evaluation. We think she suffered a concussion. Do either of you know exactly what happened?"

Seamus and I shook our heads. "I found her like that on the kitchen floor of our flat," I told Dr. Yarbrough.

"And she called me and told me to meet her here," Seamus said, nodding toward me.

"So neither one of you can shed any light on how the injury occurred."

"That's right. I'm sorry," I said. Seamus nodded in agreement.

"I'll be back in a short while. They're taking her for x-rays in a few minutes," the doctor said.

"Can we go in there?" I asked.

"Yes, but please try not to say anything that's going to upset her. I want to keep her as calm as possible. And don't turn the lights on, please. I want to shield her eyes from anything too harsh."

Seamus and I tiptoed into the darkened room.

"Sylvie?" I whispered.

"Mmm," she moaned in answer. Her swollen eyes were closed.

"It's Greer. Seamus is here with me. How are you feeling?"

"Greer?" she asked, her voice rising.

"Shh," I said, taking her hand in mine. "The doctor doesn't want you to get excited."

"What happened?" she whispered.

"I don't know. I found you on the kitchen floor in the flat. You were unconscious. No one else was there. But you're here in hospital now, and you're going to be fine."

"Do you remember anything?" Seamus asked, his voice tight.

I shook my head slightly. "I don't think we should be asking her that. It might upset her," I whispered.

"I can hear you," Sylvie said, her words thick.

I smiled. At least her sarcasm muscle wasn't damaged.

"I don't remember anything," she said slowly.

"No one in the flat?" Seamus asked. I shot him a warning look, which he ignored.

"No."

"Don't worry about any of that now. Sylvie, why don't you try to rest?" I asked, giving Seamus a hard look. "The doctor said someone's going to take you for x-rays soon."

"Could you guys wait in here?" she asked.

"Of course," Seamus and I answered together.

She closed her eyes, and very soon her breathing slowed and became more regular. She was asleep. I motioned Seamus to follow me away from Sylvie's bed. "You shouldn't be asking her questions about what happened. We don't want to upset her."

"But how else are we going to know what happened?"

"It'll have to wait until the doctor says she can discuss it."

He scowled. "Just trying to remember something can't hurt."

"Yes it can, especially if she has a concussion or some other head injury. Just leave her alone about it. We'll find out soon enough."

He slumped down in the chair beside Sylvie's bed like a chastised little boy.

I stood by the door, watching the buzz of activity in the big emergency department. Doctors and nurses hurried by, each in search of answers to the problems of their own patients, none wondering about the story behind my sister's injuries.

I tried to think of a scenario that would explain what had happened in the flat. I had been surprised to find the door unlocked, but Sylvie had probably stopped in for a few minutes and was planning to go back to work. It wouldn't be unusual for her to leave the door unlocked if she planned to be inside for just a short time. But how had someone known she would be there? I glanced over at Seamus. He was clasping and unclasping his hands as he watched Sylvie sleeping, his face taut and his eyes haggard. Did he know something?

I hated to indict him, even in my thoughts, but he had acted strangely ever since he arrived at hospital and the police had spoken to him. Had he been telling the truth about where he was when I called him? Had he been nearer the flat than I thought?

I shook my head vehemently as if to get rid of those thoughts, and my sudden movement startled Seamus.

"What's wrong?" he asked.

"Nothing. I'm sorry. Just a lot going on, I guess." He looked at me and I held his gaze for a long moment. What was going through his head?

An x-ray technician came into Sylvie's room, interrupting our staring match. "I'll be taking her for tests, then I'll bring her back here. I think they're going to put her in a room after that." Sylvie's eyes fluttered as the tech spoke.

"How're ye doin', lass?" the tech asked her.

"I've been better," she said.

"Can I go with her?" Seamus asked the tech.

"Yes, but you'll have to wait outside the room."

Seamus nodded. I wondered if he was going to put up an argument, but he kept silent. Sylvie smiled weakly at him, and he held her hand.

"I'll stay here," I said to no one in particular. The tech wheeled Sylvie out of the room, and Seamus followed.

I was suddenly exhausted. I sat down in the chair vacated by Seamus and told myself I would just shut my eyes.

* * *

I must have fallen asleep. I woke up with a start when I heard a voice.

"Dr. Dobbins, there's an officer here to see you." The nurse stared down at me, a kind look on his face. Behind him was one of the police officers who had questioned me earlier.

"Dr. Dobbins, we've been having a look at your flat. Do you know someone by the name of Gerard?"

I sat up straight. Had I heard him right? I gulped. "Yes, I know a Gerard. My former brother-in-law is Gerard Gramercy. Why?"

"I spoke to your landlord. He says a man named Gerard came to him asking for a key to the flat because he wanted to surprise you."

"And he gave Gerard a key?" I was aghast.

"No, apparently not. But it was interesting that someone was asking for the key."

I was confused. "So was Gerard the one who attacked Sylvie?"

"We don't know that. What is your relationship with Gerard?"

"I haven't seen him in several years, since long before I divorced his brother."

"How would you characterize your relationship with him?"

I didn't want to discuss ugly family dynamics with the officer, but I had no choice. "He and I did not get along."

"How so?"

"He didn't want his brother to marry me. He never liked me."

"Why not?"

"It's simple. My ex-husband's family has always felt I wasn't good enough for him. And they took it out on me."

"How did they take it out on you?"

I hesitated. "By being unkind."

The officer looked askance at me, as if he knew I wasn't telling the whole truth. "That's all? Just being unkind?"

I nodded, not meeting his eyes.

"If you think of anything you'd like to tell me, let me know," he said, handing me his card. I put it in my pocket and thanked him. After he left,

I curled up and tried to rest, but my mind kept returning to the bad time I'd spent in Alistair and Janet's house.

Chapter 16

It was the darkest period of my life. "Center" was the euphemistic word for a psychiatric hospital where, I later learned, Janet had insisted I be taken in order to "ensure the safety of both poor Greer and her wee bairn." My plan to call my mother and pretend I was talking to Ellie was foiled when I realized I was not allowed to ring up anyone myself. The nurse had to make the calls for me, and she was only permitted to call the number she had been given—Neill's mobile phone. I begged Neill to call my mother and tell her where I was, but I knew he would call her and tell her more lies. She didn't come to visit.

I hated Neill and his family more every day for letting me be imprisoned in such a place, where the patients terrified me, the nurses were aloof and uninterested in my plight, and Dr. MacDonald was rarely to be seen. I was subjected to endless tests of my neural and mental abilities and spent a good deal of time sleeping off the effects of the sedatives they must have put in my every meal. Every night I dreamed of Ellie and the McTaggart painting that had captivated me for so long the day and the night before I was sent away.

As hard as I tried, I couldn't understand why I was in this place. I wasn't as sick as the other patients—in fact, I wasn't sick at all. I wasn't noisy, though I did raise my voice in frustration and anger several times during the so-called therapy sessions. I didn't fight when it came time to eat or exercise or watch television, though the food was terrible, the exercise consisted of walking in endless circles around a small track in a courtyard, and the TV shows were mind-numbing.

I was in the center for three weeks. I was let out after realizing the wisdom of behaving meekly and engaging in the therapy sessions without complaining about my hard-luck situation or blaming anyone for my stay at the center. I feigned contrition and told my therapy group I had come to understand how the entire incident had been my fault, though I didn't believe a word I was saying. One day I heard the doctor who led the group therapies tell Dr. MacDonald that I should be allowed to go home because I "no longer exhibited signs of anxiety and self-aggression." I could have hugged her.

When Neill came to pick me up, he didn't have Ellie with him. It was a blow I hadn't seen coming. He had left her with his parents. Though I didn't mention it to him for fear he would take me back to the center, I fretted all the way back to Candlewick Lane that they would mistreat her while she was in their care. I had no idea how much time she had spent alone with them in my absence, so I could only pray it had been a very short time indeed.

"What did you tell my mother?" I asked, breaking a long silence in the car.

"I told her you had been taken to a mental hospital and were not allowed to have any contact with family except for me and Ellie." So he had told her the truth. Somehow that seemed even worse than a lie.

I nodded, trying to keep my anger from exploding in an eruption of cursing and hate-filled vitriol. I could barely stand to look at Neill. My mother must have been beside herself with worry.

It seemed like hours before we turned down the long drive leading to my in-laws' home. As we pulled up in front of the dark, dismal structure, Janet appeared in the doorway, holding a crying Ellie in her arms. Janet looked as cross as Ellie did.

I leapt from the car and ran up the walk, took Ellie from Janet without so much as a hello, and held my baby for a long time. When I looked up, Neill was going into the house. I was sure Ellie recognized me, but I felt a lurch of alarm and jealousy when she reached out her chubby arms for Janet. Janet gave me one of her sly smiles, and I took Ellie with me into the house. I went directly upstairs and sat with Ellie in our rocking chair and held her until she fell asleep in my arms.

My daughter loved me, and I was never going to let Janet near her again.

It seemed even Neill had had enough of his mother by the time I was released, so he was all too happy to pack up the car and head for Dumfries. We didn't speak to each other on the way to my mother's house, but we both concentrated on keeping Ellie entertained.

Mum was thrilled to see me when we arrived in Dumfries. She cried and sniffled while we all piled into the house. Even Sylvie was happy to see me, though she came forward to hug me tentatively, as though she actually believed I had belonged at the center.

Mum and Sylvie gushed and exclaimed how much Ellie had grown in the weeks she had stayed at the farm, while I basked in their love of her and the comfort I felt in their home. Even Neill seemed more relaxed than he had been at his parents' house.

We stayed with my mother for a few days before returning home. We needed to get back into the routine of work and home, but we couldn't do that until we had sorted out the many problems with our marriage.

We both knew we were headed for divorce, but for some reason we put it off as our jobs, our individual lives, and spending time with Ellie got in the way of talking to each other.

And something about Neill had changed. He stayed late at work quite often, or at least he said he did. I would have thought he was seeing another woman, except that he started to care less and less about his appearance. He obviously wasn't trying to impress someone else. Not that I would have cared—I was beyond feeling any love for him. I cared about him only as Ellie's father. Our marriage was more like the relationship between roommates who only ran into each other occasionally.

I never questioned Neill about coming home late from work or letting his physical appearance deteriorate as the next several months passed. I probably should have felt some concern, but I just couldn't.

The phone rang late one evening when Neill was out. Ellie was asleep and I was grading papers. Assuming it was Neill, I never checked the caller ID. It wasn't Neill—it was a man looking for Neill. When I told him Neill wasn't home, the man hung up on me. I didn't really think much of it, but when Neill finally came in about an hour later, I told him he had missed a call.

"Who called?" he asked, suddenly alert.

"I don't know. Some guy. He hung up on me when I told him you weren't home."

"You should have told him I was working late."

"How was I supposed to know what to tell him? I'm not your secretary. Who do you think it was?"

He shook his head as he checked the dead bolt on the front door. It was unnerving to watch.

"Who was it?" I repeated.

"Just a guy who wants to talk to me about something." I could see sweat forming on his upper lip. He rolled his head, cracking his neck.

"About what?"

"It's better if you don't know."

Now I was worried. "Is this something that could harm Ellie? Is someone coming over? What kind of trouble are you in?"

"Just don't worry about it, okay? I'll take care of it." He went upstairs without another glance at me, and I heard the guest room door close. I tried to get back to grading papers, but my concentration was broken and now I had another priority.

The next day I woke early to talk to Neill before he left for work. He had gotten into the habit of leaving before I went downstairs in the morning, probably to avoid me. I found him in the kitchen, drinking a cup of coffee. His shoulders slumped when I walked in.

"Neill, we need to talk about last night."

He sighed. "I told you I'd take care of it. What do we need to talk about?"

"I need to know that Ellie and I are safe in this house when you're not here, which is almost always lately. I need to know if you're in some kind of trouble. I have a *right* to know. We're still married, even if we don't act like it."

"I can't tell you about it. I have everything under control."

"Then why did the mere mention of a telephone call last night give you the sweats?" I lifted my chin, challenging him to answer me truthfully.

He spread out his hands and shrugged. "I don't know."

I sat down across the table from him. "Neill, I know something's going on. Maybe I can help you if you'd tell me what's going on."

He stared at me for several seconds. I could see he was at war with himself over whether he should tell me his secret. Finally, he drew in a deep breath. "I lost some money to a guy, and I don't have enough to pay him back right now."

"How much?"

Silence.

"Neill, how much? And who is this guy? Is he the one who called last night?"

Silence.

"Neill, we have some money in the savings account. You can use that to pay him back."

He shook his head and spoke in a barely audible whisper. "That money is gone."

I wished I had misheard him, but somehow I knew I hadn't. "Gone?" I asked, matching his whisper. My stomach lurched.

He nodded and looked away.

"Where did it go? And why didn't I know about it?"

"I took the bank statement from the mailbox a couple weeks ago." I could barely hear him.

I hadn't even realized the statement was missing. I lowered my head. "Neill, there was a lot of money in that account. It's all gone?"

He nodded again.

"You've got to tell me what's going on. Where did the money go?"

"I owe some people."

"Who? And why do you owe them money?"

"Greer, I don't have time for this conversation right now. I have to go to work." He stood up and walked out of the room. I sat for several minutes in the semi-darkness of the kitchen, my head in my hands, wondering how we lost our savings *and* our marriage. Truth be told, I knew why our marriage had failed. I hadn't forgiven Neill for hitting me at his parents' house, and I hadn't forgiven anyone for forcing me into the center. Neill never apologized, and I didn't like to speak about either of the ugly subjects. He must not have felt anything was wrong with his detestable behavior or that of his family, but at least he hadn't hit me again.

I could hear Ellie calling me from her bedroom, so I went upstairs and cuddled with her for several minutes. Eventually I put her down so she could toddle behind me as I began our morning routine. Neill had been sleeping in the guest room since our return from Scotland, and I always started the morning chores by opening the blinds in there. *He should be doing this himself.*

Ellie sat down on the floor in the guest room and busied herself with a small piece of paper she had found. I turned around just in time to see her put the paper in her mouth, and I grabbed it out. She started to cry. I picked her up and bounced her on my hip, glancing at the paper before setting it on the nightstand next to Neill's bed.

IOU. $5388. Neill's signature was scrawled across the bottom of the paper.

My knees started to fail. Neill owed someone over five thousand dollars? Was this amount part of the money Neill had withdrawn from our savings account, or was this over and above that? We had had more than that in the account, but if Neill owed this on top of the money in the savings account, how was he going to pay it?

While Ellie ate her breakfast, I called Neill at his office. I was a bit surprised when he answered his phone. Given his recent behavior, I suppose I hadn't expected him to be at work.

"I found an IOU on the floor in your room," I began.

"Oh, that's nothing. You don't need to worry about that."

"Don't need to worry about that?" I repeated. "How can I not worry about that? Did the money from the savings account cover it?" The long pause that followed answered my question. "You owe this to someone *and* our savings account is empty?" I said slowly. Again, silence. That's when I knew he had a gambling problem. "Neill, have you been gambling?" He cleared his throat. "That means yes," I accused. "What are you thinking? What about Ellie?" I knew how angry I sounded, but I didn't care. "I can make it up. I just need some time." "You've put our daughter's future in jeopardy because of a silly *bet*?" My voice was icy. "It's not like that. I can make that money back, plus more." "You haven't done a great job of it so far." "Just give me a little time," he pleaded. "I'm going to see a lawyer," I told him. "You can take all the time you need. You cannot do this to me and Ellie." I hung up on him. He tried calling back right away. Ellie looked at me, then looked toward the phone, but I ignored its relentless ringing. Instead, I found my mobile phone and called our lawyer, who recommended a divorce attorney.

That afternoon I had my first appointment with the divorce attorney. And after that things moved quickly. Neill moved out, and within a year, our divorce was final.

Chapter 17

Everything that had happened in the past several years had brought me to Edinburgh in search of my little girl and my ex-husband, neither of whom had been heard from since the late-night phone call from Neill warning me to leave town. And now Sylvie was hurt and Seamus was acting strange. I didn't know how to begin sorting out the threads of events.

My thoughts kept coming back to Gerard. Thankfully, my dealings with him had been limited and terse. If, as he had told my landlord, he really wanted to surprise me, it would certainly not have been a good surprise.

Why did he want to get into my flat? Had he been in touch with Neill?

Neill…was it possible *he* had been in my flat, not Gerard? Had Neill been trying to get in touch with me, and been spooked by Sylvie? If Neill had been in my flat, Ellie would have been close by, too. What could Neill have wanted?

Then there was Seamus. He had not been acting himself since I told him of Sylvie's accident. It was possible he knew more than he was saying. Would he have hurt Sylvie? What if he knew she had told me about his past and exacted revenge on her?

I shook my head. Anyone watching me would have thought I was arguing with myself, and I suppose I was doing exactly that. Seamus wouldn't risk going to prison again, and certainly not just because I knew about his past. *Would he?* But why was he so keen to figure out if Sylvie had seen someone in the flat?

And what of the man who had attacked me in St. Giles Cathedral and in the Gardens? He remained a mystery. He said he knew where I lived, and perhaps he'd even been there once before Sylvie's attack. Could he have been the one who hurt her?

The tech wheeled Sylvie back into the room a few minutes later, Seamus right behind them. Frowning, he shook his head, muttering to himself. "How'd it go?" I asked the tech.

"Just fine. The doctor is looking at the films right now, and he'll be in to talk to you soon." He turned to Sylvie. "You take good care of yourself, lass."

She gave a wan smile. "Thanks," she croaked. She turned her head to look at me, and I took her hand in mine. Seamus walked quickly over to the bed and took her other hand. He looked at me over her bed. Was he challenging me?

I ignored him. "Sylvie, do you need anything? A drink or some food?"

Seamus answered for her. "The tech said she shouldn't eat or drink anything because of what they might find on the x-rays. I guess in case she needs surgery or something."

"Oh. Are you warm enough, Sylvie? Do you need me to help you with your pillow?" I didn't know what to say, and I felt I needed to do *something* for her, whether it was to make her warm or more comfortable. I had a strong hunch her condition was somehow connected to me and Neill, and I couldn't shake the guilt, which was invading my ability to think clearly and focus only on her.

She shook her head. Seamus busied himself tucking in the sheets at the foot of her bed, as if he, too, needed something to do to feel useful.

Sylvie waved her hand at him. "Stop. I'm fine." He stopped, but stood looking around, probably wondering what to with himself. Finally, he sat down in the chair on the other side of the bed. The three of us waited in silence for a doctor or a nurse to come in and tell us what was happening. It seemed ages before Dr. Yarbrough came in to tell us that Sylvie had suffered some head trauma and deep bruising on her neck, back, and torso. I had seen the bruises on her neck; they had darkened and spread since arriving at hospital.

"I can't hear you," Sylvie slurred to the doctor.

"Are your ears ringing? Can you hear me if I talk a wee bit louder?" he asked, raising his voice. He took a penlight from his pocket and examined Sylvie's pupils. Clicking off the light, he turned to me. "She is displaying all the signs of a concussion, and perhaps a serious one. As I mentioned earlier, we're going to keep her here for observation. The tests we've run so far are showing no acute damage to her brain, but we need to know more about the extent of the neurological impact before we know for sure how best to treat her."

I cleared my throat. "Can one of us stay with her?"

Dr. Yarbrough looked from me to Seamus. "Sure. But only one. You two decide. In the meantime, we're going to follow a strict concussion protocol for Sylvie. That means," he started ticking off on his fingers, "no stress for Sylvie, no arguments, no reading, no watching the box, no computer, no texting. She can't even *think* too hard about anything. It has to be quiet around her. I don't want her to go back to work for at least a week and certainly not until a neurologist has seen her again."

Seamus nodded, watching Sylvie out of the corner of his eye, while I typed on my tablet, trying to keep up with the doctor's orders. After he left, the two of us avoided looking at each other. I brought up concussion treatment sites on my tablet and read them while Seamus pulled out his phone and began to text.

Why aren't we talking to each other? I trust Seamus…don't I?

It wasn't long before a nurse and another tech came to take Sylvie to her room upstairs. Sylvie remained asleep for the short elevator ride and woke up as we entered her room. Panic surfaced in her eyes. "Where are we?" she asked, her voice raspy.

"The doctors are going to keep you here for a wee bit," Seamus told her. "This is your room."

She turned to look at me. The irises of her eyes were almost black from her enlarged pupils. "Where is Mum?"

"She's on her way. Don't worry about a single thing. She'll be here very soon," I told her quietly. The last thing we needed was for Sylvie to start worrying about our mother.

She closed her eyes again, and I looked down at her. My own unbidden tears started to fall. Seamus looked at me in surprise.

"Why are you crying?" he asked in a loud whisper. Sylvie's eyelids fluttered. I motioned Seamus to follow me into the hallway.

"I don't want her to know I'm crying," I said in a low voice. "I'm just a bit at sea, I think. It's my fault she's hurt and I feel terrible about it. I want to help her and there's nothing I can do." I cried harder, embarrassed that Seamus should see me like this.

He put his arm around my shoulder. "Don't fret about it, Greer. You couldn't have known Sylvie would be hurt. Besides, maybe it had nothing to do with you. Maybe it was a random break-in."

I shook my head. "Thanks for trying, Seamus, but we both know it has something to do with me. And Neill." I sniffled and wiped my eyes on my sleeve. Seamus handed me a box of tissues he had grabbed on his way out of Sylvie's room. I smiled my thanks. *How could I have doubted him?*

While we waited for Mum to arrive, Seamus and I took turns sitting with Sylvie. When my mother finally got there, she had a flurry of questions. I shooed her into the hallway so she wouldn't wake Sylvie. I answered her queries as best I could, but I didn't have much useful information for her. As I had anticipated, she wanted both of us to come back to Dumfries.

"I can't do that, Mum. I have to stay in Edinburgh to look for Ellie and Neill. I know they're here somewhere, and I can't leave until I have Ellie back. As for Sylvie, she'll have to choose for herself, but I don't think making a decision like that right now is a good idea. The doctor doesn't want her upset or stressed or even to think very hard about anything."

Seamus wanted to stay overnight in Sylvie's room, so I went home later that evening. The door was locked when I got there, so the landlord must have come by. The police had finished looking around the flat, but blood still stained the kitchen floor where Sylvie had fallen. I cleaned it up and tidied the living room and kitchen, all the while looking for anything missing or out of place. There was nothing.

I poured myself a rather large glass of wine and called James. I sank onto the sofa cushions and told him the whole story. I felt better after telling him everything, and he came over right away. After he asked all the questions I couldn't answer, we talked about nothing in particular for hours. He knew I needed a break from the constant stress caused by Neill and his behavior and from the threats and danger and violence that had enveloped me lately. I finally fell asleep leaning against him on the sofa, and it was almost noon the following day when I woke up to find him making pancakes for my breakfast.

"You can cook, too?" I asked, rubbing my eyes.

He laughed. "Not like Seamus, but I could prevent myself from starving if I had to." He put two plates of steaming pancakes on the table and bowls of soft butter and berries.

After enjoying a big brunch together, James went back to his house to get ready for work. I decided to spend a bit of time doing research. I had planned to take my laptop and work at another of Edinburgh's museums, but instead I stayed home and did some research on the Internet.

The research was about McTaggart, one of my favorite subjects. I was trying to get a closer look at one of his paintings on my computer screen when I got a niggling feeling in the back of my mind. I didn't know what was causing it, but I couldn't shake it off. Something was wrong. Something about McTaggart and his paintings.

I closed my browser and went in search of a textbook I had bought on Scot impressionists. I found the page where the painting I had seen online had been reproduced, and I examined it closely. That uncomfortable feeling was still there, but I couldn't put my finger on it. I read the paragraphs associated with the picture, but they didn't shed any light on my unease.

It was mid-afternoon when I headed out to visit Sylvie. Mum had texted me earlier that Sylvie had slept poorly during the night and was awake but a bit dazed and had a bad headache. When I arrived, I found Mum sitting in silence, watching Sylvie. A newspaper that looked unread sat on the bedside table. Seamus, she told me, had gone to the cafeteria for some take-away lunch. He appeared before long, looking tired and unkempt. He couldn't have slept well in the chair next to Sylvie's bed. I greeted him with a smile and he held up his lunch, offering me a share.

"No thanks," I whispered. "I'll get something in a bit."

Seamus and I relieved Mum while she went next door to her hotel to rest and eat. Sylvie woke up and told us she also wanted something to eat. I was only too happy to call the nurse to ask for food. Sylvie hadn't eaten in over twenty-four hours. Seamus and I went for dinner in the cafeteria as dusk gathered outside.

"When do you think they'll send her home?" Seamus asked, poking at his gluey-looking potatoes.

"I don't know. I hope it's soon. She'll be more comfortable there than she is here, I'm sure."

"Do you think she'll be afraid to go back to the flat?"

I shrugged. "If she doesn't remember anything, maybe she won't realize there's any cause for concern."

"But she knows she was hurt there, even if she doesn't remember exactly what happened."

"True." I didn't know what else to say. I hoped Sylvie would feel safe in the flat and decide not to return to Dumfries with Mum, but I had no idea what the future held.

Dr. Yarbrough sent Sylvie home the next morning. She had a severe concussion and the bruising on her neck, he said, indicated somebody had tried to strangle her. In addition, she had been beaten about the torso and upper body and would be sore for several days. The first time she looked in a mirror, she cried. The purple bruises had become a mottled chartreuse and deep blue, and they covered every visible part of her.

Seamus and I took her back to the flat. Mum came with us, I think to satisfy herself that Sylvie was safe and with the hope that she would decide to return to Dumfries. But Sylvie never said a word about leaving Edinburgh. She was exhausted; I'm not sure she was even thinking about anything except getting into her bed as soon as we got home. The nights in hospital hadn't been restful, with nurses coming in and out, bells and alarms ringing, and people coming and going into nearby rooms. She needed a good long sleep.

Mum left with reminders that we were welcome to come and stay with her at any time, and with promises to visit soon to check on Sylvie.

It was getting dark when Sylvie woke up. She appeared in the kitchen doorway, looking dazed and rubbing her head. "How long have I been sleeping?" she asked.

"Hours upon hours," I answered with a laugh. "Seamus made dinner. Want some?"

She sat down at the table. Seamus served her a piping hot bowl of stew and some bannock. She ate slowly, almost as if she thought she might break if she made any sudden or quick movements. She winced when he patted her shoulder, and he drew his hand away with a grimace.

"Sorry, love."

She smiled up at him. "It's just that everything hurts," she said. He handed her a cup of tea, and she drank it in just a few gulps. "The tea in hospital was never hot enough," she said. Judging from the look on Seamus's face, she had said exactly the right thing. He needed to feel necessary, to feel wanted. The only way she could do that was to show him how much she appreciated what he was doing for her.

She sat on the couch until it was time for bed. The three of us talked quietly of unimportant things, the doctor's reminders to keep her calm uppermost in our minds. We talked about the weather, a new exhibit at James's museum, and some of Seamus's ideas for new paintings.

As bedtime drew near, Sylvie kept glancing at the front door. I knew she was checking and double-checking to make sure it was locked. She might not remember the attack, but she knew instinctively to be concerned about someone coming into the flat uninvited. I made a point of rattling the door handle and pulling on the locks, and I could see her shoulders relax when she was convinced we were safe.

The next morning, Seamus took care of Sylvie while I went down to the police station. I hadn't heard anything about Neill and Ellie since Sylvie had been attacked, and though it had been necessary for me to be with Sylvie, I felt I had been away from the search and the investigation for too long.

I spoke to Officer Dunbar, one of the officers with whom I had met previously. She told me two policemen had returned to Candlewick Lane to see Alistair and Janet and had learned nothing new, though they had found my former in-laws surly and rude. I shook my head, knowing full well just how surly and rude they could be.

"Did the officers look through the house?" I asked.

"No. They didn't have a warrant. There's no evidence to suggest that a crime took place on the property."

"But my daughter is missing and she has to be somewhere. Did they know there's a soundproof room on the third floor of Janet's house?"

The policewoman looked like I had struck her.

"Do you know this for a fact?"

"Yes."

"How do you know?"

And so I was forced to tell her the story of being locked in the third-floor bedroom with Ellie, and how that imprisonment and Janet's subsequent lies about it had led to me being placed at the center for several weeks. The officer scribbled notes furiously while I spoke. When I finished, she stared at me, her mouth agape and her eyes wide.

"I wish you had informed us of these events earlier," she scolded. "This may be enough for us to get a warrant." She picked up a phone and spun around in her chair. I couldn't hear what she was saying, but when she hung up, she smiled at me. "I think we can get one. Now we can have a look around the farm, and with a little luck we'll find something useful."

I was elated. My face must have betrayed my excitement, because the officer cautioned, "Don't be getting your hopes up just yet. We may not find anything. We're just having a wee look around."

"Do you think maybe Ellie is there?" The moment I asked the question, my hands began to shake. My heartbeat quickened, and I could feel myself getting faint.

"Dr. Dobbins, you have to relax. Go get yourself a strong cup of tea, and I'll call you as soon as the officers get the warrant." Her stern eyes looked into mine, and her voice softened. "We're doing everything we can to find Ellie. You have to keep your wits about you, though. I'll be in touch soon, I promise."

Outside, I took several deep breaths in the cold, bracing air and pulled out my mobile phone. A moment later James's voice came on the line, strong and sure. I told him what had happened, and he suggested we meet for lunch.

We met in the pub where we had first had dinner together. He held my hands as we sat across from each other in a snug booth, listening as I related the entire conversation I had had with the police officer. I even found the courage to tell him about the bad time at the farm, the time I had spent at the center, and the gambling addiction that developed after we returned to the States. He was shocked.

"Janet and Alistair are beasts!" he cried. "I can't imagine the horror of it! And then, to have to face Neill's addiction..." His voice softened. "I'm so sorry you had to endure that."

I could only nod, grateful that it was all in the past and that James was in the present.

"It sounds like the police are taking this very seriously," he said finally. "Maybe they're suspicious of Neill's parents, and were looking for a reason and opportunity to get back into their house."

"Do you think so?" I could hear the hope rising in my voice.

"It seems that way to me. At the very least, maybe they can glean more information about where Neill might have taken Ellie."

We ate our meal in comfortable silence. The gentle clanking of silverware against plates and the low conversations taking place around us, punctuated by occasional raucous laughter, provided a warm, peaceful feeling I carried with me the rest of the day.

But it wouldn't last.

Chapter 18

James had taken the rest of the day off, so after lunch he surprised me with an outing to Georgian House, a quaint historic home not far from the Princes Street Gardens. I knew of Georgian House, but had mentioned to James at one time that I had never had a chance to visit.

Georgian House was located on Charlotte Square, which had originally been designed by a young architect who won a contest focused on building a residential area outside Old Town in the 1760s. Conditions in the city had become so overcrowded and dirty that affluent citizens naturally moved to the new open square. First owned in the late 1700s by John Lamont, eighteenth Chief of the Clan Lamont, Georgian House had seen many owners over the years, including a judge, a minister, a wealthy widow, and a Marquis.

The inside, lovingly restored over a period of years, was breathtaking. The period furnishings, textiles, silver, and china were an art history professor's dream. I don't know if James had intended to spend four hours at Georgian House, but that's what we did. Every room held a special beauty and luxurious utility that would have been the height of fashionable decor in the eighteenth century. I could barely tear myself away from the dining room clock, which dated from the 1600s and still kept time. The artwork was gorgeous, too, and perfect for the setting. I gazed at the paintings on the wall and was reminded of something, something about the McTaggart, but it was beyond my grasp and disappeared as a wisp of fog.

We continued our tour below stairs, which was as interesting as the floors above. The rooms where the servants worked in Georgian House had also been restored and featured a Murphy bed, lovely utilitarian furniture, and items that the servants would have used on a daily basis.

I couldn't bring myself to leave until we were gently but firmly told the house was closed for the day.

Georgian House was exactly what I needed to occupy my mind and remind me of the beauty and grace of Edinburgh. Lately I had seen some of the city's ugliness, and James had known exactly what to do to keep me grounded for an afternoon. I checked my phone only a handful of times to make sure I hadn't missed a call from the police.

We were walking about Charlotte Square when the phone finally rang. Yanking it out of my pocket, I checked the caller ID and answered, breathless.

"Hello? This is Greer."

"This is Officer Dunbar. I have some news for you. Could you come to the station?"

"Yes, of course." My words came out in a rush. I covered the mouthpiece and looked at James. "Can you come to the police station with me?"

"Of course."

I spoke into the phone again. "We'll be there as quickly as we can."

James grabbed my hand, and we made our way to the police station, dodging pedestrians who were obviously not in a hurry and darting across streets where it probably would have been smarter to wait for traffic. We arrived at the police station in record time, though, and rushed headlong into the vestibule.

My heavy breathing clearly alarmed the officer at the desk. "What's wrong?" he asked, reaching for the phone. "Is there trouble?"

"No, no," I assured him, holding up my hand to get him to stop talking for a moment. He looked at me, waiting for me to speak.

James must have had stronger lungs because he was able to talk calmly to the officer while I was still catching my breath. "This is Dr. Greer Dobbins. She received a call on her mobile phone from Officer Dunbar asking her to come to the station to receive some information. We've been running," he added.

The officer reached for the phone again and dialed some numbers. He spoke in a low voice into the receiver and hung up in just a moment. "Officer Dunbar will be right out to fetch you."

We waited in the vestibule until I saw Officer Dunbar coming toward us, and I rushed forward. "What have you found?" I asked.

"Come back to my office where we can talk," she answered.

We followed her back through the warren of cubicles and offices until we reached hers. She motioned for us to sit in the two chairs opposite her desk.

"We got a warrant to check out the Gramercys' house and the officers were very interested in some evidence they found in the soundproof third-floor bedroom you told us about."

"Yes?" I could barely contain myself.

"It looks like someone has been in there. Staying in there. The bed was unmade and there were books on the floor. Children's books."

The tears started almost before she had gotten out the last words. I blinked rapidly to stop the flow so I could concentrate on what she was saying. James reached for my hand and held it in his.

"There was a pair of jeans in the closet and a sweatshirt."

"What did the jeans look like?"

"I've got photos here," she said, turning her computer toward us and hitting the arrow key. She landed on a picture of the jeans. Blue denim, green Xs on the back pockets.

I began to cry again, harder this time. "Those are Ellie's jeans," I told her, trying to choke back my sobs. "They were the only jeans missing from our house."

Officer Dunbar picked up a phone and dialed. She murmured a few words to the person on the other end and hung up. She hit the other arrow key several times. "I'm going to take you back through these photos to see if there's anything else you recognize."

When the officers searched the third-floor bedroom at Janet and Alistair's house, they were thorough. They had pulled out drawers, taken the bedding off the bed, and looked under the thin carpet. Photos showed the process of their search. Officer Dunbar paged through them one by one. The bed, bedding, floor, carpet, fireplace, chamber pot, Ellie's jeans, books on the floor. The last photo made me cry again—her favorite pajamas, the missing ones. She had tried to fold them just like I did at home.

"I recognize those," I told Officer Dunbar, wiping my eyes. "They're Ellie's. Ellie wasn't there, though?"

"She wasn't. But your former in-laws are at the police station near their home now, answering questions about what's been going on in their home and where they think Ellie and Neill may be."

"They must know something," I sniffed. "She was there. They *have* to know where she went."

"Hopefully we'll come up with something, but we have to wait until the police get back to us. I just wanted you to have the information. We're getting closer. I'll call you the minute I hear anything."

James and I stood up, and I shook the officer's hand, thanking her over and over. We left the police station and James put his arm around me. "See? They'll find her in no time, I'm sure of it. We just have to have a little patience. What do you say I walk you home and hope Seamus has made something wonderful for dinner?"

I settled into the hollow of his shoulder as we walked back to my flat in the drizzle. Soft yellow light from the streetlamps reflected off the wet cobbles, lending a romantic air to the cold evening. Leaves swept across the streets, and lights came on in flats that lined the sidewalks as people came home from work. People going about their own business, oblivious to the heartaches around them. It was like being inside a painting—a warm, dark impressionist painting. I would have enjoyed it more if I hadn't been so worried about Ellie.

Seamus had, indeed, made a delicious dinner. I wish I could have enjoyed it a bit more, but my stomach was too tightly wound to eat very much. The salmon had a sweet, mild flavor that paired well with a spicy yogurt sauce. Creamy mashed turnips and buttered leeks completed the meal. I couldn't even think about dessert, which was shortbread. James and Sylvie pronounced it flaky with just a hint of sweetness. I did manage a cup of tea after dinner while we sat around the table in the warm kitchen.

I wanted desperately to tell Sylvie and Seamus of the search warrant and what the police had found, but I knew such excitement and worry wouldn't be good for Sylvie. I tried to stay quiet and calm while we all chatted quietly. I had to sit on my hands to keep from biting my nails.

When Sylvie went to her room to lie down, James and I told Seamus all about our visit to the police station. He gave me a broad smile, his beard lifting right off his chest. He put his burly arm around my shoulder. "See? We knew this would happen. They're getting close now. You'll have your bairn back with you before you know it."

"I hope you're right," I said, reaching for my napkin. My eyes were starting to tear again,

"None of that, now," Seamus cautioned. "It's happy news. Let's celebrate with a dram."

He poured three short glasses of the golden whisky he kept on a bar cart in the kitchen and brought them to the table. I couldn't bring myself to drink it, but he and James clinked their glasses together and offered a traditional Gaelic toast:

"Beannachd Dia dhuit!"

"Greer," Seamus said in his lilting voice, "I expect you to join us when Ellie's back with you!"

"I will," I promised, then laughed. "Seamus, I'd stopped crying and now you're making me start again!"

He joined in with hearty laughter, and James beamed at us. "I've got to get to work early tomorrow morning, so I'm going to head home. Still have some work to do before I can turn in." He took my face in his hands, and Seamus made his exit. "You've had a long day. I want you to get a good night's sleep so you're ready for whatever tomorrow brings. Maybe it won't bring anything, but maybe it will. We're close, Greer. I know we are. Just keep your chin up." He kissed me, making my stomach flutter. Feeling the flutters was better than feeling the twisting nerves. He finally pulled away from me and touched my nose. "I'll see you tomorrow."

I fell asleep quickly that night, feeling warm and hopeful.

* * *

Sylvie was up when I went into the kitchen the next morning. She looked unfocused and confused.

"Sylvie? What's wrong?"

She turned and looked at me like she didn't know who I was. Keeping my eyes on her, I went to the kitchen door and called softly for Seamus. He came out of the bedroom, toweling his hair.

"What's the matter?"

"Sylvie's acting funny," I whispered. He set down the towel and went into the kitchen, where Sylvie was standing by the sink, staring out the window.

"How are you feeling, love?" he asked.

She turned to him, her eyes devoid of expression. "My head hurts."

He took her hand and led her into the living room. "Sit down. Greer, can you get her a cup of tea? I'll stay in here with her."

I put on the kettle and stood in the kitchen doorway, watching Seamus and Sylvie. She said nothing, just stared straight ahead. Seamus was stroking the back of her hand. She appeared calm, but without warning she cried out and a look of horror crossed her face.

"Sylvie, what is it?" I asked, reaching her side in a few steps. Seamus tightened his hold on her hand.

She shook her head several times, as if to rid herself of an ugly thought. "Don't do that, Sylvie," Seamus said. "You'll make the concussion worse."

Her breathing became fast, erratic. I glanced at Seamus, who was staring at her. "Lie down, Sylvie," I told her. Seamus guided her shoulders onto the sofa.

"I see him! He's behind the door!" she cried.

I looked up. There was no one in the room other than the three of us. "There's no one here, Sylvie. It's just us."

"No, he's there!"

I looked again. I was spooked, and I think Seamus was, too.

"Sylvie, close your eyes and try to rest. Getting upset isn't good for you. Seamus and I will protect you. No one will hurt you. I promise."

"You couldn't protect me before," she moaned.

Her words hit me like a fist. She was right. Seamus must have seen my distress, because he responded for me. "Sylvie, she couldn't protect you because she wasn't here. But now she's here, and I am too, and we're going to make sure you don't get hurt again."

I had a thought. "Sylvie, what did the man look like?"

She shook her head. "Brown hair, I think. A beard. I can't see his face."

Seamus motioned for me to take his place on the sofa. He went into the bathroom and brought back the bottle of pills Sylvie had received from hospital. He shook two into his big hand.

"Take these." He tipped them into her hand and gave her a glass of water from the coffee table. She swallowed them and lay back on the pillow, closing her eyes. Seamus and I sat watching her. It didn't take her long to fall asleep. We tiptoed back into the kitchen.

"She's remembering something," he said.

"It doesn't sound like there's much to remember," I noted, "if she didn't see the man's face. Lots of men have brown hair and beards."

"Maybe she'll think of something that will help."

Seamus stayed with Sylvie that afternoon, and I returned to Georgian House. I wanted to tour it a second time, this time focusing on the artwork. I still had a restless feeling that something wasn't right. I took a brisk walk to Charlotte Square in the sharp afternoon brightness. The trees waved in the wind and the passersby barely looked up, bundled against the cold.

I took my time meandering through Georgian House, even more so than I had the previous day. I took notes on my tablet, preparing for a series of lectures I hoped to give next semester about the artistry of furnishings and textiles. I was in the elegant dining room, examining the paintings up close, when I heard someone sneeze in the next room.

That's when it hit me.

Chapter 19

The paintings in Georgian House were clearly given meticulous care. Both the canvases and their gilt frames were in perfect condition, clean, free of dust, streaks, fingerprints, or visible dirt. That's how it should be with all artwork. All artists know how important it is for a viewer to look at a piece of art without the distraction of imperfection.

My mind stretched back to the time I was imprisoned in the third-floor bedroom at the end of Candlewick Lane.

I was looking at the McTaggart. I reached out to touch the canvas, to feel the brushstrokes, to close my eyes and see the ridges of paint, the swirls of color. When I drew my hand away I rubbed my fingers together as if I could still feel the paint. They were covered with dust—in fact, Ellie had sneezed from all the dust. I was dismayed. How could the Gramercys mistreat such a masterpiece? Then I thought about seeing the painting more recently, over the mantel in the living room when I went to see Janet and Alistair. The painting had been clean, free of dirt, but the frame—the plain wooden frame—was languishing under a thick layer of dust. And there were fingerprints in the dust. I don't know why it took me so long to remember.

Why would the painting be clean when the frame was covered in dust and fingerprints?

Because someone had taken out one painting and replaced it with another, not bothering to clean the frame. And it had been done shortly before my recent visit to the Gramercy house, because the fingerprints looked fresh. There had been no dust on them.

The McTaggart was a fake.

Someone had replaced the dirty original with a perfectly clean fake.

I spun around, snapping my laptop shut, and made my way to the front door of Georgian House. I ran from Charlotte Square straight to the police station. When I arrived, I was still panting. I asked to see Officer Dunbar right away. It was important, I told the desk clerk.

It didn't take her long to come for me. I followed her to her office and before I could sit down, I told her my suspicion that the McTaggart hanging over the mantel was a fake.

"If I'm right, I think this is key to finding Ellie and Neill."

She looked at me doubtfully. "What makes you think that? And what's a McTaggart, anyway?"

I had to remind myself that not everyone was well-versed in the history of Scottish impressionists. "McTaggart was a famous Scot painter. Janet and Alistair always bragged about the original McTaggart they had. They never displayed it in any of the public rooms of the house because they were afraid someone would waltz in and steal it. So they kept it in that third-floor bedroom where only the family could enjoy it. Now it's in the living room. That in itself is surprising, but that's not the only strange thing. The painting itself is in perfect condition, like new, while the frame that houses it is dusty and dirty. And there are new fingerprints on the frame."

"It's quite a stretch," she said.

"I know, but I'm telling you there's something about that painting that's not right."

She sighed. "All right. I'll ask the officers who searched the house to go back and question Janet and Alistair about the painting."

"Thank you." I left the police station feeling hopeful.

I spent the evening online, researching various auctions of McTaggart's artwork. Some of his paintings had sold for large sums of money. They were usually sold through reputable auction houses, but there were a few articles about private sales of the paintings, too. It was very late when I fell asleep that night, finally feeling like I was doing *something* to help locate Ellie.

I woke up the following morning to thunder, lightning, and a heavy downpour. The raindrops sliding down our kitchen window gave the neighboring flats a softened appearance, their stone facades smudged gray and dark brown. I thought about Ellie as I always did, wondering what she was doing on this rainy day. I hoped Neill had thought to buy her a thick, warm raincoat and boots. Just the thought of venturing outside chilled me, but I wanted to stop by the police station to gently remind them I was still waiting for news.

I slipped on my heavy raincoat and pulled on my tall Wellies. Grabbing an umbrella from the stand by the front door, I was startled to see the lock already undone. I walked quietly to Sylvie and Seamus's bedroom door and knocked. Sylvie's voice answered.

"I'm awake."

"Is Seamus here?"

"No. Why?" I opened the door a crack.

"Just checking. Uh, I was going to ask him if he needs me to pick up anything for dinner." I didn't want to mention that the lock was unlatched and it had given me a fright.

"I'm sure he'll get whatever he needs. You going out?"

"Yes. Be back in a bit."

"Should you be going out alone?"

"Don't worry about me."

I hurried to the police station, enjoying the sound of the rain falling, but not particularly enjoying the cold. Officer Dunbar was in when I got there, and I waited for her in the vestibule.

"No news," she said in greeting. My shoulders sank.

"Is there anything I can do to help or speed things along?"

"No." She used her authoritative police-officer voice. "We always advise people to be patient and let the police do their jobs."

"I know. I'm trying."

She softened, smiling at me. "I told you—we're getting closer. Believe me, you'll be the first to know the minute we find anything useful."

"Thanks." I went back outside, where the rain was coming down harder. I debated whether to spend the day at a museum, gathering research ideas, or going home to read. I settled on the latter.

I picked my way around puddles and rivulets of rainwater coursing through the streets alongside the curbs. At one busy corner I glanced up and was startled to see Seamus standing across the street. An umbrella hid his face, but I recognized him right away. His sheer size and red beard gave him away. I was just about to call out to him to wait for me when another man walked up to him and slapped him on the back.

I didn't want to interfere, so I crossed the street a short distance from them. The other man didn't have an umbrella, so I could see his face— swarthy, pockmarked, with a short black moustache and beard. He had an enormous tattoo on his neck, similar to the one Seamus had. He kept wiping rain from his eyes as he talked to Seamus. His eyes darted from side to side, as if he expected trouble from any direction at any moment. He made me nervous.

I wondered briefly if the man knew Seamus from prison. Maybe those tattoos were a sort of prison fraternity symbol. I had heard about such things in books and on television crime shows. I chided myself for thinking such prejudicial thoughts about Seamus and his acquaintance. I stood under the eaves of a pub nearby and watched them. I didn't like what I saw.

Seamus kept his face hidden under the umbrella while the other man pulled something out of his coat pocket, something wrapped in a plastic grocery bag. I pulled my hat lower over my forehead so neither man would recognize me if either turned in my direction.

It looked like the men were arguing. I couldn't hear their voices over the noise from the rain and the traffic, but their bodies tensed, they leaned into each other, and they both gesticulated vehemently.

What was going on?

I didn't want to see any more. My desire to know what was happening battled with my desire to get away from the street corner, but I couldn't risk being seen by Seamus and his mysterious companion. I hastened away and walked home using lesser-traveled side streets so I wouldn't run into Seamus if he decided to go back to the flat, too.

When I finally got home, I was soaked to the skin, despite my rain gear. When I took off my coat, water poured onto the floor. Sylvie was lying on the couch. She rubbed her eyes.

"Sorry if I woke you," I said.

"That's all right," she said with a yawn. "I haven't been sleeping well."

I sat down across from her. "Why not? Has your head been hurting?"

"Well, yes. A bit. And Seamus has been so restless. He fidgets about and it's hard for me to get a good rest."

"Is everything all right with him?"

She lifted her shoulders and let them fall again with a sigh. "He hasn't said anything is wrong. He acts normally enough during the day. It's just at night he can't seem to sleep."

I wondered if his restlessness had anything to do with the meeting I had seen.

Thunder shook the flat, and I looked at Sylvie with concern. "Does the thunder bother you?"

She chuckled. "Greer, you seem to think that noise will break me in half. It's okay. The thunder doesn't bother me at all. In fact, I rather like it. I feel like something is coming to life, even if I can't yet. I wonder how much longer I'll be stuck on this couch, in this flat, not reading or looking at the box or being on the phone or on the computer. I'm so bored."

"You can talk on the phone. You just can't text."

She picked up the phone from the floor next to her. "I'll call Seamus. Maybe he'll paint this afternoon. I like to watch him paint and that shouldn't bother my doctor at all." She rolled her eyes.

Seamus came crashing through the front door, water dripping from his beard and his clothes. He snarled as his fingers slipped as he tried to undo his coat. The plastic bag was nowhere in sight.

"What's the matter?" Sylvie asked.

"Och, nothing." He stormed into the bedroom.

Sylvie turned to me and made a face. "Wonder what's gotten into him."

"Should you go see?"

"No. He gets like this sometimes. He'll get over it, but until then he needs time to himself. He'll be his cheerful self before too long."

She closed her eyes and folded her hands over her chest. I hoped she would be able to get some sleep. I went to my room and tried reading a book, but all I could think about was Seamus.

Should I tell him I saw him on the street? Should I ask who he was talking to? No, I decided. It's none of my business.

But it may be Sylvie's business, and if he causes her stress, that's not good for her.

I didn't know what to do, so I called James. Just hearing his voice calmed my nerves and I decided to wait to approach Seamus. James still didn't know Seamus's secret, as far as I knew, so I didn't want to mention my suspicions to him. He invited me to a cocktail party at the museum later that evening and I accepted. It seemed wrong somehow to be going to parties with Ellie still missing, but I supposed it was better to be with other people than to sit in my flat and worry myself sick.

That evening I skipped dinner with Sylvie and Seamus and dressed up in a black dress. I hired a car to take me to the Artists' Museum, where James was waiting for me, looking dandy as usual in a suit and bow tie. He offered me his arm, and we went into the gallery together for drinks and hors d'oeuvres.

There was already a large group of people in the gallery, chatting quietly together in small groups. James introduced me to several of his co-workers, and they were intrigued by my job as an art history professor. I felt at home among them discussing art and architecture, and the time sped by quickly.

I was stuck talking to a dreadful man from a museum in Glasgow when James was called away. The man was trying to decide which canapé to take from the tray of hors d'oeuvres. I shuddered, making a mental note to stay away from the canapés.

The man insisted on telling me his life story, pausing only once or twice to wipe some kind of sauce from his tie. James stood across the room, half a head taller than anyone around him. He glanced up and I caught his eye. He winked at me and gave me a broad smile. I felt a flutter of something intense. Was it love? I walked over to join him, grateful for an excuse to leave the boorish man muttering to himself.

James held my hand as we made the rounds to other colleagues at the party. I felt a wee bit heady from a combination of the wine, the music, and the twinkling lights. And for a brief time, a very brief time, I was able to feel a happiness I hadn't felt since Ellie disappeared. I had felt hope, but not happiness. Then, almost immediately, pangs of guilt settled in my mind and my heart. I glanced at James. He had seen the change come over my face.

"What's the matter?" he whispered, leaning close to my ear.

I squeezed his hand harder. "I was just thinking about something."

"Whatever it was, it went from good to bad very quickly."

"You're right," I said with a smile. "Don't worry about it. We can talk later when we're alone."

"I'm ready to leave anytime you are," he said. We retrieved our coats from his office and left by a back door to avoid running into more people on our way out. We went to our now-favorite pub and sat in a booth in the back. We each ordered a dram and when the waiter left, James sat back and let out a sigh.

"Now tell me what you were thinking back at the party."

I was silent for a moment. How did I tell him how I was feeling? I figured the best way to say it was to just plow through it and hope he understood and was feeling the same way.

I took a deep breath. "I was just thinking that at that party, when you smiled at me from across the room, when you winked at me, I felt a delirious happiness for the first time since Neill took Ellie. And then straight away I felt terrible for feeling happy. Do you think that's wrong?"

"Do I think it's wrong to feel happy or do I think it's wrong to feel guilty?"

"Either."

"I don't think it's wrong at all. I've been wondering how I was going to tell you how I feel about you and you've just done the hard work for me. The truth is, I think I'm falling in love." He smiled broadly, his eyes twinkling.

I couldn't do anything but smile at him. I was afraid I would cry if I opened my mouth. He reached for my hand across the table and caressed it. "When I first met you on the airplane, I figured you for a harried, stressed-out drinker."

"And you were partially right!"

He laughed. "But not in a bad way. Harried and stressed out, definitely. But little did I know how good your reason was for feeling that way. And the drinking part? This is Scotland. To find a woman to drink whisky with me was a wee bonus."

"But what about Ellie?" I asked.

"We're going to find Ellie. But you're allowed to feel happiness even in her absence. It would be strange if you were joyful and giddy all the time, but you're not. She always occupies a big part of your mind. That much is obvious, even to someone who doesn't know you. You exude a certain sadness, a certain melancholy. And that's all right. But you can miss Ellie and, maybe, love me at the same time, you know. Do you?"

I looked into his twinkling big brown eyes as a warm feeling of love and peace and hope washed over me. And a thrill of excitement, wondering what the future might hold for the two of us. For the three of us, once I had Ellie back.

"Yes, I think I do." He squeezed my hand, staring into my eyes with a look of unbridled joy.

We took our time walking back to the flat. We had just turned onto my block when my phone rang. I glanced at the caller ID and didn't recognize the number. My pulse quickened.

"Hello?"

"It's Neill. Greer, listen to me."

"Neill—"

"Just listen to me, I said. I need money. Ellie is in real danger this time. I have to meet you."

"How is she in danger?" I had stopped in my tracks. James was staring at me.

"Never mind that. The quicker I get the money, the safer she'll be. I need ten thousand pounds. How fast can you get it?"

"Ten thousand pounds? I'm going to have to call my mother. I don't have that kind of cash. And besides, I'll never be able to withdraw that much from the cash machine."

"How much do you need?" James asked.

I covered the phone with my hand. "I need about six thousand pounds," I answered. "I only have about four thousand in the bank."

"I'll give you as much as I can," he said. "Find out when Neill needs it."

"Neill, I can get the money. Where do you want me to meet you?"

"How did you get the money so fast?" he asked.

"It doesn't matter. Please, tell me where to meet you. And when."

"Meet me in an hour on the Royal Mile, in front of St. Giles."

"Will you have Ellie with you?"

"No."

"Where is she?"

"With someone I trust. It's better if you don't know where they are."

Who had Ellie? Probably a girlfriend. Damn him.

He hung up before I could say anything more. I turned to James. "I don't know how to thank you. I have to meet him in an hour in front of St. Giles."

"Let's get to the cash machine, then." He grabbed my hand, and we turned around and headed back in the opposite direction. I remembered seeing a cash machine not far from the pub. We walked quickly to the machine and I waited while James took out five hundred pounds, the machine's limit. He counted it quickly and stuffed it into an envelope that was in a box on the cash machine. I took out five hundred pounds too, then we headed toward St. Giles.

"Wait," James said, stopping on the street. "Why haven't we called the police yet?"

"We can't call the police," I said. "It'll spook him and he won't come. And then how will we find out where Ellie is? And then what if his girlfriend—he has a girlfriend, apparently— takes her?" My voice was rising; my throat constricted.

"They can make him tell them," he suggested.

"But what happens if he doesn't tell? They can't torture him. As much as I wish they could."

"Greer, I think this is a bad idea."

"I just don't think there's any other way. Why don't you stay here and I'll meet Neill by myself?"

He shook his head. "No way. You're not going to St. Giles by yourself in the dead of night. I'm going with you."

We hastened to the cathedral. Only a few people milled about the street outside. Soft light from the magnificent High Kirk pooled on the cobbles, making the atmosphere quite bright, even in the cold darkness. I turned to James. "I'm surprised Neill wanted to meet here. It's very bright. I expected him to want to meet where it was dark, where fewer people would be able to see us."

"I don't see him, do you?"

We looked in every direction in front of the cathedral, but Neill wasn't there. "I guess we should wait for him."

I had the unsettling feeling of being watched. It was likely Neill was somewhere quite close, observing us as we waited for him. I had a sudden chilling thought. "James, what if Neill isn't showing up because you're here with me? He didn't say to come by myself, but maybe that's what he expected."

"Don't you think he'd call if he wanted me to leave?"

"I really don't know. Maybe he'll just not show up."

"He'll show up if he needs the money badly enough."

"But what if he thinks you're the police?"

James sighed. "You win. I'll leave, but I'm not going far. I'm going to a place where I can see everything." He looked around, then pointed to a tartan shop. "That's as good a place as any. I'll park myself in the front window and watch from there. Just hand him the money, try to find out where Ellie is, and get yourself out of there." He leaned in to kiss me and then hurried away.

I stood by myself in the cold, scanning the people around me for a sign of Neill.

When he walked up to me several minutes later I was shocked.

"Greer."

Chapter 20

I knew that voice. But I would never have recognized the man. Neill's hair was too long and greasy. His face was dirty, and it looked like he hadn't shaved in weeks. His clothes were tattered and disheveled. Pushing his stringy hair away from his face, he approached me slowly.

"Do you have the money?"

"Neill?" I was incredulous.

"Shh. No one can know I'm here. Do you have the money?" he repeated.

"I have a thousand pounds. That's all we were allowed to withdraw from the cash machine. Where's Ellie?"

"That's all you brought?" he asked with a groan. He ran his hand across his forehead, then shook his head. "I can't tell you where Ellie is. It's safer for both of you not to know."

"You can't keep doing this, Neill. Give her back to me and I'll protect her."

"You can't protect her, Greer. This is my mistake. Only I can protect her right now."

"*You're* the reason she's in danger," I said, jabbing my finger toward his face. "You smell terrible. Just look at yourself. She must be scared to death."

"It's a disguise, Greer."

"Don't give me that. It isn't a disguise. It's a tragedy and a nightmare for our daughter. James was right. I should have called the police. Maybe they could talk some sense into you."

"Please, Greer. As soon as I give the money to the people I owe, Ellie and I will be safe, and I'll bring her back to you. But I need that money. And the other nine thousand pounds, as soon as you can get it."

"Did you gamble all the other money away?" I asked with a scowl.

"Yes," he answered in a whisper, looking at the ground.

"Who do you owe money to?"

"His name is Arnie."

"Once you give Arnie the money, this will all be over and you'll give Ellie back to me?"

"I hope so."

"What's that supposed to mean?"

That familiar beading of sweat had formed on Neill's upper lip. He glanced in each direction, his gaze shifting rapidly. This was a hunted man.

"Neill?" I shook his arm.

"It means I hope so." He looked over his shoulder. "If anything happens to me, find Beatrice."

"Beatrice? What's she got to do with this?"

"Someday maybe I'll tell you everything, but for now please just give me the money."

The money was in the bank envelope. I slipped it out of my coat pocket and handed it to him. "This is all I have, and it's all my friend has. Please give it to Arnie and don't gamble with it. I can't get you more. And Ellie needs to be with me."

He scowled. "Don't preach at me, Greer. I know all that."

"I'm not preaching at you," I hissed. "Don't screw it up."

He turned and took off running. I hedged for a moment, then ran after him. He looked behind him and sped up when he saw me following him. I heard a shout that sounded like James. *He'll just have to try to keep up.*

James had indeed fled the shop when he saw me run after Neill. It wasn't long before his long strides caught up to mine, and he grabbed my arm. "Greer, what are you thinking?"

We were both breathless, but I felt I could have kept running all night. "I'm going to find out where Neill's headed." He let go of me, and I raced off. I could hear James's feet pounding the street right behind me. Neill was ahead, and he was pulling away. When I saw him duck into Friar's Wynd, I didn't hesitate.

Two passersby stared as James and I chased Neill down the alley. He was quite far ahead. There was a shout, and suddenly Neill was gone.

I tried to run faster, but I was winded. James loped past me as I stood in the alley, my hands on my knees, trying to catch my breath. Up ahead, he stopped and looked around. "There's another alley, but no one's down there," he called.

"Never mind. We've lost him," I answered, shaking my head.

"Let me go down this way and see if I can spot anything," he said.

I waited against a wall, still breathing heavily. It was only a moment before I heard James shout. "Greer, come here!"

I hurried over and found James leaning over Neill. My ex-husband lay on the ground, his face covered in blood. An angry gash had split his forehead; jagged bits of skin glowed dark red in the lamplight.

I covered my mouth to keep from screaming. Whoever had done this could still be close by. With my ex-husband was quite possibly lying dead in front of me, Ellie could be with some woman she barely knew, waiting for her father to return to her.

There was so much blood. James recovered first. He pulled me back to the Royal Mile, and we stood together against the side of a building while he called the police from his mobile phone.

"We need to get out of here," he whispered. "The person who did this can't be far away."

"But we can't just leave him here," I said.

"We'll just walk a bit up the block. Find some people. The dispatcher told me to get out of the area. They'll be here quickly, I'm sure."

We jogged back the way we'd come, toward the cathedral, pausing only to look behind us a few times. Several people stood talking on the sidewalk. The image of Neill's body lying in the alley, blood pooling around him, went through my mind again and again.

We could already hear the sirens. Sirens were common in this city, but somehow I knew these particular ones were for Neill.

Once we stopped, the worry set in. "James, what about Ellie? She'll be so afraid when he doesn't come back! She'll panic!" I was panicking myself.

"Let's wait until the police examine him. Maybe there's something on him that will tell us where he's been hiding. Maybe they can even figure out where Ellie is now."

He was right. I allowed a tiny glimmer of hope to burst through the vise encircling my chest. "Do you think so? Maybe they can find something in his mobile phone."

Three police cars pulled to a stop, and several officers fanned out in front of St. Giles. James strode over and explained quickly what was going on. One officer shouted, and several more police moved quickly and cautiously toward the alley where Neill lay. James and I followed them, ignoring the suspicious looks and shouted questions from the group nearby.

"Say, what's going on?"

"Where are the coppers going?"

Before we knew it, an entire gallery of people crowded down the alley, pointing and staring at Neill's body. Several of them whipped out their mobile phones and began to record the chaotic scene. The police pushed the crowd back and put up caution tape. I elbowed my way to the front of the crowd, pulling James behind me.

The officer lifted the tape so James and I could pass underneath and get closer to Neill. An ambulance had driven down the Royal Mile, and two paramedics with a gurney were making their way through the crowd, shouting for people to let them through.

James and I stood off to the side to watch the police and the paramedics do their work. One paramedic was listening to Neill's chest with a stethoscope and the other was feeling Neill's neck for a pulse. He glanced at his partner and shook his head. The partner looked at his watch for several long seconds before taking the stethoscope out of his ears and hanging it around his neck. Then he started CPR. I could feel the pressure of James's hand on mine, but nothing else was registering.

The paramedic worked for what seemed like an hour, but in fact it was probably only a few minutes. Several police officers had gathered round and were watching. Finally the paramedic looked at his watch and noted the time. His partner wrote it down on a piece of paper he was holding. They spoke to the police officers briefly, and one of the officers nodded in my direction. The paramedics turned to look at me, and one of them started walking toward me and James. I already knew what he was going to say.

Neill was dead.

I let go of James's hand and stepped toward the nearest paramedic.

"Is this man your ex-husband?" he asked.

"Yes."

"I'm afraid he didn't survive his injuries."

I nodded. I couldn't speak. I felt like I should be remembering the good times, the love we felt for each other when we were much younger and less wise, the home we shared as a family. But I couldn't. I didn't want to remember those things.

I was angry. Angry that Neill had caused all of this himself, angry that he had a gambling addiction, angry at his family, angry that I was powerless to prevent any of this from happening, angry that I had to witness the immediate aftermath of his brutal death. I would never get the picture of his bloody face and forehead out of my dreams.

But most of all, I was angry at him for dragging Ellie into this, for introducing her to a world of thugs and violence, for taking her from me, for hiding her from the rest of the world in her time of greatest need.

And I was scared, too. Where was Ellie?

But through the anger and fear, I felt a sudden and unexpected lightness as my new reality began to dawn on me—a shameful feeling of contented acceptance that Neill was gone. I would never have to deal with him again, never have to take his panicked call in the night asking for money, never have to worry that he would take Ellie from me again. And as guilty as I felt for having such thoughts, I couldn't shake them. But I pushed them aside—we had to find my daughter.

What if the girlfriend had left her alone, or with a member of his horrendous family? If Ellie were alone, it wouldn't be long before she would expect him back and begin to wonder where he was. My eyes watered thinking about my little girl, confused and lonely, upset and possibly hungry. It was past her bedtime. Was she sleeping, only to wake in the morning and discover her daddy never came back? Was she awake, too afraid to fall asleep without an adult there to protect her? The tears spilled down my cheeks, and I walked over to where James was talking to one of the police officers.

"Love, I've been telling the officer what led us to chase Neill down this alley." He looked at the tear streaks on my face and squeezed my arm. "Darling, let's sit down somewhere. This has been a lot for you."

I wiped my eyes on my coat sleeve and nodded. "It's not Neill I'm crying about, it's Ellie."

The officer looked at us questioningly. "Who's Ellie?"

Too drained to speak, I looked at James, and he launched into an explanation of my relationship with Neill, our complicated reasons for being in Edinburgh, and my missing Ellie. The officer whipped out his radio, which hadn't stopped squawking and said something unintelligible into it. Then he motioned another officer over to him.

"We've got a missing child. Five years old. The deceased is the non-custodial parent. He took the child from the child's home in the States and brought her here. Have you been through his trouser pockets? His jacket? We need to find out where he was staying."

The police started to move faster. One reached into Neill's pants pockets and began sorting through everything in them. Another officer did the same with Neill's grungy overcoat. He shook his head. "Nothin' in the pockets, sir," he said.

The officer who had gone through Neill's trousers found a mobile phone. He stood under a streetlamp, and I could see him scrolling on the phone's screen. He walked over to me and James.

"It's a throwaway. Looks like he's only dialed one number." He read the number. "Recognize it?"

"Yes. That's mine. He called me earlier to ask me to meet him at St. Giles with ten thousand pounds."

The officer looked up from the screen. "Did you give him the money?"

"I gave him a thousand. That's all I could get on short notice."

"It's not on him." He ran over to Neill's body, now covered with a white sheet and surrounded by a bevy of officers and the paramedics. I could see the police looking around the circle at each other, some shrugging, others with questioning looks on their faces. James and I edged a bit closer to them.

"There's no evidence of any money here," one officer was saying.

"So the person who hit Neill must have taken it," I said, walking up to the group.

"Probably, but we'll have to take a closer look around the area."

One officer asked me to accompany him to his police car, and another officer took James to the other car. We were apparently going to be questioned separately. I was furious.

"My daughter is missing and this is what you do? You separate me from my friend and question us like we're the people who did this? I'm the *victim* here!" I continued my rant while the officer waited for me to finish. Then he explained in his most patronizing voice that this was "protocol."

"It's the second time in recent memory that I have been made to feel like a criminal by your so-called *protocol*," I said, trying to keep my voice even. The last thing I needed was to be arrested for talking back to the police. I looked over to the car where James was standing. He was waving his hands, and I suspected he was having the same conversation.

I calmed down long enough to answer the officer's questions, which weren't too painful but felt like a waste of time. The officer left me in the back of his car while he consulted with James's questioner and was back in a few minutes to release me.

"Your story checks out with his," he said, jerking his head in James's direction. "I told you, this is just protocol. We need to ask you these questions to cover all our bases, so to speak."

"I understand. Now can we please get back to my little girl? She's missing and quite possibly alone and scared somewhere in Edinburgh." And suddenly I remembered what Neill had said. "Neill told me if

anything happened to him, I should find Beatrice. That's his sister." My
words tumbled out in a rush.

"Do you think his sister might know where your daughter is?"

"I don't know." I gave him the Gramercys' phone number. He promised
to send another officer to make the call.

The crowd surrounding us had largely dispersed. Only the die-hard
stragglers remained, the ones obsessed with trying to get one final
glimpse of the body, to hear one final expression of disconsolate grief
from a family member. I glared at them in disgust and noticed that one
had a mobile phone on which he was recording everything.

"You want a show?" I screamed, walking over to him. "I'll give you a
show! Get out of here right this minute or I'll give the paramedics another
reason to be here!" I shook my fist at the man with the camera. James ran
over to me and put his hand on the small of my back.

"I'm taking you home, Greer. You've had enough." He turned to the
man with the mobile phone, still recording every word. "Please. You
heard her. What you're doing is coarse and insensitive. Please go away
and leave us alone."

The man took more kindly to James's plea than mine and, grimacing,
put his mobile phone in his pocket. I turned to James and buried my face
in his chest, sobbing. "Why do people do that? Why do they have to
intrude?" He said nothing, but put his arms around me and let me cry.

After several minutes, my tears dried and I was able to think more
clearly and breathe more easily. "Let's get you home," James finally
suggested. He spoke to one of the officers who was buzzing around the
scene and came back to where I stood. "He said we can go. They'll be in
touch in the morning." We left without a final glance behind us, leaving
the police to their gruesome task.

Seamus and Sylvie were asleep when we got back to my flat. It was the
middle of the night. James hadn't planned to spend the night with me, but
I asked him to stay and we fell into bed, exhausted. When we went into
the kitchen in the morning, still in the clothes we had been wearing the
night before, Sylvie and Seamus gaped at us.

If I had been in a better mood, I would have toyed with them about
why James had spent the night, but my mood was still foul. "What on
earth happened to you two?" Sylvie asked, her mouth still hanging open.

"Shut your mouth," I said crossly, then felt immediately sorry. If I
looked half as bad as James, I must have indeed looked a fright.

James and I took turns telling Sylvie and Seamus all that had happened
the night before. They were incredulous. I wondered if the news would be

too much for Sylvie, but she and Seamus both assured me she was strong enough to bear the stress.

When we told them Neill was dead, Sylvie stood up and hugged me. "I can't say that I'm sorry," she said, "because I never liked the bugger, but I'm sorry for Ellie's sake. For everything she's been through and will have to go through until we find her."

I nodded, suddenly overcome with gratitude for Sylvie's decision to stay in Edinburgh with me and for her kind words about Ellie, the niece she didn't know very well.

"We're waiting to hear from the police about any evidence they may have found last night after we left," James said. "We're hoping they were able to find something that would tell us where Neill was staying or where Ellie might be."

After breakfast, James returned to his flat to shower and get ready for work. I also got cleaned up and sat at the desk in my room, intending to do some reading for my research, but I ended up simply staring out the window.

An anguished cry from the living room jerked me out of my own thoughts. Seamus came running in from the kitchen as I arrived from my bedroom. Sylvie had been watching television.

She wasn't supposed to be watching television due to her concussion, but I knew she watched it sometimes when Seamus and I were out.

"Are you all right?" I cried. "Is it your head?"

"No! Look!" She pointed at the screen, where grainy video from the alley the night before was playing on a news channel. And there was my face, close up and contorted in anger and grief, screaming at the owner of the phone to leave me alone, threatening him with bodily harm if he didn't listen.

The three of us watched, stupefied, as we heard James firmly ask the man to stop filming. The video went black. Then the news report cut back to the anchor in the studio, who reported that a brutal murder had taken place the night before in an alley close to St. Giles. No one mentioned the missing money. When the anchor moved on to the next story, I buried my face in my hands.

"Now you know how it looked last night," I said, my voice muffled by my hands. "It was just like being there. How horrible."

Seamus put his pink, beefy hand on my shoulder. "Nay, don't be worryin' about it, Greer. It's just a news report, sensationalist as always. Nobody'll give it a second thought."

I chewed on my thumbnail. I didn't want my neighbors to recognize me from the report. I didn't want them to think I was mixed up in anything nefarious. I silently cursed Neill again for getting me into this mess.

I needed fresh air. It was chilly outside, but crisp and clear. The blue skies belied my dark mood. I told Sylvie and Seamus I would be back in time for dinner and left the flat.

The walk was what I needed to clear my mind and focus. I walked slowly and idly, ignoring the other people in the park. Had I paid more attention, I would have noticed a familiar face watching me from a bench.

When the sun disappeared behind the clouds, the sudden darkening of the sky lifted me out of my own thoughts. I glanced around and saw people leaving. I hadn't heard the weather for the day, but I assumed rain was on its way. I turned and headed back toward Bide-A-Wee. Only one person remained in the park. He didn't move from his spot on the bench as I drew closer. I recognized him with a jolt of alarm.

It was Gerard. I must have looked startled, because his lips curled in a reptilian smile, hitching up each side of his dark, scruffy beard. He was happy to have taken me by surprise.

I had had enough surprises to last a lifetime.

"Gerard. How did you know I was here? What do you want?" I glanced around to see if any other people had come into the park, but we were alone.

He stood up, ignoring my question. "What're ye doin' here, Greer?"

Why did he care what I was doing when his brother's body lay in the mortuary?

"I was just out for a walk." I decided to take the high road and offer him my condolences, in spite of my fear of him. "Gerard, I'm sorry about what happened to Neill."

He gave me a quizzical look. "What happened?"

"You haven't heard?"

"No. What?"

"Neill was killed last night in an alley not far from St. Giles."

The color drained from Gerard's face. "Liar!" he accused.

"It's true. I'm sorry you had to hear it from me."

"What happened?"

"Someone hit him in the head."

He stared at me. "How do you know?"

"I got there just after it happened."

"Why were you there?"

"He had asked me to meet him by St. Giles, but he took off running. I chased him and got to him just a few seconds too late. I'm surprised you hadn't heard."

"I dropped my mobile phone last night. Can't get calls or texts." He turned suddenly and ran off.

"Gerard!" I yelled after him. He must have heard me, but he didn't turn around.

What was Gerard doing here in the first place? Was he living nearby? I doubted it.

Had he been following me? If so, why?

He knew where I lived, since he had asked the landlord for a key to my flat. He hated me, which I had known for years. He was strange, which I had also known for years. There were several reasons he could have been following me. But what did he want?

My mobile rang as I walked into the flat. I listened to the person on the other end and let out a cry.

Chapter 21

"They found Ellie! The police have her!"

Sylvie stopped short and her eyes widened. "You're kidding!"

I shook my head and bent down. I didn't know whether to laugh or cry, so I did both. Sylvie did, too. We slid down onto the floor and laughed and cried together. When Seamus walked through the door a few moments later, he was shocked.

"Girls! What's the matter?" He dropped the bags he was carrying and knelt down beside us.

"They found Ellie!" Sylvie sobbed.

"What?" Seamus looked from me to Sylvie and back again.

"It's true! The police called my mobile and told me. She was alone, watching TV, and she saw my face on the screen. It must have been that mobile footage that was on this morning. Anyway, Ellie found a phone and called the number that was flashing across the bottom of the screen. I can't believe it!"

"Well, what are you sitting here for?" Seamus asked. "Go get her!"

I nodded, tears running down my face. "She's at a police station in Bell's Loch, in East Lothian. I'll get James to drive me." I rang him on the mobile.

He couldn't believe the news. He left work right away, picked up his car, and we were on our way to the police station in less than thirty minutes. Sylvie and Seamus had offered to go with us, but I felt so many people gawking at her might be a bit overwhelming for Ellie. I wasn't even sure of the wisdom of taking James along, but he had a car and it was much quicker for him to drive than for me to try to hire one. And, I confess, I needed and wanted him with me.

We didn't talk much on the way to the police station. I chewed my fingernails—I couldn't help it—but stopped temporarily every time James glanced in my direction.

When we pulled up to the police station, I turned to James.

"I'm nervous. What if she's angry with me for letting Neill take her?"

"You're being silly, Greer. She's going to be beyond thrilled to see her mum. Now get in there and let's take her home! I'm not going in because she needs to see just you first."

I squeezed his hand gratefully and hurried into the station.

It seemed ages while I waited in the lobby for one of the officers to usher me down a long hallway and into a small, cheerless room. There he indicated a chair where I could sit and wait for my daughter.

And when I saw her, I knew the meaning of joy.

I heard her before I saw her. She was asking a question. I could tell from the inflection of her voice. I stood up, waiting for the door to open. And when it did and my daughter stepped tentatively into the room holding the hand of an officer, my cheeks ached from the huge smile on my face. I choked on a sob and stepped forward as she let go of the officer's hand and threw herself into my arms. My worry that she would be angry at me had been for nothing.

I knelt on the floor, my arms wrapped around her little body, and we both cried the happiest of tears. My eyes were closed, but I heard the door click softly as the officer left the room so Ellie and I could be alone for a little while.

I held her at arm's length and sniffled. Her wide smile told me everything. She was happy to see me, she was healthy, and she was with me to stay.

She wiped her eyes and let out a loud hiccup. We laughed. I reached out to touch her hair. I knew Neill had shaved it into a buzz cut, but seeing it was still shocking.

"Daddy said he had to do that so I would be safe," she said. She looked away. "It's not long anymore."

"It's beautiful," I whispered. "I missed you so very much, and I was so worried about you. Are you all right?"

"I'm a little hungry," she said, smiling.

"Then we will get you some lunch just as soon as we leave here." The police station seemed a sterile place to talk, so I poked my head into the hallway and waved down a nearby officer. He helped me get the paperwork ready so I could take Ellie back to Edinburgh. Before I left, the officer I had spoken to on the phone earlier came into the room where

Ellie and I were waiting. She shook my hand and touched the top of Ellie's head. She asked me to call her when we were settled back in the flat.

As Ellie and I walked to the car, I explained that James was my friend and that he would be joining us for lunch and driving us home. When he knelt down to introduce himself, I could have kissed him. He seemed to know just what to do.

Ellie climbed into the car. I sat next to her in the back seat, holding her hand until James pulled up next to a small restaurant in the next village. The three of us enjoyed a simple meal while James and I told Ellie about the flat in Edinburgh and about Sylvie and Seamus, waiting there for her. She asked about Neill, but we sidestepped the issue by telling her she wouldn't be seeing him for a long time. She didn't ask any more questions about him.

I was dying to pepper Ellie with questions about where she had been staying, the people she saw there, and how Neill had treated her, but I knew such an interrogation would have to wait. She needed time to absorb all that had happened and to get used to her father not being around anymore. I had no idea how and when to tell her that he had died. She didn't seem to understand the chaos she had seen on the television screen, other than to recognize me and know she had to call the number provided.

After lunch, we drove back into Edinburgh. Ellie seemed fascinated by the beautiful old buildings, the bustle of the city, and the traffic. She commented several times about being in "the big city." It led me to believe she had not seen much or even any of Edinburgh since coming to Scotland with Neill. When James pulled to a stop in front of Bide-A-Wee, Ellie was enchanted.

"This looks like a house from a book!" she cried. James and I laughed.

"It is lovely, isn't it?" I asked. "Let's go inside and see Sylvie and Seamus." James promised to stop by later, after Ellie was settled in.

Ellie took my hand and we walked up the front steps together. Sylvie must have been watching from the window upstairs, because she swung open the door and stood, smiling, waiting for us.

"Ellie, you may not remember Sylvie, but she's my sister. Your aunt. She has been helping me while I've been in Edinburgh."

Ellie gave Sylvie a shy smile and Sylvie bent down. "Ellie, we've been waiting a long time to see you! I'm so glad you've come! Welcome to Bide-A-Wee."

Ellie gave me a confused look. "That's the name of this house," I told her. The three of us went upstairs into the flat. Seamus was in the kitchen, but he came into the living room when we opened the door. Ellie took one look at him and glanced up at me quickly. I realized how imposing Seamus must look to a small child, with his beard and tattoos and big limbs. I hastened to introduce them.

"Ellie, this is Sylvie's friend Seamus. He's a wonderful cook and a painter. Maybe in a little while he can show you some of his paintings." Those seemed to be the right words, because Ellie stepped forward and took the hand Seamus was holding out to her.

"I'm pleased to meet you, lassie," he said. She smiled up at him. "I hope you like cake. I'm making a special cake for dessert tonight."

"What kind of cake?" she asked.

"Chocolate!"

She smiled at him again, and I knew I was watching the beginning of a friendship form before my eyes.

It was late in the evening when James came to the door and we all finally sat down to dinner. Conversation was light, as I didn't want to mar the happy occasion with a mention of anything dark or sinister in front of Ellie. My fear of her being overwhelmed by people and attention had been allayed. She was quiet, but she smiled often and seemed keenly interested in the things we talked about at dinner.

When Seamus brought out the chocolate cake, her eyes widened and she grinned. "Wow!" was all she said. And Seamus had outdone himself. The cake was slathered in chocolate frosting, dotted with green leaves and pink rosebuds made of sugar. I was touched by his thoughtfulness and the time he had obviously put into making such a magnificent dessert.

Ellie practically fell into bed after dinner. Her eyelids started to droop before we finished eating, and she yawned several times. She lay down in her new room, and I lay on my side next to her as she snuggled in for the night.

"I'm so glad to have you back," I told her for the thousandth time that day. "I'm a very lucky mum."

"I missed you, Mummy," she said, nestling her head against my arm. "Daddy got angry sometimes when I was scared and didn't know where you were."

"I know. I'm sorry you were scared. I was trying very hard to find you. So was James."

She nodded, barely awake by then. I kissed her on the forehead and watched in the dim glow from the nightlight as she fell into a deep sleep, her breathing slow and regular. It took all my willpower not to wrap her in my arms and hug her all night. But she needed a good, long sleep. I could spend the rest of my life hugging her.

James, Sylvie, and Seamus were waiting for me when I went back into the living room. They were full of questions.

"Is she afraid in there by herself?" Seamus asked.

"Did she ask for Neill?" asked Sylvie. "Did you remember to turn on the nightlight?"

I rolled my eyes. Has any mother ever forgotten to turn on a nightlight? Would any child let her forget?

"She's fine. Sleeping soundly already. And yes, I checked the window latches three times to make sure they're locked. She didn't ask about Neill, but I assume we'll talk about him soon."

We kept our voices down while Ellie slept. I had planned to sleep in my bed, but I couldn't. I pushed an armchair into the narrow hallway by her bedroom door and slept there instead. Or rather, tried to sleep. As tired as I was after the exhausting day, I couldn't rest. I wanted so much to sleep next to Ellie that night, but it was more important that she rest without interruption. And I was still a bit nervous about crowding her too much. After all, it had been a while since we had seen each other, and I wondered whether she still harbored some latent resentment that I didn't come for her while she was with Neill.

Before Ellie awoke the next morning, I called the police station in Bell's Loch. When I spoke to the constable who had called me—had it really been less than twenty-four hours since that call?—she told me a little more about what transpired when Ellie called the police.

She had been alone in a small flat in town. Her voice had trembled as she spoke to the officer who answered the phone. She had told him she saw her mummy on television, and she wanted to know where her mummy was. She said she lived with her father, but he had gone somewhere and wasn't back yet.

When the police arrived at the flat, it was clean and bright. It was also clear Ellie had been well-fed while she had been staying there. When the officers asked her how long she had been there, she didn't know. She told them her home was in the United States. She hadn't been to school since arriving in Scotland, and the circumstances of her arrival had been unclear to the police. They asked her how she had seen me on the television, and she responded that it was something bad and that I was yelling. When they asked her the channel she had been watching, she just pointed to the box.

"The one that's playing now?" the officer had asked. She nodded. The police took her with them and made a call to the television station. After a little research, someone at the station had discovered the video footage of the crime scene and notified the police, who tracked down who I was, why I was in Scotland, and that the girl was, indeed, my daughter.

"Here's what confuses us, though," the officer said. "The flat is not in your ex-husband's name, and we haven't been able to learn who it belongs to or who has been paying the rent. According to the landlord, the rent arrives in an envelope under his door once a month, in cash, and the signature on the lease is unreadable. It appears the person who signed the lease was using an alias and it was sent by fax, so he's never actually met the leaseholder. Do you know who might be renting the flat?"

I thought for a long moment. "I know Neill has been in contact with the loan sharks since he arrived in Scotland, but I doubt any of them would have paid for his flat. Maybe his girlfriend? How long has the person been renting it?"

"Several years. Who's the girlfriend?"

"I don't know. She doesn't live there?"

"It seems not."

I told the officer I would try to find out, then thanked her again for finding me. The officer said she would email photos of Neill's flat to the police station in Edinburgh. I could peruse them there to see if there was anything I recognized that could give them a clue as to who rented the flat.

Ellie wandered into the kitchen a few minutes later and greeted me with a yawn and a hug. How I had missed that! We had breakfast together, then I shooed her to the bedroom to get dressed because I had plans for us to spend the day together.

Ellie was still wearing the same clothes she had worn the previous day, so our first stop was Jenners to buy her some new clothes. Laden with bags of skirts and dresses, leggings and tops, and two cute pairs of shoes, we stopped for lunch at a café and then dropped off our purchases at James's museum. He promised to meet us for dinner, and we continued our fun.

Ellie was delighted with Camera Obscura, a popular tourist attraction. At the top of its 150-year-old observatory were panoramic views of the city, enhanced by telescopes revealing miles of countryside. We had fun exploring the mirror maze, the holography exhibit, and the optical illusions all throughout the magnificent building. Ellie especially loved the room where small people become large, and tall people become tiny.

We also took a long walk through Princes Garden, where she had fun chasing squirrels and playing peek-a-boo behind trees. Clouds of worry darkened her face a few times throughout the day, but each time I asked her if she wanted to talk, she shook her head.

She did tell me that she had spent much of her time indoors, though Neill took her to playgrounds and parks in the late afternoons occasionally.

I asked Ellie if people ever came to visit them at the flat where she stayed with Neill. She nodded. I didn't want to scare her, so I spoke as casually as I could.

"Oh? Were they nice?"

She shrugged.

"Did you know them?"

"No."

"Were they ladies or men?"

Ellie squeezed her eyes shut and pursed her lips. "Both."

"Do you remember their names?"

She scrunched her mouth up and looked up. "No."

I didn't want to upset her, so I stopped my questions.

"When can I go back to school, Mummy?"

I had been waiting for that question. I had pondered it often in the quiet moments since Ellie came back to me, but I was still undecided. I knew how important it was for her to go back to school, but part of me held back. Neill had been able to take her from her supposedly secure school back in the States, and I had no idea what school security was like in Edinburgh. I wasn't yet ready to return home to the U.S. when there were still too many unanswered questions in Scotland: Who killed Neill? Were Ellie and I still in danger? What had Neill needed the ten thousand pounds for, and who had the money now? I didn't really care about the money since I had Ellie back, but if it meant we were still in danger, then I had to get the answers before I could feel safe anywhere.

"I don't know, Pumpkin."

"When are we going home?"

I smiled as I reached out to touch her short spiky hair. "I don't know that, either. We need to stay in Edinburgh for a while."

"Okay." She didn't seem to mind. I was relieved.

"Do you like Edinburgh?"

She shrugged. "I think so. It's big."

We held hands on the way back to the flat, where Seamus had made a scrumptious chicken tikka masala for dinner. We could smell the warm spices even before we went through the front door, and Ellie turned to me with a big smile.

"I smell Indian food!"

I laughed, knowing Seamus was trying his best to impress his littlest diner. He said a little bird had told him Ellie liked curries and Indian food, so he wanted to surprise her with a special treat. James arrived not long after we did, and our "family" enjoyed a leisurely dinner together while Ellie regaled everyone with the things she had seen during the day.

Not long after dinner, I put Ellie to bed while the others talked in the living room. I joined them for a dram of whisky, and eventually Sylvie and Seamus retired to their room to watch television. James and I were left alone in the living room. I snuggled next to him on the sofa. He put his arm around me and we sat in silence for several quiet, blissful minutes. Finally he spoke.

"When do you think you'll be going back to the States?"

I looked up at him in surprise. "I don't know. There are still a lot of unanswered questions here in Edinburgh. I don't want to leave until I know for sure that Ellie and I will be safe no matter where we are, and I know how and why Neill died."

James nodded.

"Why do you ask?"

"I was thinking how nice it's been with you here. I don't know what I'm going to do when you leave."

He had just spoken the words I was afraid to hear. I shifted out from under his arm and faced him, my knees crossed under me. "I don't know, either. But we *are* going to have to leave eventually. Ellie has to go back to school, and I have to get back to my students. And our home."

He sighed. "What do you think we should do about it?"

"Do we have to do anything?"

"I don't want to continue like this. I've given it a lot of thought. You know I love you, but I hate to think of how much it's going to hurt when you're gone."

"So what should we do?"

He was quiet for a moment, then he spoke, a touch of hesitation in his voice. "Maybe we shouldn't be seeing so much of each other. I mean, the more time we spend together, the more it's going to hurt when we're apart. And not just apart, but separated by an entire ocean. Thousands of miles."

I was stunned. Did he just say what I thought he said? Was he suggesting we break up? I cocked my head and struggled for the right words, my mouth working silently.

"Um, what?"

He stared straight ahead. "I can't keep spending all this time with you, knowing in the back of my mind that it's all going to end, and I'm going to be alone when you leave. I think it's best if we cut it off now."

"So it's better to be alone and suffer loss now, than to experience the good times and suffer loss at some point down the road?" I scoffed.

He shrugged. "It sounds silly when you put it that way, but yes, I suppose that's basically what I'm saying."

My head was already starting to hurt from my clenched teeth. "How can you honestly believe that? I thought we were a couple!"

"We are. I mean, we were. Hell, I don't know what I mean anymore." He ran his hands through his graying hair. "I need some space right now to figure out what to do next."

"We just sat here for a long time with your arm around me! It was comfortable and perfect! And you were thinking about breaking up with me the whole time?" The heat was rising in my face.

"I don't know. It sort of popped out of my mouth, though I admit it's something I've been thinking about for a while."

A sudden thought struck me. "Does this have anything to do with Ellie?"

His eyes widened, and he shook his head vehemently. "Absolutely not. I think she's a darling little girl, and I'm thrilled for both of you that she's back."

"Are you sure you're not feeling jealous because of all the attention Ellie's been getting? Or mad because now you have to share me with her?" I sounded petty even to my own ears, but I couldn't help myself. "Or maybe you just don't like her and want an excuse to get away?"

He stared at me, his jaw slack. Finally he recovered himself. "Greer, you know that's ridiculous. I'm very fond of Ellie, and I've always assumed I'd have to share you once you found her. I'm not jealous at all."

"I think you should go." I walked to the door and held it open.

"Greer, this doesn't mean we have to stop seeing each other completely. We can still get together sometimes."

"Forget it."

"I'm doing this because I love you, Greer. I'm trying to spare us more pain in the future."

"Yeah, I know. Now please leave." I motioned to the doorway. He picked up his coat and sighed.

"I'm sorry, Greer."

I said nothing.

After he left, I shut the door a little too forcefully and sat down on the sofa. I wanted to cry, but no tears would come. My insides were twisted, my head ached, and there was a hard lump growing in the back of my throat. It hurt to swallow.

Sylvie came out of her bedroom. "Is everything all right?"

I didn't answer.

She furrowed her brow and asked, "Did James leave?"

I nodded. "For good."

She gasped. "You're kidding!"

"Do I look like I'm kidding?" It was unkind, but I couldn't help it. I wasn't in the mood to feign niceties.

"What happened?"

"He said he *loves me too much* to keep seeing me," I answered, making air quotes with my fingers. "Do you believe it?"

Sylvie put her hand over mine. "I'm really sorry, Greer. I thought you two would end up married."

"Well, that's not going to happen." I laughed bitterly.

"You know, maybe it's not over. Maybe he just needs some space."

"It's over. He suggested we get together sometimes, and I told him to forget it."

"Why?"

"Because it would be too hard. I couldn't do it."

"I wish there was something I could say or do to make you feel better."

"Thanks, but there isn't." I mustered a quivery smile for her.

Sylvie went into the kitchen, then returned a moment later with a tall glass of water. She gave me a sympathetic look before going into her room. I was staring at nothing and pretended not to see her.

When she had shut her door, I was finally able to let the tears come. I cried silently, not wanting Sylvie or Seamus to hear, or to wake Ellie.

There were so many emotions at war in my heart. Embarrassment, anger, disbelief, confusion. I still loved James and he said he loved me. So why were we doing this? Sure, it would be hard to go back to the States, but maybe we could have worked out an arrangement.

There was also guilt. I had come to Edinburgh to get Ellie back and I had her back. Shouldn't I be consumed with joy over that? Shouldn't that be good enough for me? How could I be concerned about my love life when I had just been lucky enough to get my daughter back? How could I be thinking about myself at a time like this? But I *was* thinking about myself, and I couldn't help it.

I was suddenly exhausted. I needed more than anything to lie next to Ellie with my arms around her. I crept into her bed and put my arm gently around her, trying to banish thoughts of James from my head. I thought I would never fall asleep.

But I did sleep, and I didn't wake up until Ellie stirred in the morning. I lifted my head with a groan, my neck muscles protesting, and Ellie rubbed her eyes, touching my arm.

"Mum, why are you sleeping here?"

"I wanted to make sure you're safe, that's all."

"I'm safe. Don't worry." I rested my cheek against her downy head and closed my eyes as I breathed in her scent, the fragrance of soap and shampoo filling my nostrils.

I hugged her and rolled out of bed. "Mimsy is coming to see you today," I said. "She can't wait to get here. What shall we do with her?"

Ellie loved her Mimsy and was very excited to hear she would be visiting. She jumped up and down and clapped her hands. "Let's take her to Camera Obscura!"

I laughed. "You want to go back there?"

"Yes!"

For just a short while that morning, Sylvie and Seamus looked after Ellie while I dashed over to the police station to have a look at the photos from Neill's flat. To no one's great surprise, I didn't recognize anything in the pictures. They were mostly shots of furniture and small kitchen appliances and bedding. I returned to Bide-A-Wee, excited to see Ellie. I felt sorry for having to leave her so soon after she was returned to me, but I couldn't very well take her to see the photos.

When Mum arrived, she broke down and cried when she saw Ellie. She couldn't stop touching Ellie's head. Eventually Mum regained her composure, and the three of us walked down to Camera Obscura. We spent a few hours going through the fascinating place, and Ellie was delighted to show her grandmother all the exciting things she had found there.

We went home after a light lunch. Ellie retreated to my room to read some picture books Mimsy had brought her while Mum and I talked in the living room.

"What's next for you and Ellie?" she asked.

"I don't know," I admitted. "I want her to go back to school— *she* wants to go back to school—but I'm not comfortable with the idea until I know we're not in danger anymore."

She nodded. "I agree. You can't be too careful. At the risk of repeating myself, why don't you two come down to stay in Dumfries while you figure everything out? I'd love to have you stay with me until you know what you're going to do."

My first instinct was to stay in Edinburgh. After all, there was James. But then I remembered he had ended things. There was no one to keep me in the big, beautiful city. Sylvie and Seamus were here, but their lives would continue without great interruption if I moved out. *Maybe Ellie would be better off in a smaller town.* But I loved living here, with the magnificent museums and the gorgeous old buildings and the endless possibilities for study. And I was sure Ellie liked being in Edinburgh, too.

"I don't know yet. I'll think about it," I promised Mum.

My mother ended up spending the night. She couldn't bring herself to leave, she said, because she was having such fun with Ellie and because she wanted to fuss over Sylvie a while longer. Coincidentally, she had packed overnight bags "just in case" and left them in the car. Sylvie and I exchanged knowing glances, having expected Mum to do just that.

The flat was full, warm, and happy that night. Three generations of the Dobbins family, plus Seamus, enjoyed a delicious meal, then Mum, Ellie, and I watched a movie. Ellie fell asleep midway through it. As I lay down with her later, I realized that I hadn't thought of James even once during the movie. I had become so used to having him at the flat, watching movies and sitting in front of the fireplace, that I thought I would miss him terribly, but I didn't. Perhaps it was because there were so many people around.

As I tried to sleep, though, thoughts of him crowded into my mind. How I wanted to see him again. Silent tears fell again, but thankfully they weren't as fierce as they had been last night.

I dreamed of him. We were walking hand-in-hand through Princes Gardens. I turned because I heard a noise, and there was a man rushing toward me. James yelled at me to run, and together we ran until we found ourselves trapped in a dark alley near St. Giles. A body was lying on the ground. It might have been Neill, but I couldn't tell because it was face-down. I jerked my head around in desperation, looking for an escape. I could hear the footsteps of the man from Princes Gardens thudding closer and closer behind us. I caught a glimpse of another person standing in the shadows, but I couldn't make out who it was. James was bellowing something in my ear, but I couldn't understand the words. A moment later, the man from the Gardens ran up to us. He grabbed my sleeve and James reached for my hand as it was pulled from his. We separated in the darkness. . . .

I awoke with a start, in a cold sweat and panting. My eyes were moist. It took me a second to realize where I was, and I peered over at Ellie to make sure she was still sleeping. I wondered if I had made any noise while I dreamed. When my heartbeat finally slowed and I felt composed, I sat in bed listening to Ellie's regular breathing and the silence of the flat.

It didn't take me long to fall asleep again after that. My dream still tingled in the back of my mind, but I tried my best to steer my thoughts away from it, focusing instead on the spectacular lochs of the Scottish Highlands, where I had spent so much time as a child on holiday and where I wanted to take Ellie before returning home.

But I didn't forget the dream completely. There was something about it... something that bothered me, but I couldn't quite put my finger on it.

When I woke up again, Ellie was still sleeping. I made a pot of tea and sat at the kitchen table while it steeped, my head in my hands. Part of me wanted to forget the dream, but part of me wanted to search it until I figured out what I was missing.

And it didn't come to me. At least, not right away.

The next several days were a maelstrom of activities. I wanted above all else to stay busy—not just for Ellie, but for myself, too. I knew the busier I was, the more likely I would forget about James, and maybe I would even stop missing him so much. But when I wasn't chasing Ellie around the park or talking with her as we walked the streets of Edinburgh or looking through a textbook while Ellie sat nearby reading one of her own books, my mind was consumed with thoughts of James. A couple of times, I took out my mobile phone, intending to call him, but each time I stopped myself just in time and put the phone away.

My mother ended up staying in Edinburgh for almost a week, and spending time with her helped me keep my mind off James, too. Twice we drove out of the city, visiting the seaside and the small villages dotting the Scottish countryside. There were so many charming places to visit. Ellie was delighted, and I rediscovered places I hadn't been to since I was her age.

When it came time for Mum to return to Dumfries, we were all sad to see her go. Even so, I was content with my decision to remain in Edinburgh. As much as I would have scoffed at the notion when I first arrived in the city, I enjoyed all the time I was spending with Sylvie.

And Seamus too, of course. Though there were moments when I was unsure of Seamus—when I remembered his hurried "transaction" on the Edinburgh street with a man I didn't recognize, when I pondered the questions he had so intently asked Sylvie about the break-in at our flat just after she arrived at hospital—I mostly trusted him and enjoyed his company. I still wondered whether Sylvie had told him that I knew of his past, or when she would decide to break it to him.

As the days passed and winter turned to spring, the weather began to turn from foggy, blustery, and chilly to sunny, warmer, and glorious.

Trees were in bud all over the city, softening the ancient buildings with showers of white, pink, and yellow petals. Ellie and I delighted in visiting our favorite places with the patina of spring glowing all about Edinburgh.

It was on one of those beautiful days when we ran into James. He was coming out of a pub around lunchtime when Ellie and I were walking by.

He stopped short in the doorway of the pub; the person following him out the door bumped into him from behind. After apologies by both parties, the man continued on his way while James stood on the sidewalk, fiddling with the lapel of his sport coat.

"Hello, Greer. Hi, Ellie. It's good to see both of you."

Ellie answered first. "Hello, James. Why don't you come to our flat anymore?"

James's face flushed, and he looked down at his feet. I was almost amused, waiting to hear his answer. "Uh, well Ellie, I... I've been very busy, and I know your mum waited a long time to be able to spend time just with you."

That seemed to satisfy my inquisitive little girl, and she turned her attention to a double-decker bus driving past. Puffing out his cheeks and releasing his breath slowly, James looked at me. "How have you been?"

"Fine, thanks."

"How are Sylvie and Seamus?"

"They're fine, too."

"I miss Seamus's cooking." He let out an awkward laugh.

I nodded, unsure of what to say next.

"How's work going?" he asked.

"Work's fine. I've been doing lots of research in museums around Edinburgh."

"Any word on, uh, Neill? You know, what happened that night?"

I glanced down at Ellie. She still hadn't asked about her father. "Nothing yet. I'm sure the police will tell me as soon as they know anything."

"Have you two eaten lunch yet?"

"Not yet."

"Do you want to join me?"

I pointed to the pub he had just exited. "Didn't you just eat?"

"No. Too crowded in there. I'm going up the street."

Before I could answer, Ellie chimed in. "Yes! I'm hungry!"

I gave James a grim smile. "Okay. We'll join you." I most certainly did *not* want to join him for lunch, but I didn't want to suffer a barrage of questions from Ellie if I refused.

The three of us walked in silence to a nearby café. James held open the door, and Ellie and I ducked under his arm. A fleeting memory of his arm around my shoulders skittered across my mind, but I shook it off quickly.

Lunch was an uncomfortable affair. Ellie didn't seem to notice. Her legs dangling from the chair, she was absorbed in coloring the pages the server had given her when we sat down. At first James and I didn't say much, but finally I thought I would go mad in the silence.

"Mum came to visit recently. She was thrilled to see Ellie and to satisfy herself that Sylvie's healing well."

"She sounds great. It's a shame I didn't get to meet her."

Now what?

James spoke next. "I've been working on a great new exhibit on impressionism. You'll have to come by and see it. I know you love the Scottish impressionists."

"Sounds interesting."

He gave me the details about the exhibit and told me the opening date. "At the cocktail party the night before the exhibit opens, we'll have several modern impressionist artists, as well as curators from two other museums. Perhaps you'd like to meet them."

I swallowed hard. "I don't know. I'll have to get back to you."

"Oh? Do you have plans?"

"I'm not sure. I'll let you know."

Another uncomfortable silence. It was finally broken by the server bringing our lunches. Ellie picked at hers, despite her earlier insistence that she was hungry. I was finished eating in no time, and waited a bit impatiently for her to push her plate away. James seemed overly interested in the food on his plate, staring at it intently. I couldn't wait to leave the restaurant.

When we emerged from the café into the sunshine of Edinburgh, James smiled and kissed my cheek. "Thanks for lunch," he said.

I smiled. "Thank you." Then, turning to walk in the opposite direction, I muttered under my breath, "That was awful."

"What was awful, Mum?" Ellie asked, her voice seeming much louder than usual.

I glanced behind us and wasn't surprised to see James watching us. Had he heard Ellie? I sighed. It didn't really matter, did it?

"I didn't like my lunch, that's all," I told Ellie with a smile.

Chapter 22

Ellie and I had just finished reading a story, and I was settling down to watch television when my mobile phone rang. I looked at the caller ID. It was the police.

"Dr. Dobbins, we have some information for you about the flat where your ex-husband was staying with Ellie."

"Yes?"

"We still don't know who rented the apartment, but we found some items that we were hoping you could shed some light on."

"Such as?"

"Was Neill a painter?"

"No. Neill never showed any interest in art. Why do you ask?"

"There were a lot of painting supplies in the flat. They were in a large box in one of the closets."

"Maybe they were Ellie's. Maybe he bought them for her to play with, since she didn't go to school."

The officer sounded doubtful. "These were an adult's tools. They're too big for a child's hands."

"Maybe Neill's girlfriend?"

"We haven't been able to find out anything about a girlfriend," the officer replied.

"Well, I'm sorry I can't help. I'll ask Ellie if she remembers anyone painting. Is there anything else?"

"We found the passports belonging to you and your daughter."

"Wonderful! We can go back to the States as soon as all this is cleared up."

"You can go back now if you'd like."

"I need to see this through to the end before we go. To ensure that Ellie isn't in danger anymore."

"We'll be in touch as soon as we know more about the night your ex-husband died."

"I have a quick question. Was there anyone else at the scene that you remember? I mean, besides me and James and Neill?"

"The onlookers, but our officers talked to most of them, and they've been cleared of any suspicion. I'm not aware of anyone else in the area."

After I hung up, I thought about the dream I had had about the night Neill died. Why had my subconscious conjured a person lurking in the shadows? Was it possible someone had really been there? Could I have caught a glimpse of a person and didn't register it at the time?

When I tucked Ellie into bed that evening, I tried to find out more about the painting supplies. "What sort of things did you do at the flat when you were staying with Daddy?"

"Played."

"Did you ever paint?"

"No. But sometimes that lady did."

I gripped the sheets a little tighter. "What lady?"

Ellie screwed up her lips, her characteristic thinking-hard look. "I don't remember her name. But she painted."

"What did she paint?"

"Pictures of outside."

"Were they pretty?"

Ellie shrugged.

"Was she nice?"

"She never said anything. Just painted."

"Do you know her name?"

Again the scrunched-up mouth, then Ellie said, "No."

Another dead end.

It was a good thing we got outside during the nice weather, because it quickly changed to rain, which fell steadily for the next several days. I only heard from the police once, when they called to tell me they had spoken to Beatrice and she had no idea why Neill had suggested contacting her before he died.

I had almost forgotten about the opening exhibit cocktail party James had mentioned, but then I got a text from him.

Would you like to go to the cocktail party for the new exhibit?

I took my time answering his text. I still hadn't decided whether to go. I was torn—if I went, would I wallow in self-pity afterward, wishing James hadn't decided to break off our relationship? Would I be angry? On the other hand, if I stayed home, would I regret it? Would I wish I had gone to meet new people and show James that I was perfectly happy without him?

I decided to go.

When the evening arrived, I was nervous. I spent way too long trying to decide what to wear, finally settling on a navy blue dupioni silk dress with a wide sash, flared skirt, bateau neckline, and scooped back. I paired it with navy suede pumps and simple gold jewelry, and pulled my hair into a French chignon. Seamus whistled as I checked myself in the mirror next to the front door one last time before leaving the flat.

"James is going to take one look at you and beg for forgiveness," he said.

Laughing, I thanked him and Sylvie again for watching Ellie for the evening and left for the waiting cab. I smiled to myself, pleased that I had taken so much time and care to dress. *Was Seamus onto something? Did I really want that from James?*

I thought the answer was yes.

At the museum, several groups of people stood in the atrium, talking quietly, sipping champagne and nibbling on appetizers that were being passed around by tuxedo-clad butlers. I accepted a flute of the sparkling citron-colored champagne, then nodded greetings to several museum employees I knew as I made my way through the throng in search of James.

I found him talking to a man near the reception desk. He glanced over at me, then did a quick double take, his eyes widening. I smiled to myself.

"You look beautiful tonight," he said.

"Thank you." I suddenly felt shy.

"Have you met any of the artists here?"

"Not yet. I've only talked to you."

He put his hand on the small of my back and guided me toward a small group of men and women. He introduced me to everyone, and we talked for several minutes. They were all artists whose works were being featured in the new exhibit or elsewhere in the museum. Several of them asked me about my work and the research I had done on Scottish impressionists.

"Aye, that McTaggart was a wonder," one man said. "He had a vision, and his hands just followed what was in his head and his heart." As much as I agreed with him and could have talked about McTaggart all night, the conversation in this small group was slow and ponderous. Not surprising, really, since many artists approached their art in the same manner.

The talk of impressionists, and McTaggart in particular, had me thinking again. And the more I thought about it, the more I was sure that faked painting had something to do with what had happened to Neill. And to me and Ellie, too.

James suggested we leave early and get a drink. We went to our favorite pub and slid into a booth.

"We couldn't really talk the other day with Ellie at the table," James said. "How have you been?"

"Fine. And you?"

"You know, busy at work."

Our conversation continued in the same stilted manner as we talked about Seamus's painting, a new exhibit at the Scottish National Museum, and several of James's co-workers.

Finally, our safe topics had been exhausted, and we fell silent. Both of us looked around the restaurant awkwardly until our server brought our orders. We ate in silence until James set down his knife with a loud clink and announced, "I've missed you."

I must have betrayed my surprise, because he continued in a rush of words. "That shouldn't take you unawares. Of course I've missed you. I didn't leave your flat that last time because I wanted to. I left because I couldn't bear the thought of the pain if I stayed. I was devastated." He spread out his hands. "I didn't want us to stop seeing each other. I've had an awful time of it, Greer. I just didn't want to feel this way, or even worse, later on."

I opened my mouth to speak, but closed it when I realized I didn't know what to say.

"Do you understand why I had to make that decision?" he asked.

I nodded slowly. "I think so. But you know the old saying, 'It's better to have loved and lost than never to have loved at all.' Don't you agree with that?"

"I do. But that doesn't really apply, does it? We've loved *and* lost."

"But why did we have to lose each other?" I blurted out without thinking.

He put his hand over mine. "Maybe it was a mistake."

"Maybe *what* was a mistake?"

"Maybe we should stay together for now."

"But you're right—it *is* going to end someday, when Ellie and I go back home."

He closed his eyes and sighed. "I know. But you have a point, and I confess I've been thinking the same thing for these past days. Why should we both be miserable now, while you're still in Edinburgh, when we can postpone the misery until you leave? A complete turn-around from what I felt not long ago, but I've missed you so much."

"I've missed you, too."

He picked up my hand and raised it to his lips. "I'm glad we've talked. So am I going to see much more of you and Ellie until you go back to the States?"

"That would be nice." My eyes were hot with tears, but I blinked them back and smiled at James. "I'm very happy."

"Me, too."

James walked me home after we left the pub. It felt right to be encircled in his arm, my head against his shoulder. The moon, full and round, lit our way back to the flat. He accompanied me into the living room, and Sylvie and Seamus looked up in surprise.

"Hi, Mum! Hi, James!" Ellie cried, running over to hug me.

"What's this?" Seamus asked, rising from the floor where he had been playing dolls with Ellie. He walked over and pumped James's hand several times.

"We had a wee talk and decided the whole thing was silly," James answered, smiling at me. "Why feel terrible now when we can postpone it and feel good?"

"That's what I would have done," Sylvie said.

"This calls for a celebration," Seamus boomed. "Drams all around!" Then he looked down at Ellie. "Except for you, little bairn. You get ginger ale!"

It was like we never skipped a beat, the five of us, sitting in the living room, talking and laughing and enjoying the company. We steered the talk away from any discussion of Neill or the police investigation surrounding his death so Ellie wouldn't be upset. But as soon as I put her to bed, James began asking questions about what had happened since we had last spoken of Neill.

"The police haven't made much progress," I said with a sigh. "Beatrice had no idea why Neill suggested we look for her after his death. And though they found paint supplies in the flat where Neill was staying, that hasn't been much help. They don't know who the supplies belong to, and they still don't know who owns the flat. Ellie says a woman would come over to paint, but she doesn't know the woman's name. Or she can't remember it, if she ever heard it. I suspect it was Neill's new girlfriend."

James grimaced. "I'm torn. On the one hand, there must be something the police can do to hurry this up and bring Neill's death to a conclusion. You and Ellie will both be safer. On the other hand, once it's cleared up, you and Ellie leave to return to your lives in the States."

"I just don't want the police to forget about it," I said.

"Have you told them what Ellie said about the woman who painted in the flat?"

"No. I didn't even think to do that. I'll call them first thing in the morning and let them know. Maybe that information can help them in some way."

When James left later that evening, after Sylvie and Seamus had gone to bed, I walked him to the door and he gave me a long, lingering kiss. I felt goose bumps on my arms and legs, so happy to be back in his arms. He released me and held me away from him.

"I don't even want to think of what the future holds. I'm just grateful for what we have now."

I nodded, too happy to speak, and he left. I slept well that night, even though I was curled up in Ellie's bed. It was probably time for me to start sleeping in my own room again and stop worrying about Ellie being spirited away in the night, but I wasn't ready for that yet.

Early the next morning, I called the police department in Bell's Loch. When I told the constable that Ellie had remembered a woman coming to the flat to paint, she said it made sense.

"What do you mean?" I asked.

"Just yesterday we found evidence at the flat that a woman had likely been there."

"What kind of evidence?"

"A piece of hair, quite long."

"How do you know it was a woman's, not just a man with long hair?"

"We don't know, that's why I said 'had *likely* been there.'"

"Do you think you can find out who the woman was?"

"We can do a DNA test on the hair, but it will take some time. If Ellie could remember the name of the woman,that would be a big help."

"I'll do what I can to encourage her memory, but I don't want to put too much pressure on her. She's more likely to remember if I'm not trying to force the issue."

"You're right. Just do what you can on your end, and we'll keep working on our end to figure out who we're dealing with."

That day, I took Ellie to the Edinburgh Zoo. We wandered around the exhibits for hours, doubling back to see her favorite animals and enjoying lunch outdoors. Ellie seemed happy, her thoughts far away from Neill's flat. I tried casually to bring up the subject of the unknown woman.

"You know, it would be fun to have a painting of some of these animals, don't you think? I wonder who we could ask to paint them for us."

"Hmmm. I don't know," Ellie replied.

"How about that woman who painted those pictures in the flat where you used to stay?"

"Yeah, I guess she could do it."

"If only we knew her name…"

"I can't remember her name. Just that she had kind of long hair."

So the hair the police found probably did belong to our mysterious painter.

"If you think of her name, tell me and maybe we can find her."

"Okay. How about Seamus?'

In the end Ellie thought it would be best if Seamus painted the animals for us, but at least I had wedged a thought into her head about the woman at Neill's flat. Maybe Ellie would remember her name when she least expected it, as adults often did.

That night after I had put Ellie to bed, I was sitting in the living room with Sylvie when the phone rang. Sylvie answered it and handed the phone to me.

"Who is it?" I whispered.

"I don't know."

"Hello?"

A voice growled on the other end. "I know where you live, and I'm coming after you and that kid of yours."

"Who is this?" I demanded. My heart skipped a beat.

"You're in this just as deep as the rest of us. You're never out of my sight."

I hung up and leapt off the sofa. Rattling the front doorknob, I made sure it was locked. Sylvie looked at me in amazement. "What on earth's goin' on?"

I told her about the phone call.

"Where's Seamus?" I asked, my voice tight and tense.

"I don't know. He went out for a walk, I guess."

"When's he coming back?"

"I don't know," Sylvie snapped. "I'm not his keeper, you know."

I ignored her sarcasm, well aware that she was as nervous as I was. I opened my bedroom door a crack to check on Ellie; she was fast asleep.

When I returned to the living room, I rang up the police. Though I now dealt with two police departments—one in Edinburgh and one in the Lothians—I left a message for Officer Dunbar in the Edinburgh station, whom I was told was outside taking a break. When she called back a few moments later, I told her about the threatening phone call and asked her what I should do about it.

She thought it was a prank, someone who had gotten my home number somehow and was trying to scare me. When I disagreed and suggested it was someone connected with Neill, she sighed and said she would ask someone to check it out and get back to me. I hung up thoroughly dissatisfied and, for the first time, dismayed at the lack of interest being shown by the police.

Sylvie had rung up Seamus on her mobile phone. I could hear them talking, her voice urgent and tense. She hung up and turned to me. "He'll be home soon. He ran into some old friends and they're having a drink in some pub. I told him to hurry up."

We sat on the sofa, listening for every tiny sound. We must have looked timid and pathetic, but we were scared. I wished I hadn't worried her by telling her about the phone call, but she had a right to know.

As the minutes turned into an hour, I began to wonder where Seamus was. Why wasn't he home yet? Had the person who called me gotten to him? Was Seamus lying, hurt, on a sidewalk or in an alley somewhere? Had he met the same fate as Neill?

Then something much worse occurred to me: What if Seamus had something to do with the phone call? What if he was behind it? What if all my suspicions about his recent behavior were justified? My mouth ran dry as I tried to swallow. I fidgeted with my hands until Sylvie, ashen and still, finally snapped, "Stop that!"

"Stop what?"

"Fiddling with your hands, that's what!"

"Sylvie, I can't help it. That's what I do when I'm nervous. I'm sorry."

"That's okay," she said, giving me a small smile as a peace offering. "I just can't believe Seamus isn't home yet. Where in the world is he?"

She didn't intend for me to answer, and I couldn't hurt her by sharing my dark thoughts with her.

We sat in silence for several more minutes, until we heard a scraping sound at the door. I shot up like a rocket, running to look through the peephole.

It was Seamus. I unlocked the door and held it open. He stumbled over his feet on the way in.

"Seamus, are you *drunk?*" Sylvie asked, her hands on her hips. I hadn't seen her eyes blaze like that since we were teenagers.

"I am, lassieeee," he slurred.

"You make me sick! And you reek of alcohol. Get out of those clothes and take a shower."

Seamus waggled his finger at her. "You can't tell me what to do. We're not married."

Sylvie stood facing him, her nostrils flaring, and pointed at their bedroom door. "Get out of my sight. We needed you here tonight, and what do you do? You get filthy drunk! I'm disgusted." She threw up her hands and spun around on her heel. I followed her into the kitchen with a last glance at Seamus.

"What do you think is wrong with him?"

"He's drunk!" she spat.

"I know that. What I mean is, what made him go out and get drunk? That's not like him."

She threw up her hands again. "I don't know. He's not been himself lately." She took a deep breath and blew it out slowly, looking down at the floor. "Maybe I'm too hard on him. Maybe he's going through something he doesn't want to talk about." She looked up at me. "What do you think?"

I didn't know what to think. I had seen Seamus behaving strangely, but something had kept me from telling Sylvie about it. I didn't want to burden her with it now. And I trusted him. I hated to think my trust may have been misplaced.

"I don't know what to think, Sylvie. Maybe you should have a talk with him." I lowered my voice. "Does he know that I know about his time in prison?"

"No," she said, shaking her head vigorously. "So don't mention it to him."

"I won't."

"You know, you might have something there. That time in his life is something I never really think about. But maybe he's gotten back into that crowd. Maybe someone got in touch with him, and he didn't have the willpower to say no. I'll talk to him about it. Not now, though. He's a mess."

I could hear Seamus singing in the shower as I checked and rechecked the front door lock and peeked in on Ellie. I was still shaken over the phone call, but Seamus's drunken appearance had at least given me something else to focus on.

My little girl was still sound asleep. I couldn't stand the thought of anything happening to her again. I traced my finger across her cheek, then crawled into bed with her. I held her in my arms all night. She stayed asleep, but I laid awake, going over the phone call a thousand times and wondering who was behind it. I didn't believe for a single second that it had been a prank.

I woke up the next morning with a headache and a sour feeling in the pit of my stomach. I couldn't stop worrying about the phone call and whatever was causing Seamus to act so unlike the happy, grounded man I knew. As I was pouring my tea in the early dawn, Seamus walked into the kitchen and sat down heavily at the table.

"You okay, Seamus?"

"Och, I'm in trouble. Sylvie's fair ragin' at me. And my head's killin' me. Got any more tea, Greer?"

I poured him a cup and sat down across from him. "Want some unsolicited advice? Leave Sylvie alone for the day. Go somewhere and paint. She won't be as angry as time goes by, but the more she sees you today, the more she'll think about last night and get mad all over again."

He looked at me, his eyes bloodshot and his hair standing up in all directions. He looked like a hawthorn bush.

"I've learned that about her. I wanted to sleep this off, but I think you're right—maybe she'll be in a better mood if I disappear for the day." He stood to go.

"Wait, Seamus. Just one thing. Did Sylvie tell you about the phone call I got last night?"

His eyes narrowed, and he scratched his beard as he shook his head slowly. I searched his face for any sign that he knew what I was talking about and was trying to stall for time. I didn't see anything.

"If she did, I honestly don't remember it. I'm sorry, Greer. What phone call are you talking about?"

I told him. His eyes grew wide and his moustache twitched. "I'm such an eejit. I never should have gone out last night."

"You couldn't have known what would happen, Seamus." I hoped I was right, and that he hadn't been behind that phone call. "You're entitled to go out once in a while and blow off some steam."

He shook his head and left the room, returning a few moments later, his painting supplies tucked under his arm and a bag slung over his shoulder.

"I'm goin' out. I'll be back in time to fix dinner." He left with a dejected look, his gait slow and his shoulders drooping.

I was still sipping my tea when Sylvie came in. She grabbed the small pitcher of milk and slammed the refrigerator door shut.

"Have you seen Seamus this morning? I wanted to talk to him."

"He just left."

"Where'd he go? He knows I wanted to talk to him."

"You wanted to talk *at* him. I sent him out for the day to paint. You two can talk tonight, after you've had a chance to calm down and think this through. Besides, all this drama isn't good for you while you're still recovering from a concussion."

"I didn't ask for this drama," she said, raising her eyebrows and nodding in my direction. Meaning, of course, that it was my fault.

"You're right. I take full blame. Or, at the very least, I share the blame with Neill. I'm sorry about that, but I didn't ask for this, either. If I hadn't gotten that phone call last night, you wouldn't have been quite so angry at Seamus for going out and coming home drunk. You were just scared because he wasn't here. So was I. I'm *still* scared."

* * *

"I didn't mean those things I said," Sylvie mumbled. "I'm sorry."

Sylvie, Ellie, and I spent the day at home. It was a beautiful day, and I knew Ellie longed to play in the park nearby, but I wasn't comfortable with the idea. I suggested that we spend some time in the garden behind the flat instead. She was delighted. She brought a doll and a stuffed sheep James had given her and played with them while I sat on one of the uncomfortable wrought-iron chairs and watched her. I kept a constant eye on the walls around the garden—I didn't want anyone surprising us out there. Only one person came by—James. He had called the phone in the flat. Sylvie told him about the call the night before, and he stopped over to see if we were all right.

While Ellie sang to her doll and sheep, James and I sat at the table, talking quietly about the phone call. He, too, thought it was probably someone connected with Neill, probably trying to get more money from me.

"I'm worried about your safety. And Ellie's, too. I don't think you should be going anywhere alone. Make sure Seamus or I am always with you."

"What do you think of Seamus?"

"What?!"

"Shhh. What do you think of Seamus?" I repeated, lowering my voice so Ellie wouldn't hear us. "I mean, we really don't know him very well, do we? What if he's behind the phone call? What if he's behind some of the other things that happened, like the attack on Sylvie? He acted strangely after that."

"I'm so surprised to hear you say all this. I had no idea you suspected Seamus of anything. You think he had something to do with the phone call? Or Sylvie's assault?"

"I don't know. I hate suspecting him, but he hasn't been acting normally lately."

"What do you mean?"

"He came home stinking drunk last night, a full hour after Sylvie called him in a panic and asked him to come home. It was like he didn't realize she was upset. And I can't help but go back over the day Sylvie was hurt and Seamus met us at the hospital. He kept asking her questions, even after the doctor told us she had to stay calm, about what she may have seen at the flat before she was hit."

James leaned back in his chair. "I don't know that those actions rise to the level of being a suspect in this whole affair. Maybe he was just out with friends, having a drink, and time and good sense got away from him. Maybe the day Sylvie was hurt, he was just concerned about her and wanted to find out if she had any more information that could help catch the person who did it. Have you mentioned these things to the police?"

"No. I don't know if I should. Maybe you're right. Maybe I'm seeing things that aren't there. But I do know that I'll be keeping a closer eye on him now." I wondered if James would feel differently if he knew more about Seamus's past. But I couldn't tell him. As much as I wanted to, I couldn't betray Sylvie's trust.

James left, but Ellie and I stayed in the garden. It wasn't long before my fear began to get to me, and I told her it was time to go inside. She didn't want to, but I promised her we could watch a movie.

Sylvie was still annoyed at lunchtime, but she seemed to have mellowed a bit. At least she wasn't slamming doors and swearing under her breath. I hoped she could lose the last of her anger before Seamus came home for dinner. And though it was against her doctor's orders, she sat on the sofa with Ellie and me and watched movies all afternoon.

Shortly after our last movie ended, I got a text from Seamus.

Is it ok to come back?

Yes, I texted back.

Is she still mad?

Not 2 bad.

Be there soon.

Seamus was back at the flat within thirty minutes, bearing all his painting supplies and two bags of groceries. He set everything on the kitchen counter with a thump. He turned to Sylvie, Ellie, and me, rubbing his hands together. "A real treat for dinner tonight, my ladies. Cottage pie, cauliflower, pickled onions, and Empire biscuits."

"What are Empire biscuits?" Ellie asked.

Seamus tweaked her nose. "They're biscuits with jam and icing. How does raspberry jam sound?"

"Good!"

"Then we shall have raspberry Empire biscuits. I think we should call them raspberry Ellie biscuits, don't you?"

Ellie threw her head back and laughed.

Seamus got to work on the cottage pie first. He dry-fried the lamb while the potatoes boiled, then added the vegetables and other ingredients to the meat. Ellie watched in fascination as Seamus deftly sliced mushrooms and diced carrots. He showed her how to thicken the meat mixture with flour, butter, and broth, and let her help stir everything together. The pie was assembled and in the oven in no time. Sylvie announced that she had a raging headache, most likely from watching movies during the afternoon, and was going to lie down until dinnertime.

Seamus was ready to make the "Ellie biscuits." He let Ellie help him make the dough, then they rolled it out and cut it into rounds. He left them next to the oven to pop in when the cottage pie was ready. He turned to Ellie. "Next we'll put some raspberry jam in a bowl, and we scoop a bit of it onto each biscuit when it comes out of the oven."

He opened the refrigerator door and rummaged around, then closed the door and went to the cupboard. After rifling through its contents, he looked at Ellie again. "I'm sorry, lass, I don't seem to have any raspberry jam. How about strawberry-rhubarb? We have some of that."

Ellie wrinkled her nose. "That's okay. Maybe we can have the cookies without jam."

I jumped up from the kitchen table. "I'll run over to the shop and get some raspberry jam. Ellie biscuits won't taste the same without it."

"Och, Greer, you don't have to do that," Seamus said. "I'll go." He untied the apron he always wore around his waist while he worked in the kitchen. "Wait. I've got to cook and mash the cauliflower. Are you sure you don't mind going, Greer?"

"Not at all. Be back in a jiffy."

I took a raincoat from the hook by the front door, gave Ellie a peck on the cheek, and hurried out into the fine mist that was falling from the sky.

I had already forgotten my promise to James that I wouldn't go anywhere alone.

Chapter 23

It was dark and the pavement was slick. Tiny raindrops fell into my eyes, so I pulled my hood over my face and walked briskly toward the closest market.

I didn't see the man behind me.

I paused at the corner to check for cars before stepping into the street. That's when I felt the first hammering blow from behind. My shoulder exploded in pain and, out of sheer surprise, I turned around to see what had hit me.

I somehow knew what was coming next, but I didn't have time to duck before he punched me full in the face. I heard a loud cracking sound, and pain shot through my jaw like a burst of flame. I fell to the ground and the man, who had so far made only grunting sounds, kicked my ribs, then yanked my arms behind me. I closed my eyes against the pain and heard moaning—*was that me?* I wanted to fight, but my body wasn't mine. Then I heard duct tape ripping. My assailant bound my hands, then my elbows, tightly in front of me. He grabbed my upper arm and jolted me to my feet.

I got my first good look at him—it was the man from St. Giles Cathedral. The one who had followed me into Princes Street Gardens and assaulted me. As I struggled to free myself, he glanced up the street toward my flat.

A car pulled up to the curb. My momentary flash of hope was dashed when a person jumped out and opened the back door. I couldn't see a face, but the figure was too big to be a woman. My assailant shoved me into the back seat and crowded in next to me. He pulled a strip of cloth from his coat pocket and tied it over my eyes. Everything went black. The coarse fabric rubbed against the skin around my eyes. I heard that ripping sound again, and I jerked my head from side to side to keep him from taping my mouth closed. The kidnapper slapped my face. As my jaw exploded in a fresh wave of pain, he taped my mouth shut. I had no more fight left to give.

My attacker got out of the car and slammed the door. A moment later, he was in the driver's seat. His companion said one word: "Go."

I must have drifted in and out of consciousness while we drove. I tried breathing slowly and deeply, but the pain was excruciating. I wanted nothing more than to go to sleep until it was gone.

I don't know how long we drove. But when the car slowed and I could feel it making several turns, I knew we were reaching our destination. When we stopped, rough hands pulled me out of the car. I could feel myself being propelled through a doorway. A flight of stairs, then a series of steps in a straight line, then another flight of stairs. Another doorway, then someone pushed me onto a piece of furniture. The door closed with a bang.

I stood up gingerly, using the backs of my knees to feel my way along the surface where I sat. The duct tape still held my wrists and elbows. Sensing I was on a sofa or a bed, I sat down again, then lay down on my side and curled into a fetal position. I couldn't hear anything but the blood rushing in my ears, the sound of my fear and pain. At some point, I must have passed out.

The moment I awakened, the pain came back in a sickening rush. I took a few deep breaths to keep the bile from rising in my throat. Thoughts of Ellie crowded my mind. What was she thinking? After everything that had happened with Neill, how would she be able to handle my disappearance? How long had I been missing?

I heard a door creak open. Soft steps became louder as someone crept nearer. I tried to sit up and must have cringed, because I heard a low chuckle. Seconds later, a hand reached out and ripped the duct tape from my mouth, then removed my blindfold.

I blinked in the dim light of the room, pain and darkness blurring my vision. When everything came into focus, I found myself staring into a face that looked like Neill's. My mind churned in slow motion. It wasn't Neill—it couldn't be!

It was Gerard.

I glanced around the small room that was my prison. It was a familiar cell—the same third-floor room at the house on Candlewick Lane; the room that had haunted my dreams since the last time I visited with Neill.

What was happening?

"Greer, you've made it impossible for me," Gerard said, shaking his head and clicking his tongue.

"What are you talking about?" I croaked. "Can I have a drink, please?"

"Of course. Anything you want." He smiled at me like a crocodile might. Goose bumps spread over my body.

He went to the doorway. "Mum, Greer wants a drink. Would you please bring up a glass of water? Oh, and a straw. I think she's going to need it."

Gerard turned back to me. "Now, where were we? Oh, I remember. You've made it impossible for me to continue my business because of your refusal to help Neill."

"Help Neill how?"

"By giving him the money he needed. The ten thousand pounds."

"But I did! I did give him the money."

"Greer, Greer. Don't play games with me. I think you've seen how things end up when you try to deceive me." He wagged his finger at me.

"I'm not trying to deceive you." *How could I make him understand? And if he did, would he let me go?* "I gave Neill the money he asked for that night in front of St. Giles." The pain in my jaw kept me from speaking clearly. I hoped Gerard understood me anyway. "How did you know about that money?"

"Who do you think he owes the money to? Myself, that's who."

I stared at him, dumbstruck. "Then who's Arnie?"

"Someone who works for me."

Janet came in, carrying a glass of water. She thrust it onto the table next to the bed. "Haven't seen you in a while, Greer. How have you been?" She laughed and turned to Gerard. "What does she have to say for herself?"

"Not much. Broken jaw, I'm pretty sure."

"We'll have to get a doctor out here. How's that sound, Greer?" She laughed again.

Dr. MacDonald's face swam in front of my eyes. I shivered in fear. Janet smiled with malicious glee. "I think Dr. MacDonald would be a great help at a time like this. Don't you think so, Gerard?"

"Yes, Mum. Now go. I want to talk to Greer alone."

With a smirk, Janet closed the door firmly behind her.

"Now you're going to tell me where that money is or I'll hit you again."

"Gerard," I murmured, "I gave the money to Neill the night he was killed. I don't know where it is now. Someone took it from him. Probably the same person who killed him."

Gerard gave me a long look. *Did he believe me? Did he know who killed Neill?*

He clearly didn't know what to believe. He didn't hit me, as I feared he would, but he didn't ask any more questions, either. He turned on his heel and stalked out of the room, slamming the door behind him. I heard the key scraping in the lock and knew I was again a prisoner in the third floor room.

Even if I hadn't been bound in duct tape, banging on the soundproof door would have been useless—I knew that from bitter experience. At least now I could see, but I couldn't reach the glass Janet had left. It sat there as a tantalizing mockery of my pain and thirst.

By now, it was completely dark. There was no clock in the room, and I had forgotten my mobile phone when I left the flat. I was hungry, but even if Janet brought food for me there was no way I could eat it, as my jaw was in racking pain.

My thoughts returned to my family. They must be wondering where I was. I hoped Sylvie or Seamus had called the police. Was Ellie afraid? Was she wondering why first Dad, then Mum, had gone away? Imagining my daughter's fear and pain, I could barely breathe.

I lay back down on the bed. Tears of pain, of fear, of anger slipped over the bridge of my nose and pooled under my face. There was no way out of this, except for sleep.

I awoke hours later when someone opened the door. The room was in utter darkness, so I couldn't see who it was. The person did not speak, but shined a flashlight into my face. I squinted to avoid the blinding light. The figure shifted the light and sliced through the duct tape on my wrists and arms with a small sharp knife. Then I was alone again in the inky blackness.

I reached for the glass of water and tried to drink, but I couldn't open my mouth wide enough because of the pain in my jaw. The liquid dribbled down my chin. I felt around for the straw and pulled off its paper wrapper. This time I was able to sip some water and despite the pain it caused, I felt a trickle of relief as the water made its way down my parched throat.

I lay back down on the bed and stretched out on my back to ease my cramped muscles. But the pressure on my face from lying on my back was too much, and I rolled over on my side again.

Dawn was creeping through the high window in my prison when the door opened again. It was Janet. She stood in the doorway with a plate of scrambled eggs.

"You'll just have to eat soft foods until you can get that jaw looked at."

"Thank you," I mumbled.

She set down the eggs on the table next to me and handed me a fork. "It's your fault Neill's dead. You're lucky you're getting any food from me at all. If Gerard hadn't asked me to bring this to you, you'd starve for all I care."

I was in no mood or condition to have a discussion about Neill, his death, his brother, or my feelings about any of it. I looked over at the plate, refusing to acknowledge Janet's words. Eventually, she left.

Who had sliced off the duct tape last night? I doubted Janet would have done such a thing. That left only Alistair and Gerard—and possibly Beatrice, though I didn't even know whether she still lived on Candlewick Lane.

As the morning dragged on, no one else came to my prison. When I tired of lying on the bed, I shifted to the floor, sitting against the bed and hugging my knees. Everything still hurt, and I couldn't bear to touch my swollen face. I could only imagine how it looked.

I had nothing to do—nothing to look at, nothing to read, nothing to think about but my daughter, my family, and my misery. And James. I wondered if he were looking for me. I could picture Sylvie calling him, asking whether I had stopped at his flat.

But James and Sylvie wouldn't be able to find me here. I knew that already from hard experience. I was hidden from the entire world, in a terrifying room of silence, alone with my bruises and heartaches.

Janet came upstairs twice with plates of food. In the middle of the day she brought *neeps and tatties*, then in the evening, she brought a barley pudding. I had to spit out the raisins and currants. I imagined her downstairs in the kitchen, mixing the hard fruits into the pudding with glee.

Gerard came upstairs as night fell. He yanked me to my feet. Janet stood behind him in the doorway. "What're ye doin'?"

"None o' your business, Mum. I have to take her somewhere."

Janet stood aside as he pushed me through the door and down both sets of stairs to the front hall.

"Get in the car," he told me, jerking his head toward the driveway. Janet had followed us, and she finally dared to ask her son another question. "Are ye bringing her back here?"

"I don't know what I'm doin' wi' her, Mum. Stop asking questions."

Interesting. Even through the fear clouding my thoughts, I could tell that whatever Gerard's plan was to hurt me, Janet wasn't privy to all of it.

The man from St. Giles was in the driver's seat. He hit the gas, and we drove off into the twilight. We made several stops—the bank, the grocery store, the liquor store. After the last stop, Gerard opened the back door and slid into the seat beside me. He unfurled the blindfold from his pocket and tied it around my face. I winced as the cloth dug into my skin and tightened against the bones that hurt so badly.

We drove in silence for what seemed about thirty minutes. I tried to guess where we were headed by noting how often the car seemed to turn or go around bends in the road, but I quickly lost track. Finally, the car pulled to a halt and Gerard, in a surreal repeat of the previous night, took my arm and steered me through another doorway. Once indoors, he ripped the blindfold off.

I recognized the place immediately from police photographs. I was in Neill's flat. So Gerard had known about this place. Was he the owner?

He locked me in the bathroom, where there were no windows and no other means of escape. At least this was better than having to use the chamber pot as I had been forced to do at Janet's house.

I slumped onto the floor with my back against the door. Not much sound came from the rest of the flat. I could hear the two men moving around and murmuring to each other, but I didn't know if anyone else was with them or what they were discussing.

Eventually I heard the television come on, and then smelled the distinctive odor of cooked cabbage with vinegar. I could hear the *tink* of ceramic plates and cutlery. And before long, the men's voices could be heard above the news program on TV.

They were arguing. And probably drinking, since their words became more slurred and more belligerent as they talked.

"What are we going to do with the good doctor?" It sounded like the man from St. Giles.

"I dunno. Maybe keep her here until everything dies down. Then we'll decide where to put her."

Put her? What were they going to do with me? My breathing was becoming heavier and more labored. I couldn't think straight for worrying about Ellie. Who would take care of her if something happened to me? I remembered the quick peck on the cheek I had given her before I headed out—was that the last time I would ever see her? Hot tears fell from my eyes and my nose started running, but I didn't want to sniff and miss any of the conversation. My lungs longed to hyperventilate, but I forced myself to take long, slow breaths to keep from blacking out.

The men appeared to have forgotten me because their words were unguarded now.

Or maybe it didn't matter what I heard. Maybe I wouldn't survive to tell anyone.

"Are we getting rid of her?"

"Maybe. She can identify both of us and she's no more use to us if she doesn't have the money."

"Can she get it?"

"Maybe that boyfriend of hers can get it."

I froze, straining to hear the rest of the conversation. Would they try to harm James as well?

"He'll pony up if we tell him we'll release Greer when he pays. Maybe we'll take the kid, too, for extra insurance."

I couldn't believe what I was hearing. Neill had been right—we were still in danger and there was no way I could help any of us.

"Can the sister identify you?" the man from St. Giles asked. "From the day you beat her up?"

"I don't think she got a good look at me. Damn those sisters—they look so much alike."

So it *had* been Gerard who attacked Sylvie, thinking it was me. Fiery anger burned in the pit of my stomach.

I had to think of a way to get out of this mess. I had to find some way to contact Sylvie— to tell her where we were, to tell her to protect Ellie and to warn James that these monsters might be coming for him.

But how?

I struggled to stand, then hobbled over to the sink and drank from the faucet. Dazed, I watched the water swirl down the drain.

Slowly, an idea emerged from the blurriness of my mind.

I sat back down against the door and listened for any talk between the men, but they said nothing more. I heard the clunk of their dishes in the sink and then shuffling movements, but after that there was silence. I could hear a toilet flushing; there must have been a second bathroom in the flat. A door closed somewhere. I hoped they were going to sleep. I tried to peer under the bathroom door to see if any lights were on, but I couldn't get down far enough to see. The pressure in my face was too painful.

I turned on the water in the bathtub. How I longed for a nice, long, hot bath.

Instead, I slumped against the porcelain and waited.

A couple hours later, the phone rang, its trill screeching through the flat.

"Who's 'at?" the man from St. Giles yelled.

There was mumbling, then a shout. "Arnie! Open the door! Get her out of there!" More shouts as I could hear footsteps pounding toward the bathroom.

So Arnie was the man from St. Giles.

"What the—?"

The door swung open. Arnie's face was twisted in pure rage.

"What the hell do ye think ye're doin'?" he yelled.

I sat on the toilet seat, not wanting to get my feet wet. The bathtub faucet still ran full force. The water cascaded down its sides, coursing across the floor and into the hallway. I suspected the phone call had been from the downstairs neighbors, complaining of a flood coming from their ceiling.

There was a banging at the front door. Arnie ran to get it, pointing at me. "Stay there!" Gerard answered the door; voices went back and forth in anger. I looked around, then spied what I had been looking for. A mobile phone lay on the kitchen table.

I sloshed through the water as quietly as I could. The voices still yelled at the front door, the thick Scottish accents becoming stronger as the anger became more heated. I dialed the police, set the phone on the table, crossed my fingers and said a prayer, then waded back to the hallway in front of the bathroom just in time. Gerard and Arnie got rid of the people at the door and came charging through the flat back to the bathroom.

In the confusion, neither man had thought to turn off the water. Gerard pushed past me and wrenched off the faucet. Then he, came back and stood before me, his nostrils flaring and eyes glittering black.

"Think ye're pretty smart, do ye?" Before I could move away, he punched me in the torso. I groaned and doubled over, trying to breathe. I feared he had broken a rib.

He hit me again. This time I landed on the floor, my head lolling into the water. I couldn't catch my breath. He drew his foot back, but Arnie grabbed his arm.

"Ye better not," he warned. "We don't want the nosy arses downstairs to hear and make more trouble."

Gerard glared at me, then reached down and jerked me to a sitting position. I covered my head in a pitiful attempt to ward off any blows he might give me, but he didn't hit me again.

"Get off the floor, ye soppin' eejit. You're becoming a real problem. No wonder Neill couldn't stand ye."

"What do we do now?" asked Arnie.

Gerard closed his eyes and rubbed his temples. "I don't know. Just let me think a minute, will ye?"

The three of us stood in the hallway, the water swirling around our feet. Finally Gerard said, "We'll take her back to Mum and Dad's. No one'll find her there."

"Yer mum'll know."

"Who cares? Mum'll do what I tell her to do, and I'll tell her to keep quiet."

"What about yer father? And Beatrice?"

"We'll take her in when they're not home. Beatrice must have felt bad for her after you beat her up. She took the duct tape off 'er when she was there. Can't take the chance she'll let her loose or something."

Gerard grabbed my arm, then pushed me in front of him toward the front door.

"Wait, I forgot my mobile," Arnie said. I froze as he reached for the phone on the kitchen table and pushed it into his coat pocket without even glancing at the screen. I breathed a quivery sigh of relief.

Gerard went first down the stairs, then I followed him. Arnie came down last. As soon as we were outside, I glanced quickly in each direction, praying I would see lights from an approaching police car. There was nothing but darkness.

Arnie seemed to be the designated driver. He slid into the front seat while Gerard opened the back door and pushed me inside. Once Gerard was in the front seat, Arnie started the car. He was pulling out of the parking space when the first red-and-blue swirling lights appeared against the side of a building at the end of the block.

The police were coming.

Arnie hit the brake and the car lurched forward, then backward. My head was flung against the window, and Gerard's lip hit the dashboard. Blood ran down his chin.

"Punch the gas and drive!" Gerard yelled. I hung on to the back door while the car shot forward, hitting the car in front of it.

"Dammit, man! Can't you do anything?" Gerard screamed. Arnie put the car in reverse and backed up. The police were speeding up the street toward us.

Gerard grabbed the wheel and yanked it to the left, but Arnie had taken his foot off the gas pedal. "Go!" Gerard yelled.

"The police are *right there!*" Arnie exploded.

"But they're not here for us," Gerard said, trying to stay calm. "You panicked because you saw the lights, but they're not here for us. They don't even know we're here."

"Yes they do," I said in a voice that seemed too loud.

Both men turned around and stared at me. "What do ye mean? You're off your nut," Gerard sneered.

"I called them."

"Nice try, Greer," Gerard answered in a triumphant tone. "Now go," he told Arnie, turning back to face forward. "They're not here for us."

"I called them from his phone," I said, pointing to Arnie.

"How'd ye do that?" he asked.

"You left it on the kitchen table when you went to answer the door. I called them and left the phone on."

Gerard let out a scream that seemed to come from the depths of his very soul. He was reaching for the door handle when a police officer tapped on the car window. Arnie was already getting out of the car.

One of the officers looked into the back seat. "You okay back there?"

Without warning, the tears started to fall and I shook my head. The officer spoke a few words into the radio clipped to his shoulder and opened the back door. He took one look at me and shouted for his partner. "Call for an ambulance." As soon as he spoke, the two officers who were talking to Gerard and Arnie said something to each man. They put their hands in the air.

The police officer turned to me. "Are you the one who called?"

I nodded, still crying and unable to speak. He led me to one of the police cars and eased me down onto the back seat, leaving the door open.

The two men were being led to the other police car. Gerard sat in the back and one of the policemen stood beside Arnie, presumably waiting for another police car to arrive.

It was finally over.

Chapter 24

In the confusion that followed, I gave a statement about everything that had happened over the previous two nights. It seemed a lifetime ago that I had left my flat in Edinburgh to fetch raspberry jam for Ellie's biscuits. I cried again thinking about her, wondering when I would get to see her.

The ambulance arrived a few minutes later. I was whisked to the hospital, where I was diagnosed almost immediately with a broken jaw, a broken bone around my eye socket, two cracked ribs, and bruises and lacerations too numerous to count. I was dozing on painkillers when James strode into the room.

"Greer!" The relief in his voice was palpable. His eyes moist, he swept over to my bed and kissed my forehead.

"The doctors told me not to give you a proper kiss because of the damage to the bones in your face," he told me, gently running his finger along my hairline.

I smiled, my eyelids heavy with sleep. I lifted my hand to reach for his. I was so happy he had come.

"Ellie?" I whispered, my mouth dry.

"She's back at the flat with Sylvie and Seamus. They all want to come visit, but they sent me as the advance team because they wanted to know what shape you're in. They didn't want Ellie to see you and be afraid if your injuries were severe. And it looks like they are."

I nodded sleepily.

"Would you like them to visit?"

I mumbled incoherently, unable to speak. How bad *did* I look?

I was vaguely aware of James pulling up a chair and holding my hand as I drifted off.

When I woke up to the sun streaming through my window, I was still groggy and in pain. Even closing my eyes against the sunlight hurt. I opened them a slit and turned away from the window. James watched me from the side of the bed. Had he been here all night?

I smiled and squeezed his hand. He stood up to close the blinds, then came back to me.

"How are you feeling this morning, my love?"

I groaned, unable to open my mouth. Lying on a comfortable bed in the relative safety of the hospital room, I had finally been able to sleep deeply for the first time since my kidnapping. Rather than benefitting from the rest, though, my face had stiffened up, my ribs throbbed, and the rest of my body felt lame and sore.

A doctor came into the room. In a quiet, soothing voice, he explained the surgery that would be necessary on my jaw. That would happen right away, he said, so the jaw would start to heal properly. Normally, such news would have sent me into a frenzy of anxiety, but the painkillers were doing their job and my nerves stayed calm.

James held my hand. After the doctor left, he pulled out his mobile phone. "Why don't I call Sylvie and Seamus, and have them bring Ellie out to visit? They're all dying to see you, and I know Ellie must be beside herself with worry. Sylvie and Seamus haven't been able to give her a good answer about where you went after you left the flat the other night and I'm sure she realizes something is up."

"Okay," I mumbled.

James dialed, and soon was speaking to Sylvie. She must have asked to speak to me, because he put the phone on speaker and pointed it toward me.

"Greer, thank God you're safe! We're bringing Ellie out to see you later today, after James calls and tells us the surgery is over. Love you."

I tried to smile. James hung up and sat with me in the darkened room until the nurses came to get me ready for surgery. I couldn't go under anesthesia with all the painkillers still in my body, so I had to wait until they wore off. By the time I was wheeled into the pre-op, I was in a great deal of pain.

When I awoke from the surgery, my jaw had been wired together. I couldn't eat, but the nurses helped me drink water from a straw. While I was still in recovery, James called Sylvie and Seamus and told them to bring Ellie to the hospital within the next few hours.

The tears burned and stung my face when Ellie, followed by Sylvie, Seamus, and my mother, walked tentatively into my room just before dusk that evening. Ellie saw me and gasped, but then ran over to my bed. She took my hand, rubbing my dry skin with her finger, and told me everything would be all right. Sylvie, Seamus, and James watched from the doorway. Sylvie and Mum cried openly, James blew his nose, and Seamus blinked rapidly, pretending he had something in his eye.

Ellie seemed to know I was trying to smile through my wired jaw. James stepped forward to explain to Ellie, probably not for the first time, that I wouldn't be able to talk for a few weeks until my jaw healed. She nodded solemnly. I didn't know how much the adults had shared with her about my ordeal, but I hoped it wasn't much. It would be best if Ellie thought I had been in an accident.

The others came closer. Mum leaned over and kissed my forehead. James watched the reunion, a wide smile on his face. Then he drew Ellie away and asked her if she'd like something from the hospital cafeteria. She nodded and took his hand, and the two sauntered off.

Sylvie took Ellie's place in the chair next to me, and Seamus stood on the other side of the bed. Mum stood nearby.

"What really happened?" Sylvie asked, leaning forward on her elbows.

I gestured to a notepad on the table next to my bed. I scribbled a short paragraph for her to read aloud.

The man from St. Giles is named Arnie. He works for Gerard. He grabbed me when I left the flat to get the jam and then he took me in a car. Beat me up.

She gasped after she read the note to the others and Seamus curled his fists into balls. "What a beast!"

"Do you know why he grabbed you?" Sylvie asked.

I wrote again. *Gerard wants more money.*

"Money? What does he need money for?" she demanded.

My wrist was getting tired from writing. *The money I gave Neill was supposed to go to Gerard. But he doesn't have the thousand pounds.*

"So who has it?" Seamus asked.

I don't know. I was too exhausted to continue.

"What are you talking about?" Mum asked, clearly bewildered.

"Never mind. We'll talk about it when Greer's feeling better. Thank God Arnie and Gerard are in jail. You just concentrate on feeling better," Sylvie said.

While we waited for James and Ellie to return, Seamus told me all about what they had done with Ellie while I was missing.

"We wanted to keep her mind off missing you. It wasn't easy. But we took her to a park, a playground, a museum, and two restaurants. And we baked enough goodies to last a lifetime!"

I nodded my thanks, hoping they would see the gratitude in my eyes. Before long, James and Ellie were back and it was time for everyone to return to Edinburgh. Mum explained they had told Ellie this would be a short visit so I could get some rest, but they promised to come back in the morning. Ellie kissed my hand and waved good bye as they left the room. I missed them as soon as they disappeared down the hallway, but I had happy dreams that night—no Neill, no dark alleys, no strangers, no Gerard, no Arnie.

Two days later, I was released. My injuries were all under control, and my jaw was healing nicely from the surgery. I still could only mumble, but I was getting pretty good at getting others to understand me. Mum returned to Dumfries, promising to visit soon.

I was thrilled to be home and back with my daughter. Eventually the wire was removed from my jaw, allowing me to talk a bit more clearly. I hired a tutor to provide lessons for her at our flat because I still wasn't prepared to send her to school—not in Edinburgh, nor back in the States. Gerard and Arnie had insisted they hadn't killed Neill, and the police apparently believed them.

So Neill's killer was still unknown and out there somewhere.

Ellie and I were quite possibly still in danger, the police told me, until that person was apprehended. They advised me to stay local, where they were familiar with the circumstances surrounding Neill's death and they could protect us. I hoped we wouldn't need protection.

James was trying his best to convince me to stay in Edinburgh. His incessant requests—more like pleading—were better than his previous decision to walk away from me entirely, but I was undecided. My job was in the United States, as were my friends, my colleagues, and my home.

But as the days passed and there was no word from the police, Ellie and I began to meet people—at the park, at the playground, at the museums we visited. Ellie's tutor had two daughters, and the three of them would play together in our flat for hours. Ellie began to ask questions about going to school in Edinburgh, and I found my insistence on returning to the United States wavering.

And it wasn't just because Ellie was making friends. I, too, was meeting people—other mothers, friends of James, friends of Sylvie and Seamus. I began to weigh the pros and cons of living in the States or staying in Scotland.

And, of course, there was James. The more time I spent with him, the more I loved him and the harder it was to imagine my life without him in the United States. When we'd been apart, I felt like part of myself was missing. Having Ellie back would have been enough for me to be happy for the rest of my life, but now there was the possibility of even more—of a permanent life with James if I decided to stay in Edinburgh.

One night when I went to check on Ellie, I switched off the nightlight and sat on the bed, watching her sleep. As I looked around in the dappled moonlight, my gaze fell on each piece of furniture, each doorway, each irregular floorboard that had become so familiar over these past long weeks. *I love this flat. I can't see myself living in Dumfries, back in Mum's house, even for a short time. I want to stay in Edinburgh, with or without James. This is the first place Ellie came to when I got her back—I want her to stay here.*

I stood up and switched the nightlight back on. If Ellie had awakened, she would have asked why I was smiling so broadly. And I would have told her: *because we're going to stay in Edinburgh.*

When I told James a few days later that I had decided to stay, he was the happiest man I had ever seen. We were walking through Princes Street Gardens when I gave him my decision.

"James, I have some news."

He stopped walking and turned to face me, squeezing my hand. "Is this the news I hope it is?"

I grinned. "I think so. I've decided to sell my house back in the States and stay here in Edinburgh. With you."

He let out a whoop that startled all the people around us. Strangers smiled and pointed as he picked me up in his long, strong arms and swung me around, my feet leaving the ground in happy flight.

He kissed me for a long time in the sunshine underneath the cherry trees. I couldn't wait to get home to tell Ellie. I knew she would be thrilled. We would miss our friends in America, especially Dottie and her family, but we could visit them and they could visit us. I could seek a position with a university in Edinburgh or apply for funding to establish a new position through my university to teach long-distance from museums and historic places in Scotland. James thought the idea was brilliant and started making plans immediately to introduce me to everyone in the Edinburgh art world I hadn't already met.

We walked back to my flat hand-in-hand, smiling for all the world to see. Sylvie knew the moment we walked through the front door.

"You decided to stay." It was a statement, not a question. A huge smile spread across her face.

"Yes," I said, squeezing James's hand. "Ellie and I are going to stay in Edinburgh."

"Does Ellie know?"

"Not yet. We're going to tell her now."

"She's taking a nap. Can I be there when you tell her?"

"Of course!"

She ran into her bedroom and dragged Seamus back into the living room. "What's going on?" he grumped.

"Tell him," Sylvie directed me.

"Ellie and I are staying in Edinburgh," I told him.

A smile to rival Sylvie's lit up his face. He threw back his head and started laughing. "I knew it! I knew you'd stay!"

"This calls for a dram," James said.

Seamus went to the cupboard. He took down four whisky glasses, poured a generous measure of the golden liquid into each one, and passed them around. We stood in a small circle in the kitchen, the late afternoon sun streaming through the window and the scent of Seamus's herb garden perfuming the air.

"*A h-uile la sona dhuibh 's gun la idir dona dhuibh*!" Seamus cried.

We all repeated the toast and clinked our glasses together.

It was a wonderful memory to carry with me in the terrifying hours that followed.

Chapter 25

I couldn't wait for Ellie to wake up to share my decision with her. I went into the bedroom and shook her shoulder gently. "Ellie," I whispered, "James and Seamus and Aunt Sylvie are out in the living room waiting for you. We want to tell you about some exciting news."

She sat up slowly, rubbing her eyes. She brushed a strand of hair from her eye as she sleepily asked, "What is it?"

"We'll tell you when you come out to the living room," I teased.

She took my hand, and we went down the hallway together. James, Sylvie, and Seamus stood facing us, smiling. "Ellie," I said, kneeling down so I could look her in the eye, "I've decided we should live in Edinburgh. What do you think? Should we make this our home?"

She was still groggy, but the fog was lifting and her eyes widened. "We're staying here? With my friends? And with Aunt Sylvie and Seamus and James?"

I nodded.

"Yay!" she yelled, twirling around the room and hugging everyone. The joy in our living room was palpable. Ellie's happy shouts echoed off the old walls and through the open windows, announcing her excitement to everyone outside. She had endless questions.

"Can I go to school now?"

"Are we going to live in Bide-A-Wee?"

"Are Aunt Sylvie and Seamus going to keep living with us?"

"Is James going to live with us, too?"

That last question made me blush. James and I hadn't discussed marriage, but the thought hadn't been far from my mind lately, and if I knew James, he had given it much thought, too.

"Maybe someday," I answered, looking at James. He winked.

"This calls for a dinner celebration," Seamus boomed.

"Let's go out," I suggested. "Seamus, I want you to have a night off. We're going to let someone else do the cooking for once."

He smiled. "You know I'd be happy to cook on this braw occasion, but it would be nice to enjoy a meal out to celebrate."

"Then it's settled." While Sylvie and Seamus changed their clothes, James, Ellie, and I waited for them in the garden. The light bathed the trees in a golden glow, amplifying our happiness, promising the life we might enjoy together in the near future.

When Sylvie and Seamus joined us, we set out to walk to a restaurant nearby. I was so lost in my own happiness that I didn't see the person watching us from across the street.

Ellie walked between James and me, holding both our hands. "Mum," she said, "when I was taking a nap, I thought of the name of the person who visited Daddy in his flat."

James and I stopped so quickly that Sylvie and Seamus walked right into us. "What's wrong?" Sylvie asked.

"Nothing," I said breezily. "Just tripped on a crack in the sidewalk." I didn't want to alarm Ellie. "Sorry about that," I mumbled to her. "What were you saying, Ellie?"

"I said, I remember the name of the lady who visited Daddy at his flat."

"Oh? What was her name?" I had to fight to keep my voice nonchalant.

"He called her 'Bee.' Isn't that a funny name for a person? Bee?" She laughed.

Beatrice.

Neill told me once, long ago, that he had called his sister "Bee" as a child. There was no girlfriend. Beatrice had visited Neill.

Over Ellie's head, James gave me a stunned look. I shook my head slightly, hoping he would realize I didn't want to discuss Beatrice right now.

"Is Bee who I think it is?" Sylvie whispered, pulling on my arm so I would turn around.

I nodded, my movements tight. I knew my silence would make her stop talking.

"Who's Bee?" Ellie asked.

"Just a lady I used to know," I replied. "She's not very nice." I squeezed Ellie's hand. After Neill's family had sent me to a mental institution, Ellie never saw them again. He hadn't taken her to see them in the summers, and apparently he hadn't kept pictures of them on display in his apartment back in the States. Otherwise, Ellie would have realized "Bee" was really her aunt.

Much to my relief and surprise, Ellie dropped the subject. She seemed more interested in getting dessert if she ate a good dinner, asking a hundred questions about chocolate cake and ice cream.

We were seated quickly at the restaurant, and I excused myself to go to the restroom.

I was washing my hands when the door opened. I looked up in the mirror and gasped.

Beatrice stood there, just a few feet from me. She stared at me with unmistakable hatred and malice, her mouth in a grim line and her black eyes flashing.

"Come with me," she said. I considered sprinting past her, but she was holding a razor blade. It gleamed at the end of an artist's tool in her fist.

"What do you want?"

"Money, you nutter. Money. The thousand wasn't enough, as if you didn't know."

"*You* have the money I gave to Neill?"

"It was for me anyway. He was just going to give it to me. I need the extra nine thousand pounds." She gestured at me with the blade.

I glanced in both directions, hoping we weren't alone in the bathroom, but I didn't see any feet under the stalls. My mind frantically searched for a way out of the situation. I almost screamed, but when she pushed the blade closer to my face I thought better of it. I tried talking to her instead.

"Were you there the night Neill was killed?"

"Who do you think did it?" she asked, her eyes glittering. She ran her finger along the razor blade almost lovingly. "I forgot this at home, so I hit him with the next best thing, a hunk of cement lying in that alley. Hit him pretty hard."

Beatrice killed Neill? Had I unknowingly caught a glimpse of her? Had she been the one in my nightmare, the one standing in the alley as Neill breathed his last?

"We'll be miles from here before your bairn even knows you're gone." She jerked her head toward the bathroom door and held the razor blade in front of her.

"I'm not going anywhere with you."

"Wrong. We're going to the bank. Now get going."

"How much do you need? I don't have nine thousand pounds."

"Should I get your boyfriend?"

I shook my head. I couldn't drag James into this. "I'll go with you."

She opened the bathroom door and propelled me toward the back of the restaurant, out of view of the other patrons. There was a door propped open, and I could see the alley beyond. Looking around furtively, she pushed me into the shadowy alley. I had hoped someone from the restaurant staff would be outside taking a break, but there was no one in sight.

As we turned onto the sidewalk, she got behind me on my left, where she could keep the razor blade centimeters from me while hiding it in her palm.

"Which bank?" I asked.

"Shut up. I'll tell you when we get there."

My mind was working furiously. *How was I going to get out of this? What would happen when we got to the cash machine and she realized I could only withdraw five hundred pounds? Would she kill me out of pure frustration?* My heart was thumping so hard, I was sure she could hear it.

We were walking briskly away from the more populated area of Old Town Edinburgh. The wind had kicked up, and leaves and fallen flower petals swirled around our feet. Lights were coming on behind the blinds in the flats we passed, but those flats were getting fewer and farther between. We were entering a more commercial part of town, a more desolate and empty area. Businesses here had closed for the day, their windows like wide eyes behind bars and padlocks.

We kept walking, Beatrice poking me in the back every few steps so I would keep moving quickly. I had turned my mobile to vibrate before we left the flat, and Beatrice hadn't thought to take it away from me. I could feel it vibrating incessantly in my pocket—by now, everyone knew that I was gone. I longed to answer the phone, but Beatrice made me keep my hands where she could see them. I didn't dare risk reaching for the mobile with the razor blade so close to my skin.

Eventually we slowed down. Beatrice seemed to be looking around for something. We turned a corner and started down one street, then Beatrice decided to go back and go another way.

The wind caught at my clothes, making me shiver. Presently we arrived at a store with a money machine beside it. The lights over the cash machine flickered, giving the immediate area a spooky, strobe-like effect. Two shady-looking people loitered across the street. I would have no choice but to punch in my PIN.

Beatrice prodded my back, then moved in even closer, holding the razor blade next to my ear. Her eyes darted from side to side, birdlike.

She grabbed my purse and rifled through it until she found my wallet, which she drew out with a triumphant, thin-lipped smile. "Now get out your card and punch in the PIN," she hissed.

My mind went blank out of sheer fear and I couldn't remember the PIN. She jabbed me in the back with the handle of the razor blade.

"Hurry up!"

"I can't remember the PIN. I'm trying."

"Liar!" She pushed the handle harder against my ribs, which still hurt.

Finally, the number came to me. I punched in the code, and my account sprang to life on the screen in front of us. I hit the "Get Balance" button, and the full amount of my savings appeared.

"That's not enough!" Beatrice said through gritted teeth. "Open your boyfriend's account."

"I don't have a card for his account. I don't know his account number or his PIN or anything. It doesn't matter anyway, Beatrice. We're only allowed to withdraw five hundred pounds a day."

"If you only knew how close you are to bleeding out..." She trailed off. She closed her eyes and took a deep breath.

"Call him. I'll talk to him," she seethed.

I dialed James's mobile with clumsy, shaking fingers. He answered before the end of the first ring.

"Greer? Where are you? Are you all right?"

I was about to speak when Beatrice grabbed the phone. She gave him the address of the cash machine and told him to meet us in thirty minutes. She told him she'd kill me if he brought the police. She punched the button to end the call and jerked her head around, looking up and down the block. The two people across the street still stood there, watching us. Beatrice steered me toward a dark doorway not far from the cash machine, out of sight of the only people who had seen us.

"James can't take out that much money, either," I said.

"Shut up."

"Why do you need money?"

"Do you ever stop talking?"

"You might as well tell me."

"Neill owed me money for some work I did for him."

"What kind of work?"

"You're the nosiest person I ever knew. No wonder Mum can't stand you."

I ignored that. "What kind of work?" I repeated.

"Just shut up, will you?"

We stood in silence. I was afraid to ask any more questions for fear Beatrice would use the razor blade on me. After almost thirty minutes, we left our hiding place in the doorway and walked back to the cash machine.

There were three people across the street now, all smoking and talking quietly, and I debated whether I should call out to them for help. But I dared not. The blade was pushing into my back, and it would only take a flick of Beatrice's wrist to slice me to ribbons.

A cab drove by and stopped a few meters beyond the cash machine. James jumped out of the back and hurried over to us.

"Put your card in the machine and withdraw everything in your account," Beatrice ordered.

"I can only give you five hundred pounds," he said, looking at me.

"Quit looking at her and do what I said!" Beatrice hissed. James inserted his card, and the screen appeared prompting him to enter his PIN. He pushed four buttons, and his account opened on the screen. Beatrice leaned over to look at the balance.

"Take out all you can. Now."

She looked around frantically while James pushed the necessary buttons. James took the money from the bottom of the machine and reached out to hand it to Beatrice. When she tried to grab it from him, though, he let the money go, launching it into the wind that howled around us. Beatrice let out a primal scream. She dropped the razor blade and lunged for the bills that floated around our heads.

James knelt down on the sidewalk, as if he were trying to help her retrieve the money. I was incredulous.

"James, let's get out of here!" I yelled. Beatrice looked up and grabbed at her blade, but James had retrieved it.

Steps pounded from across the street. I looked up to see one of the strangers running full tilt toward us. He dashed up to Beatrice with his long strides, reaching down and yanking her up to a standing position. In the pulsing light from the cash machine, I could see his police badge. Beatrice squirmed in his grip for a moment, but then seemed to change her mind. She hung her head and stood sullenly still.

Other police officers spilled out of the shadows and converged on Beatrice. James had called them, he said, right after he talked to Beatrice on the phone.

"She didn't strike me as particularly bright," he told me with a wan smile, "so I took a chance that she wouldn't even realize I had called the police. I hope you don't mind, seeing that she threatened to kill you if I called them."

"How could I possibly mind? You're the reason I'm still alive," I said as he put his arms around me and smoothed my hair. I was shaking. He held me until I could breathe again.

After we gave our statements to the police, one of the constables drove us back to the flat. Sylvie and Seamus had, once again, come to the rescue and looked after Ellie while I was missing. She had gone to bed, they said, after they told her I had to help a student who needed me.

They wanted all the details, but they would have to wait. I did tell them, though, that Beatrice was the one who killed Neill, so they wouldn't worry about a killer running loose on the streets of Edinburgh.

What I needed was a shower and a long night's sleep. I promised to tell them the story the next day. Before crawling into bed, I checked on Ellie, who was fast asleep. As I stroked her face, it hit me that all the dangers that had plagued us for months were gone. Really, truly gone now. Neill was dead. Beatrice, Gerard, and Arnie would never bother us again, I was sure of that. It was now time to start living again in the open, not worrying about who might be following us or whether Neill's killer had been caught. I could take Ellie to St. Giles and show her the magnificent kirk without fear of being attacked.

I slept well that night.

The next morning, the phone woke me up. It was one of the police officers who had been at the scene last night. He told me that Beatrice had confessed to everything. It was quite a story.

That night, James came over for dinner. After Ellie went to bed, we took turns telling Sylvie and Seamus everything that had happened. Was it only yesterday? It felt like a year had passed since then.

"So why did Beatrice need the money?" Seamus asked.

"That's where it gets interesting," I replied. "It turns out Neill owed money to Arnie *and* Beatrice."

"Why did he owe money to Beatrice?"

"He owed her money for artwork she had done for him."

"Artwork?" Sylvie sounded surprised.

"Yes. She had copied a painting for him. The McTaggart hanging in her parents' house. She was faking artwork, and her paintings would be sold as originals."

"She was *forging* artwork?" James was incredulous.

"I couldn't believe it when I heard," I said. "But then it all clicked. When I was in the Gramercys' house, the McTaggart was hanging over the mantel. It had always been in the room on the third floor because Janet and Alistair thought someone would steal it. The painting was in pristine condition, but the frame was covered in dust and had fresh fingerprints on it."

"So the forged painting was hanging over the mantel?" James asked.

"Right. Neill had somehow convinced Janet and Alistair to move the real painting to its spot above the mantel. Once it was there, he was easily able to switch the real painting for Beatrice's fake. Apparently Janet and Alistair never even realized their painting had been switched."

"So Neill was going to sell the real McTaggart?" Sylvie asked.

"Yes. He already had a potential buyer. He was going to use the money from the sale to pay his gambling debts, but then he owed money to Beatrice, too, for the fake she painted."

"How much did he owe her?" James asked.

"Ten thousand pounds, the same amount he owed Arnie."

"So did he sell the original?" James asked.

"No. Gerard found out Neill had it, and Gerard stole it before Neill died. Neill didn't know Arnie worked for Gerard, so even though Gerard's theft of the original painting canceled Neill's debt, Neill didn't know that. He still thought he owed ten thousand pounds to both Beatrice and Arnie. Gerard had come up with the whole scheme in order to take advantage of Neill's gambling problem."

"So what happened to the thousand pounds Neill was carrying when he died?" James asked.

"Beatrice took it when she killed Neill in the alley," I replied.

"Why kill him if she was going to get the money?" Seamus asked.

"Because she snapped when she realized it wasn't enough. She was already angry because, according to the police, Beatrice had overheard Neill telling Arnie that he would pay Arnie before he paid Beatrice. She wanted to be paid first. She figured she was getting the full ten thousand pounds, then when it wasn't all there, she killed Neill in a rage."

James shook his head. "That's incredible."

"So does Beatrice get to keep the money, or will you and James get it back?" Sylvie asked.

I grimaced. "James and I would get our money back, except Beatrice used it to send her parents on an extravagant weekend trip to London last week. She has a soft spot for her mum and dad."

I looked over at James. "I'm sorry," I said.

"Let's not worry about that now," he said. "We're all safe, and the people who belong in jail are in jail."

"How did Beatrice hide her fakes from Janet and Alistair if they were all living in the same house?" Sylvie asked.

"Beatrice was living with Janet and Alistair, but she had rented a flat where she would work on her paintings. That's the flat where Neill was staying and where the police found Ellie. All the art supplies in the flat belonged to Beatrice. And Ellie had no idea Beatrice was her aunt because she hadn't seen Beatrice since she was a baby."

"How did Gerard find out where Neill was staying? Did Beatrice tell him?" Sylvie asked.

"No. I asked the police officer the same question. After Beatrice's arrest last night, the police went to Janet and Alistair's house to question them. The officer told me that Janet and Alistair confessed that they had known all along where Neill was staying. They'll be in some trouble for that," I added.

"But how did Gerard find out where Neill was staying?" Sylvie asked again.

"Janet let it slip. She knew that Neill had a gambling problem and that he owed a lot of money to someone, but she had no idea it was Gerard. She also had no idea that the flat belonged to Beatrice, so she told Gerard one day that Neill was staying in a flat in Bell's Loch. Gerard put two and two together and found Neill at Beatrice's flat."

"What a mess," James said.

I nodded. "The whole family is rotten, but Beatrice surprised me the most. She always seemed so meek. She was never downright unkind to me when I was married to Neill—she merely followed her mother's lead. I almost felt sorry for her. Turns out Beatrice was the worst one of them all.

"But she will be going to prison for a long time, along with Gerard and Arnie, I'm sure of that," I announced. It didn't occur to me that the mention of prison might make Seamus uncomfortable. Without thinking, I looked at him. He narrowed his eyes and cocked his head at me. He knew that I knew about his past. I was suddenly sure of it.

"Ahem." Sylvie cleared her throat. "Seamus, I should probably tell you that Greer knows about where you were before we met. I told her one night when I'd had too much to drink. I'm sorry."

"What?" James asked, looking confused.

Seamus shifted his gaze between me and Sylvie for a long moment, then he nodded, his lips pursed together. Finally he spoke. "That's all right. I mean, it can't stay a secret for all time, can it? Greer, I hope you'll let me explain everything to you sometime."

I realized I had been holding my breath since my comment about jail, because I let out a long exhale of relief.

"Sure, Seamus."

He smiled kindly at me. "Did I have you worried?"

"Would someone please tell me what's going on?" James asked in exasperation.

Seamus gave him a brief history of his experiences before he met Sylvie. James was speechless.

"I hope you don't think any less of me," Seamus finally said.

"Not at all, man. I had no idea," James answered.

Sylvie reached for Seamus's hand. "I'm so sorry. I should have told you that I spilled the beans."

Seamus chucked her chin and grinned. "I see I won't be able to keep a secret around your family, eh?"

But I wasn't convinced that Seamus was completely innocent. In the back of my mind, I still carried questions about Seamus, about his behavior after Sylvie was attacked in our flat, and about that day I saw him exchange something on an Edinburgh street corner with a man I didn't recognize. I didn't say anything, but it was obvious to me that Seamus could, indeed, keep a secret.

Chapter 26

But he couldn't keep his secret forever. Ellie and I had come in from having lunch with James one weekend a short time later. I had finally enrolled Ellie in a school near our flat, and I was busy working on a new research project. Those activities filled our weekdays, so on weekends we always spent most of our time with James.

When I opened the front door, Sylvie and Seamus were in the living room. I had obviously startled them. I gave them a second to untangle before ushering Ellie into the room.

My sister and her boyfriend stood in the room smiling. Sylvie held out her hand to me. An emerald-cut diamond sparkled on her ring finger.

"You're kidding," I said.

"Can you believe it?" she asked, her face flushed.

"Did you say yes?" I asked.

"Of course!" She put her arms around Seamus and kissed him.

"What's going on?" Ellie asked.

"Your Aunt Sylvie has agreed to marry me!" Seamus answered, his voice filled with happiness.

"Hurray!" Ellie yelled, running up to hug him and Sylvie in turn. Then I hugged them, and I asked how Seamus had proposed.

"He got down on one knee, just like a knight, right in this room!" she gushed. Seamus blushed.

"Let me see the ring again," I said.

She held out her hand to me, wiggling her fingers to catch the light.

"It's gorgeous," I breathed. "Seamus, did you design it?"

"Och, no. I'd be no good at that. I'm a painter, not a jeweler. I got it from a friend who works for a jewelry shop. It's a funny story, actually. I was supposed to meet him at one of the museums one morning, but he lost the ring. I almost hit the roof! I was walking home in the rain later that afternoon and he called me. He had found it. So we agreed to meet on a street corner and make the exchange there. I'm sure anyone watching thought some kind of shady deal was going down." He laughed at the memory.

And that explained the transaction I'd seen that day in the rain.

"I probably acted a bit strange for a while," Seamus admitted. "I was nervous about the whole thing. I was afraid she'd say no. That night she called and asked for help, I was already beyond my limit at a pub with a couple friends. They were trying to loosen me up so I could pop the question that night, but when I got home Sylvie was so mad there was no way I could ask her then."

And that explained why Seamus had been drunk the night of the phone call.

I asked him about his behavior when Sylvie was taken to hospital after being assaulted. He seemed embarrassed. "I know a lot of guys from when I was in prison," he explained. "I was just thinking I could call one of them and ask him to pay a visit to the person who attacked Sylvie. That's why I was so keen on finding out if she knew who did it. I'm sorry if I worried you. You know I'd never hurt Sylvie for anything."

The two of them held hands, and we called James. This time, when the five of us went out for a celebratory dinner, there were no abductions from the restaurant, no threatening phone calls, no attacks.

James and I were curled up on the sofa in my flat the next night. Ellie had gone to bed, and Sylvie and Seamus were out celebrating with friends.

"Do you think they'll be happy?" James asked.

"Perfectly."

"Do you see us together, happy, in the future?" he asked.

I smiled at him. "Yes. Perfectly."

Glossary

A h-uile la sona dhuibh 's gun la idir dona dhuibh: May all your days be happy ones

Bairn: child

Bampot: idiot

Beannachd Dia dhuit: Blessings of God be with you

Braw: great, fine

Cock-a-leekie: a Scottish soup of leeks and chicken stock, thickened with rice or barley. Traditionally served with julienned prunes.

Crofter: a small-scale farmer. Traditionally crofters paid rent to a landlord, but many crofters own and farm their own crofts

Dinnae: did not

Dram: a measure of whisky

Eejit: idiot

Hairst bree: also known as hotch potch, a mutton stew filled with vegetables

Och: Oh, my!

Scunner: something that makes one sick (slang)

Slàinte: (slanj'uh) (To your) health!

Stovies: a traditional Scottish comfort food, usually made with leftover meat and vegetables

Tattie: potato

Verra: very

Discussion Questions

1. How do you think Sylvie changed throughout the story?

2. What do you think Greer learned about herself as a result of her experiences in the book?

3. Why do you think the author told Greer's story about her time in the house on Candlewick Lane as a series of flashbacks?

4. What is the theme of the story?

5. Is there a particular scene or passage that encapsulates Greer?

6. Who was your favorite character and why?

7. Who was your least favorite character and why?

8. Did you learn anything new from reading the book?

9. How do you think the setting contributed to the story?

10. What do you think is next for the characters?

If you enjoyed *The House on Candlewick Lane*,
be sure not to miss Amy M. Reade's

HOUSE OF THE HANGING JADE

*A dark presence had invaded the Jorgensens' house.
On a spectacular bluff overlooking the Pacific Ocean,
something evil is watching and waiting . . .*

Tired of the cold winters in Washington, DC and disturbed by her
increasingly obsessive boyfriend, Kailani Kanaka savors her move
back to her native Big Island of Hawaii. She also finds a new job
as personal chef for the Jorgensen family. The gentle caress of the
Hawaiian trade winds, the soft sigh of the swaying palm trees, and
the stunning blue waters of the Pacific lull her into a sense of calm
at the House of the Hanging Jade—an idyll that quickly fades as it
becomes apparent that dark secrets lurk within her new home. Furtive
whispers in the night, a terrifying shark attack, and the discovery of
a dead body leave Kailani shaken and afraid. But it's the unexpected
appearance of her ex-boyfriend, tracking her every move and
demanding she return to him, that has her fearing for her life . . .

Keep reading for a special excerpt.

A Lyrical Underground e-book on sale now!

Chapter 1

I knew I should have stayed home.

I bent my head as the wind whipped down Massachusetts Avenue, hurling snowflakes at my face, stinging my cheeks with hard, frosty pellets. The icy sidewalks were treacherous, making my walk to work precarious and slow. There were very few others brave or foolish enough to be out in this weather. I passed one man out walking his dog and silently praised him for being so devoted.

I finally arrived at the restaurant. I stamped on the snow that had piled up against the front door and slipped my key into the lock with fingers stiff and clumsy from the cold. Once inside, it only took me a second to realize that no one else was there. On a normal day, one without a blizzard, my assistant Nunzio would already have come in through the back and flipped on the kitchen lights before I arrived.

I groaned. Even Nunzio, whom I could always count on, had stayed home. I moved through the darkened dining room and turned on the lights in the kitchen. As they blinked to life, I heard a heavy knock at the front door.

Hurrying to open it, I recognized the face of Geoffrey, the restaurant's owner and my current boyfriend, bundled up in a thick scarf and hat.

"Kailani, what are you doing here?" he exclaimed, brushing snow off his boots in the vestibule.

"Someone has to be here to get things started," I answered testily.

"I don't think we can open today," Geoffrey said. "There's no way the delivery trucks can get through, and I don't think we'd have any customers even if they could."

"You mean I came all this way for nothing?" I whined.

Geoffrey smiled down at me. "Sorry. I just assumed you'd know not to come in on a day like this."

"Why did you come in, then?"

"To catch up on paperwork. Plus, snowstorms don't bother me."

"Ugh. They bother me. Well, I guess if you don't need me here, I'll head back home."

"Want me to stop by later?"

I didn't, but I nodded. Geoffrey and I hadn't been dating for long. He was already becoming a little too clingy.

He leaned over and kissed me on the cheek. "Be safe getting home. I'd call you a cab, but there isn't a single one on the streets."

"Believe me, I know."

I trudged home the same way I had come, the snow falling even harder now and blowing sideways, making it difficult for me to see.

When I finally made it to my apartment building, I clumped up the stairs in my heavy boots and stood inside my apartment, leaning against the door for several moments to catch my breath. It took me a while to peel off all my layers. I left them lying on the floor while I heated up milk on the stove for hot chocolate. As the milk warmed, I gazed at a canvas photo that hung in my front hall. It was a faraway view of the beach, taken from my parents' backyard, overlooking the black sand and the curling waves of the azure Pacific Ocean.

"We've got to go home," I said aloud to my cat, Meli, as she stepped daintily around me. This wasn't the first time I had expressed this sentiment to Meli, but this time she stopped and looked up at me. She blinked and twitched her ears.

It was the sign I needed.

I watched the snow continue to fall for several hours from the warmth and safety of my apartment. Meli and I curled up on the couch while I tried to read a book, but I couldn't concentrate. My thoughts returned again and again to palm trees and warm, caressing trade winds, to the faces of my mother and father, of my sister and her little girl.

Geoffrey eventually stopped by, bringing with him an icy blast of air as I opened the door to the hallway.

He laughed. "Looks like this storm may never end."

I invited him into the warmth of the apartment. "Take off your stuff. Want some hot chocolate?" I called over my shoulder as I walked into the kitchen.

"Sure," he answered, struggling with one of his boots.

I joined him in the living room a few minutes later. He was trying to stroke Meli's chin, but she apparently wanted none of that. Her ears flattened back and she squirmed out of his reach.

I handed him the mug of hot chocolate and sat down opposite him.

"Geoffrey, I have news," I told him warily, knowing he probably wouldn't be as happy as I was.

"What is it?"

"I'm going back to Hawaii." I waited for his reaction.

"That's nice. It'll do you good to get out of this weather for a while."

He obviously wasn't getting it. "No, not for a while. I'm *moving* back. For good."

I was right. He was not happy. In fact, he looked stricken, his eyes wide and his mouth agape. "What do you mean, for good?" he asked, choking on his hot chocolate.

"I mean, I just can't stand it here any longer. I'm never going to get used to the weather, I miss my parents, and my niece is growing up without her auntie. It's time to go back. This is something I've been thinking about for a long time.

"I'll miss you, Geoffrey, but this is what's best for me," I added, trying to soften the blow.

He looked like he was struggling for words.

"But . . . but . . . what will you do?"

"I'll do the same thing I do here, Geoffrey. Sous-chefs are not unique to DC."

"Okay, but what will I do? Without you, I mean?"

I felt sorry for him. He looked crestfallen.

"Geoffrey," I said gently, "there are lots of women in Washington who are looking for someone as wonderful and kind and handsome and successful as you are. I have to do what my heart is telling me to do, and that's to go back to Hawaii."

He nodded slowly, his eyes downcast. "Is there anything I can say to keep you here?"

"I'm afraid not."

"When are you leaving?"

"I don't know. I just made the decision this morning."

He sighed and leaned back against the couch cushions, holding his mug on his lap and staring into space.

"Geoffrey? You okay?" I asked.

He set his mug on the coffee table and pushed himself up from the sofa. "I guess I should get going, then. Will you keep working at the restaurant until you leave?"

I was surprised that he wanted to leave already, but I didn't mention it.

"Of course. I'll give you plenty of time to find another fabulous sous-chef."

I watched Geoffrey as he walked down the hallway of my apartment building. His shoulders were stooped and his gait slow. He looked like a forlorn little boy. Poor Geoffrey. At the end of the hallway, right by the elevator, he turned around and made a pleading motion with his hands and walked back toward me.

Uh-oh.

"Kailani, how can you just throw away all the time we've spent together?"

I was a little taken aback, but I suppose I shouldn't have been. Such dramatic statements were normal with him. "Geoffrey, we haven't really spent too much time together. We haven't been dating very long."

"But doesn't that time mean something to you?"

"Yes, of course it does. I've enjoyed getting to know you and we've had fun together. But it's time for me to go home. And I'm afraid a long-distance relationship just isn't possible. It's too far away."

"There's got to be a way, Kailani. I just can't stand the thought of losing you."

"I'm sorry, Geoffrey. I've got to go. I'll see you at work tomorrow." I closed the door gently and stood there until I heard the *ding* of the elevator.

I waited a few hours before calling my mother since there was a five-hour time difference between DC and Hawaii.

She and my father were both thrilled by my news, as I knew they would be. They had a million questions for me, like when I would be coming home, where I would be looking for a new job, and whether I could live with them for a while.

"I don't know!" I laughed. "I'm going to start putting out some feelers right away for jobs in restaurants and resorts along the Kohala Coast. Someone must need a sous-chef. Or even a head chef. But I'll be home soon, don't worry. I can't stand another day of this winter weather."

I hung up, promising to keep them posted about my job hunt. Suddenly, the winter seemed a little warmer.

SECRETS OF HALLSTEAD HOUSE

Dark secrets, dark waters...

AMY M. READE

*"You are not wanted here. Go away from Hallstead Island or you will be
very sorry you stayed."*

Macy Stoddard had hoped to ease the grief of losing her parents in a
fiery car crash by accepting a job as a private nurse to the wealthy and
widowed Alexandria Hallstead. But her first sight of Hallstead House is
of a dark and forbidding home. She quickly finds its winding halls and
shadowy rooms filled with secrets and suspicions. Alex seems happy
to have Macy's help, but others on the island, including Alex's sinister
servants and hostile relatives, are far less welcoming. Watching eyes,
veiled threats...slowly, surely, the menacing spirit of Hallstead Island
closes in around Macy. And she can only wonder if her story will become
just one of the many secrets of Hallstead House...

THE GHOSTS OF
PEPPERNELL
MANOR

The roots of evil run deep...

AMY M. READE
Author of *Secrets of Hallstead House*

"Do you know what stories Sarah could tell you about the things that happened in these little cabins? They'd curl that pretty red hair of yours."

Outside of Charleston, South Carolina, beyond hanging curtains of Spanish moss, at the end of a shaded tunnel of overarching oaks, stands the antebellum mansion of Peppernell Manor in all its faded grandeur. At the request of her friend Evie Peppernell, recently divorced Carleigh Warner and her young daughter Lucy have come to the plantation house to refurbish the interior. But the tall white columns and black shutters hide a dark history of slavery, violence, and greed. The ghost of a former slave is said to haunt the home, and Carleigh is told she *disapproves* of her restoration efforts. And beneath the polite hospitality of the Peppernell family lie simmering resentments and poisonous secrets that culminate in murder—and place Carleigh and her child in grave danger...

Photo by John A. Reade, Jr.

USA Today bestselling author **Amy M. Reade** is also the author of *Secrets of Hallstead House, The Ghosts of Peppernell Manor*, and *House of the Hanging Jade*. A former attorney, she now writes full-time from her home in southern New Jersey, where she is also a wife, a mom of three, and a volunteer in school, church, and community groups. She loves cooking, traveling, and all things Hawaii and is currently at work on the next novel in the Malice series. Visit her on the web at www.amymreade.com or at www.amreade.wordpress.com.

Made in the USA
Lexington, KY
12 February 2017